JUSTICE SERVED

JUSTICE SERVED

TERRA KRIS™ BOOK THREE

MICHAEL ANDERLE

DISRUPTIVE IMAGINATION®

LMBPN Publishing
PMB 196, 2540 South Maryland Pkwy
Las Vegas, NV 89109

Version 1.00, August 2021
Version 1.01, September 2021
ebook ISBN: 978-1-68500-403-3
Print ISBN: 978-1-68500-404-0

THE JUSTICE SERVED TEAM

Thanks to the JIT Readers

Larry Omans
Dave Hicks
Zacc Pelter
Wendy L Bonell
Diane L. Smith
Deb Mader
Kelly O'Donnell
Rachel Beckford

If I've missed anyone, please let me know!

Editor
The Skyhunter Editing Team

*To Family, Friends and
Those Who Love
to Read.
May We All Enjoy Grace
to Live the Life We Are
Called.*

— Michael

PROLOGUE

Waves rose high, twelve feet fore and aft, rolling and rocking in the darkness. In the center of it all was a vessel, tiny by comparison.

The passenger boat was sturdy, but that wouldn't mean anything without the trained skill of its captain. A young woman, only thirty years old with arms coiled like knotted rope, held the wheel and fought against the elements. Waves beat against the hull, and the boat listed to an alarming degree before she righted it and brought it back under control.

The waves were only half of the battle. Although veiled by the fog, she knew of the rocks that jutted out of the water on either side—black, jagged things that hungrily bit into the hull of any boat careless enough to clip them. Her heart beat ragged rhythms in her chest. Her cargo hunkered below deck, unable to sleep as they took the torturous journey to the island.

Rain hammered against the glass. The only guiding signs to lead her onward were the tiny luminous buoys that rose and fell with the waves. She gritted her teeth and fought the wheel while playing the throttle to fight against the latest attack. *It's like the gods are trying to prevent our passage, to hide the evidence of the island.*

The island... That was what those below deck were seeking. Only a short distance from Atlantica's mainland, Liberty Crag was almost a myth among the mainlanders. The ever-present fog that blanketed Atlantica blocked the island from view for the most part. On a particularly sunny day, an Atlantican might view the range of rocks from afar. Even then, it was only a hazy shape on the horizon.

Today wasn't a sunny day, and Kristin Jackson knew what she had gotten herself in for. One of the only sailors who not only accepted the challenge of the trek but embraced it, Kristin had been making the short trip back and forth for the last four years, bringing the island's residents to their destination. On a calmer day, helicopters were the preferred form of travel, gracefully gliding across the ocean and landing placidly on the island.

On days like these...

A head appeared from the hatch behind her. A shaky voice thick with nausea called, "How much farther?"

Kristin didn't turn. Her narrowed eyes stayed on the water. "You won't fucking make it if you don't get your ass back down and quit distracting me. We'll get there when we get there."

The pale face hovered a moment longer until the boat lurched and whatever hesitation they had faded.

Kristin grinned. It was one of the perks of the job. Her gig was one of the most highly paid in the world, given the short distance they had to travel. It allowed her to take no shit from the wealthy sons-of-bitches who ruled every other part of the island.

Money might buy you respect, fame, and notoriety in the civilized parts of this world, but out here on the seas, Kristin was king. A short round trip with enough passengers in the stormy seasons could net her enough to make the owners of the NFL teams look like beggars.

The island slipped into view, a great barrier of dark rocks directly ahead. The storm continued its assault. Kristin was undeterred as she felt the rhythm of the waves and slowly gained distance. Her arms ached, the skin prickling from the exertion, but the adrenaline kept her going.

To her, it was a win-win. If she made it to the island, her pay packet would be ludicrously high. If the boat went down, she would know how to survive, but those below...

Well, the sea would wipe them out in silence. Their competitors might even reward her.

She pulled alongside the dock and killed the throttle. The hull bumped against the wooden structure in time with the somewhat calmer waves. With a few graceful bounds, she hopped to the rail and tossed a loop of rope over a post. Temporary mooring secured, she swiftly wrapped lines around the permanently anchored cleats and knotted the ropes in place. When that job was complete, she knocked on the hatch and informed the passengers they could disembark.

A small group of green and white faces rose from the depths. Assistants held umbrellas and guided them down the walkway and onto the black sand of the small beach. The cove was only one hundred feet wide and bordered by the steep rise of black rock.

A neat stairway had been carved into the stone, trailing upward to the island's main body. The stairs were smooth and decorated in white marble, yet another egregious display of wealth that Kristin rolled her eyes at. She'd been a woman of meager means for most of her life, the world of the wealthy a far stretch from her upbringing.

She led the way ahead, lighting the torches to illuminate their passage. A small cave stood beside the bottom of the stairway, leading into darkness that Kristin had never dared to tread. She scaled the stairs, the troop grumbling behind her.

Kristin's legs burned. She couldn't imagine how the residents felt, knowing that many were hardly the exercising type. She wondered why, with all of their wealth, they hadn't found a better way to climb after the nauseating boat trip, but it wasn't her job to wonder. Her job was to lead.

As she crested the top, the community unfolded before her. High, golden fencing skirted the entire island flat, standing at least twice as high as Kristin. A gate, not unlike those she had seen in depictions of the pearly gates, barred their way.

A small, boxy office stood on either side, the silhouettes of guards inside. They stood at the arrival of powerful flashlights and emerged from their booths, assault rifles in hand. Kristin noticed the bulbous turrets stationed at intervals around the gates. The island's defenses were comprehensive and aggressive, a stark juxtaposition to the creature comforts within.

Kristin approached the guards. They were monoliths of men and women, their eyes shielded behind thick dark glasses despite the storm. Muscles rippled, the reflection of the flashlight catching the slick rain-covered flesh of arms that jutted out of Kevlar vests. One grim-faced individual approached Kristin, holding a hand out flat.

Kristin held up a badge she'd drawn from her inner pocket. "Island clearance, ID four-five-eight-nine-two."

The guard lowered his arm, then turned his head to the approaching residents. They stumbled forward, ignoring the guards as they beelined for the gate. Amber lights flickered to green as they passed. Kristin was aware that the sensors were some of the most sophisticated and powerful in the world, able to read biomarkers from dozens of feet away. The gates retracted as the bowed-over individuals clutching their coats around them-selves staggered onward and home.

Kristin stood in wait, counting each as they passed. There had been fourteen with her on the boat. Six passed through the gates with no issue.

A young man with curly brown hair that stuck flat to his head passed the scanner. The light turned red. A *beeping* sound emit-ted, informing the guards of the anomaly.

The atmosphere changed in a heartbeat. The guards turned to the individual, a man whom Kristin was certain called himself Tyger. He had a kind smile and had seemed like a good guy when he transferred the travel money into her account.

Now, that smile faded.

"On the ground, now!" a guard called.

Tyger held up his hands, eyes wide. He hesitated, whether through fear or stupidity, but that was all it took. A shot fired. Tyger's chest exploded, blood adding to the pouring rain. Tyger crumpled to his knees, then fell to his stomach. The assistant who had been holding his umbrella turned to run, fleeing away from the gates. Another well-aimed shot ended him. Two bodies lay flat on the dark rock.

The world hushed for a moment. Kristin watched, unfazed. It hadn't been the first time she'd seen intruders trying to gain unauthorized entry into the compound.

The guards divided, dragging the bodies out of sight. They would deal with them when they finished their job. One guard approached Kristin, dwarfing her with his size. His thick dark beard hid his face. "Didn't think to vet the intruder in your midst?"

Kristin shrugged. "Not my job. I deliver. You filter."

The giant smirked. "Think you're real clever, don't you?"

"I'm just doing my job," Kristin replied. "How about you do yours?"

The man's fingers flexed on his weapon. He stared at her for a moment longer before returning to his post.

It's all testosterone with you fuckers. She watched the final residents make it through security. Finally, the gates began to close. Kristin doffed her cap, then turned back to the stairs. She would wait on the boat for the next visitors wishing to travel to Atlantica's mainland.

With any luck, the storm would last for a while, forcing the islanders to realize there was no alternative except her. It was a dangerous gig, but one she embraced. Everyone found their niche in life in the end.

When she approached the top of the stairs, Kristin paused. A glance to the right had her looking down at the rough range of rocks bordering the island. Down there in the darkness, where waves pounded the shores, she thought she saw a single light.

She narrowed her eyes, shielding them against the rain with one hand. A light bobbed around in the gloom. She glanced back at the guards, wary of arousing suspicion, then made her way down the stairs.

On the boat, she ducked into the captain's quarters and fished out her binoculars. She climbed back on deck and hid from the rain behind the glass windows surrounding the boat's main controls. The light was gone, but she looked through the binoculars anyway, scanning the dark, blurred shapes of the rocks as she hunted for another sighting.

There was nothing.

Not to be dissuaded, Kristin cast off, started the engine, and crept around the side of the island. She moved as slowly as the waves would allow, listening to the creaks and moans of the vessel. On occasion, she had to move farther out, avoiding shallower water.

Twenty minutes later, the light came back into view. She idled and cut her running lights. Looking through the binoculars once more, she locked onto the light source, frowning as she tried to make sense of what she saw.

A steel structure the size of a telephone booth stood on a small outcrop of rock. It was the strangest thing, jarring against the harsh natural layout. The light was a set of green LEDs pulsing at the top corner.

Strange. They didn't look green from afar.

She glanced around, watching for the silhouettes of the guards, but could see nothing beyond the thick veil of rain. Salt stung her eyes as she narrowed her gaze at the building. She drank from her water bottle and rested her ass on the control board.

She wasn't sure how long she sat there watching the strange little building on the side of the island, but soon enough the door opened. The white light returned, coned from the flashlight's head, and a figure trudged out, hood pulled up tight around their head.

There was no way to tell who or what this person was doing, only that they took great caution in ensuring that they placed a series of locks on the door. The cold and the wet must have slicked their fingers as chains bound and locks engaged.

Once satisfied with their efforts, the figure turned, flashlight searching for a small gully which they began to climb back to the compound. Kristin wasn't sure where this person was going. As far as she was aware, the island only had one entrance in and out. When the island's residents were a mixture of millionaires and billionaires, you ensured that you could guarantee their safety.

The light faded as the figure crested the ridge. Kristin set her attention on turning the boat and returning to the cove. It might be a few minutes before another rich bitch needed passage. It might be another few hours. All she knew was that if she wasn't there to transport the residents over to the mainland, the money wouldn't siphon into her account.

She throttled up, braced herself for the fight back to the dock, and set into motion, not fully understanding the impact of what she'd witnessed.

CHAPTER ONE

Terra rested her elbows on the cool metal rail of the balcony and stared out at the Atlantica jungle.

The view was exquisite, standing four stories high with the edges of the large expanse of forest filling her sight. The fog veil hovered above the canopy like fallen clouds. The song of birds, insects, and the array of apes that populated the jungle filled the air, not that Terra had ever seen too many of them in the flesh.

"This place is beautiful," she muttered. "A perfect mix of metropolitan city and nature. Shame that it won't be long until some mogul gets the smart idea to plow the trees down and build some kind of megaplex compound to showcase their wealth."

No current plans are in place for such an operation. APRIL's voice arrived in her head, unbidden and unrequested. **Atlantican law protects the jungle. It serves as a nature reserve for the array of endangered and unique species on the island.**

Terra smirked, her nostrils filled with the scent of the coffee steaming in her cup. "When has that ever stopped anyone before? All you need is one corrupt politician and the whole thing changes. Atlantica isn't built in everyone's best interests. Its laws protect the wealthy. It's disgusting..."

Still, her eyes narrowed on the tranquil beauty before her. If she strained her ears, she fancied she could hear a nearby waterfall, though where it would be, she had no idea.

She drew a deep breath of the fresh air and sat in the wicker chair behind her. She was aware that her skepticism of the island had only grown in the last few days, what with the influx of information thrown her way by someone she had, up until that point, not been aware existed on the island.

Her body was recovering, thanks to APRIL's assistance. The adventures of bringing her former captain, Parker Garcia, to justice had taken a lot from her, physically and mentally. To find herself on a solo mission, escaping from a group of medical staff who insisted on cutting the advanced artificial intelligence technology from inside her skull was something she didn't want to revisit.

Although Terra often worked better solo, she liked the missions where she was at least still connected to the Atlantica Justice System team. For the last few weeks, she'd been a nomad, on the run for her life. That would be exhausting for even the strongest Atlantican.

Her brow wrinkled as the memories piled on her. The large woman, Nora Asplin, had divulged more information than Terra wished to bear. Yet she still only had more questions. More things to ponder and fathom.

"Tell me, Terra…What do you know about 'The Executioners?'" she had asked, smugly sitting across the table, her gelatinous muffin top straining inside her clothes.

The word had sparked a note of recognition inside her, and it took Terra a moment to figure out where she'd heard it. She thought of the jungle, of a beat-down mansion and two kind owners who had trodden the line of betrayal when Garcia arrived at the house.

"The city was darkening," Juniper Huckman had informed Terra when the AJS officer asked why her parents had abandoned the city and moved into the fringes of the jungle. "Rates of crimes were rapidly rising. Murders were up. Drugs filled the holes and cracks in the pavements. We had to get away—especially after the island introduced the public versus private rule."

Then a word slipped from her lips. Something that sounded like "Executioners," although at the time, Terra wasn't certain.

Nora had studied Terra's expression, waiting to read the signs. Terra remained tight-lipped, not knowing whether or not to trust the large woman. Although she'd rescued Terra from the rooftop and taken Garcia into custody, she had yet to reveal her credentials or the purpose of this strange, clinically minimalist facility.

Nora had leaned forward, hands clasped together, eyes flickering toward Imani, who stood by Terra's side. "The Executioners were an elite program that operated on Atlantica in the late sixties to early seventies. A prestigious band of law enforcement who helped birth justice on this strange island home we call Atlantica." Nora fixed her gaze on Terra.

"Back in the early days of the island's formation, there were a lot of…*ideas* thrown around. Opinion filled the land, with every Tom, Dick, and Sally wanting to shape the direction the island ran. This was new ground—*virgin land*—and every son of a bitch with coin to spare wanted to work this island into a playground for corruption. A safe space, a haven free from criminal justice and prosecution."

"Well, they smashed that, then," Terra replied. "They got exactly what they wanted. The island is all of those things and more, a Mecca for the twisted and the deceitful." She sighed. "We've just arrested one of the island's leading law enforcement captains for his collusion in drug rings and the APRIL program."

Terra's blood began to boil. "He was inside my head, Nora. Controlling what I could and couldn't see. If I hadn't severed that connection, who knows where I'd be right now."

"In a graveyard with a hole in your head from the extraction of the miracle technology that kept you alive." Nora's tone was stark and blunt.

It took Terra aback. Imani rested a hand on her shoulder.

Terra drew a steadying breath. "Nora, while I appreciate you rescuing me from that place, I'm still pretty beat and not in a place to fuck around. You mention this supergroup of law enforcement officers like they're common knowledge, but I've never heard of them. Even if they did exist, what's their influence now? What's the point in you telling me this?

"The AJS is fucked. There's no telling who's clean and who's dirty anymore, and even if we do, the law will protect them. We can hand Garcia over to the courts, but he'll get himself free somehow. I'm almost certain of that."

Then Nora had said something that had Terra's mind racing. It stole her breath and took her off-guard. "It wasn't always that way, Terra."

A howler monkey bellowed in the treetops. A knock came from Terra's apartment door. She called, "It's open," finding it strange that for the first time in years she felt comfortable not locking her bedroom door. Not that it was her bedroom. The white walls and the lack of homely items ensured that she was reminded of that constantly.

Footsteps sounded on the marble tiles. Imani appeared in the sliding doorway, wearing a black tank top and dark cargo pants. Her toned arms were dark, soaking in the sun as it attempted to break through the fog. "Beginning to get worried about you. You were always the early riser."

Terra checked her watch. 10:15 a.m. "I haven't slept."

Imani gave a knowing nod. She took the chair beside Terra, grabbing the second coffee mug that was waiting for her. "You always did know when to expect me."

"I'm not sure that's true," Terra replied solemnly.

Imani sat back and looked out at the view. "You know I had to, right?"

Terra nodded, although it wasn't genuine. She still hadn't fully forgiven Imani for her abandonment in their last mission. They had Garcia in their grasp. Terra had left Imani inside Garcia's apartment with Garcia to guard him. Instead, she'd disappeared while Terra had gone to fetch the car.

"I had to," Imani repeated. "Not only to keep up my cover of playing the good cop for the AJS but to alert Nora and the team to what was going on." She laid a hand on Terra's. "I would never abandon you like that. We're partners, you and I. We're a team. We tracked down Garcia, and we brought him to justice."

I did. Most of it was me.

Terra hated herself for the thought, but her head was in a thousand places, the least of which was justifying her former partner's actions. She knew without a doubt that she wouldn't have survived without Imani's intervention, but the other woman could at least have brought her into the plans. Not only that but being in this place, trusting a stranger after all that had happened…Terra didn't know what to believe.

"It's fine," she replied after a moment.

Imani watched her a moment longer, then turned back to the forest. "I know it's a lot to take in, Terra. A lot of what we thought we knew isn't true. The AJS is a house of cards, relying on a few corrupt assholes to keep the whole thing standing. Sometimes you have to topple it all to rebuild it the way it was supposed to be."

"Like The Executioners?" Terra asked skeptically.

Imani's lips thinned. "It seems impossible, doesn't it?"

Terra scoffed. "An elite group of law enforcement officers, taking on the island and performing vigilante justice to bring down the assholes ruining the place? Not only that but a group backed by island law?" She shook her head. "Imani, that's a fairytale. If this kind of shit existed, don't you think we would have at least heard about them in academy training?"

"Would we?" Imani returned. "Think about it, Terra. Why would the AJS tell us if they're trying to cover it all up?" She turned, eyes lighting with excitement. "Think of what this could mean for the city. Imagine if we could—"

"Break the system?" Terra interjected. "Tear it down, make it better?" She sighed. "It's all I've ever dreamed. It's all I've ever wanted. To see justice prevail. But it's impossible, Imani. The city is too entrenched in the grave it built for itself. There's no way."

Imani turned her gaze to the forest, relaxing into the chair, a smile on her face. Terra's words hadn't taken the wind from her sails, it seemed. Terra grumbled, feeling guilty for her negativity. She didn't like it, but how else could she feel after spending weeks on the run, battling the system and seeing just how dirty members of the AJS were. If the very system meant to protect the island wasn't functioning as it should, what hope did they have?

"I remember when I first met you," Imani mused, watching a colorful bird take wing and soar into the canopy. "It was like a lightning bolt struck. After three years on the force, I thought I knew the measure of each person here. I thought they'd set the bar. But you…" She chuckled. "You changed all of that."

Terra thought back to seeing Imani's eyes track her as she walked into the precinct and made her way to the captain's office. At the time she loathed being watched, but now…

"You were different," Imani stated. "Straight away, I knew that to be true. You weren't some chump looking to accelerate their progress, only caring about their interests. You *cared*. You wanted to make a *difference*."

"Yeah, and look where that got me," Terra replied. "Demoted and utilized as some experimental biological weapon."

Imani's grin grew. "Even then, you beat the odds." She sipped her coffee. "Those first days, I prayed to be joined with you. I prayed that we'd become partners. I begged Garcia, pleaded with him. He yielded, eventually. I've never looked back from that. Even now, with all the odds against you, you've shown that you're special.

"The system tried to drag you under, and you're still floating. A team of whack jobs tried to control you, placed physical technology in your head to direct and guide your every move. You detached yourself, pushed away from 'the man' and out on your own. They want the technology back, but you won't give it to them. You forged your path, and now here you are."

"What's your point?" Terra desperately tried not to see the truth in Imani's words.

"My point is that you've been blessed with an incredible opportunity," Imani continued. "You can pioneer a new wave of justice. All you have to do is believe. All you have to do is listen. All you have to do is open your mind and know that change is inevitable, and it lies in you."

Terra set down her cup, her desire for caffeine gone as her stomach roiled. "You sound like a shit version of Anthony Robbins."

Imani chuckled. "It's true."

Terra considered this. She'd been struggling with her initial meeting with Nora for a few days now. With the large lady out at so-called "meetings" for most of the day, Terra had barely had a chance to engage her curiosity and ask any more questions. For the most part, she had stayed in her hotel room, allowing her body to recover. On the odd occasion, she strolled on the fringes of the forest, breathing in the clean oxygen.

"Suppose I do believe..." Terra replied at last. "I can't move forward without getting the chance to speak to Nora again. Where has she been? Out doing who-knows-what while I'm sitting in here like a caged lion, toying with a future that's unfocused and uncertain."

Imani nodded. "I hear you. Good thing that Nora is back in the compound."

Terra's ears perked up.

"She wants to meet with you," Imani continued. "Tonight. Dinner. Says she'll answer anything and everything you want to know. No holds barred."

Terra took a long breath. "Just me and her?"

Imani put a hand on her chest. "You don't want your best friend there?"

Terra rolled her eyes.

Imani laughed. "Just you and her. Unfiltered, all-access pass."

Terra thought for a moment, then gave an affirming nod. "Fine. But she's paying."

Imani smirked. "I'm sure she can handle that."

CHAPTER TWO

Terra looked through the one-way glass at the masterpiece before her.

The building was huge, an almost exact replica of Caesar's Palace in Las Vegas. It made Terra smile to think of the bustling gambling city in the center of the desert. The world outside of Atlantica was fascinating, and Vegas was one of many places she'd long wanted to visit. Maybe she'd be able to by the time she basked in the glow of retirement.

Lights reflected in the water features. Men and women in glamorous gowns and black tuxedos strolled arm in arm. Valets waited outside the main doors, ready to drive patrons' cars out of sight and out of mind.

"All yours," the driver stated as he pulled the sleek black Mercedes to a halt.

Terra started, unused to having a real person driving her around instead of the typical driverless cabs which roamed the city streets. "Thank you." She took her cell phone, tapped in a figure for the tip, then looked for a touchpad to initiate the transfer.

The man chuckled. "Not necessary, ma'am. All taken care of."

Terra nodded her acknowledgment, then stepped out of the car.

The air was brisk, a steady wind rolling around the plaza. Palm trees lined the water's edge. Neons illuminated the signs on the building. Large letters read "Brutus' Palace."

Terra narrowed her eyes, thinking back to her history lessons. Julius Caesar, a dictator of the Roman people, had been stabbed to death in an operation led by Marcus Junius Brutus and Gaius Cassius Longinus. To her knowledge, the investors screwed out of building the original Caesar's Palace in Vegas owned this establishment. Bad blood spread between the greedy, and now this shining beacon of wealth was a monument standing to the real victor in that operation, a woman by the name of Prudence Tajarskin.

"Why only one name?" Terra mumbled, looking up at the shining "Brutus." She glanced to the right and saw a small annex of the building, where large glass panels jutted from the main building and formed the entrance to the restaurant. "Gaius' Gala" flickered in varying colors above the doorway, where two greeters stood in pristine white tuxedos.

"Solves that question," Terra stated.

She headed to the restaurant, feeling remarkably underdressed in her black tank top and leather jacket. She'd tied her hair back into a neat ponytail, and as she approached the two greeters, their welcoming facade remained, but their demeanor changed, plastic smiles fixed to their faces. "Welcome to Gaius' Gala," the greeter with a thick caterpillar mustache announced. "May we help you?"

"I have a reservation here," she replied. "Terra Kris, guest of Nora Asplin."

The greeters exchanged a look. "Apologies madame, but we adhere to a strict dress code here." He examined her casual combat pants. "Even with a reservation, we won't be able to let you inside."

Terra raised an eyebrow. "I'm sure you can make an exception." She glanced at the tablet held in the second greeter's hand. "Terra Kris and Nora Asplin. Look for the reservation."

Sweat pearled the second greeter's brow, although his smile remained. "I'm afraid that my colleague here is correct. It's all stated in your reservation confirmation. We have to keep up appearances here. I'm sure you understand."

Terra drew a deep breath. She became aware of the patrons waiting behind her, a small group of diners waiting for entry.

"Oh, I understand," Terra replied. "I think what you don't understand is that I don't care. I have a reservation here, and I intend to keep it."

A man who had been standing nearby, talking on his cell phone while holding a glass of champagne in his hand, turned away. Terra tracked him in her peripheral vision as he touched a finger to his ear and muttered something inaudible.

APRIL...

On it, APRIL replied.

The greeters muttered something that Terra didn't catch as the man's amplified voice met her ear. "We have a troublemaker at the front of the Gala. Requesting permission to remove."

Terra's skin bristled. *Troublemaker? They don't know the half of it.*

"Please step aside, ma'am," Mustache stated firmly, moving toward Terra.

Terra moved away from his grasp and raised her hands. "Fine. I'm sure that Nora Asplin is going to be happy that you sent away her dinner guest."

A seed of doubt appeared in the second greeter's eyes. Still, the first greeter moved ahead. "I'm sorry, ma'am."

The third man stepped forward, coming out of the shadows with a grim determination on his face. Terra sighed. *Really? Always conflict?*

APRIL. Identify.

Digital information appeared in her vision, identifying the greeters and the man by name. Graphs and charts showed their biological information including heart rate, medical history, and possible weak spots to aim for. Terra planted her feet, staring down the man as he approached her.

"What is going on here?" a familiar voice called from the glass walkway.

Terra hadn't noticed how imposing Nora Asplin was. She knew she was large but had only ever really seen the woman sitting. Now she was standing on full display, as tall as she was wide, her brow set and dark eyes boring into the staff.

"Is there a problem?" she asked.

Mustache straightened his spine. "Unfortunately, this guest doesn't adhere to the dress code. We're removing her from the premises, ma'am. Nothing to worry about."

"That guest happens to be *my* guest," Nora informed them. Her voice was commanding, an aura coming from her that sang authority. Terra enjoyed the wilting of the second greeter and the uncertainty on the man who had clearly been an undercover staffer in case of emergencies.

"She's fine as she is. If you'd like me to contact your superior, I can do that, of course. I'm more than happy to ensure that you're removed from your position and will never find another job on this island again." She turned her gaze to the others. "That goes for all of you."

The undercover staffer curled his lip, hatred pouring from his eyes.

"I didn't think so." Nora addressed Terra. "Come on. Let's get you fed."

Terra grinned, allowing Nora to lead on. She wondered how the woman could walk so quickly. The pair of them were soon in the center of the restaurant.

Terra spied empty tables and wondered when they were going to stop. To her surprise, Nora led her through the restaurant and toward a gleaming silver elevator. A woman in a sharp red uniform called the elevator and opened the doors. She stepped inside with them and requested their number.

"Sixteen," Nora replied.

The elevator started its ascent.

"Where are we going?" Terra asked. "I thought we were getting food."

"We are." Nora wore a smug grin.

The ride was silent for the most part. Terra felt the waves of heat pouring off Nora's body. When the uniformed woman opened the doors, Nora led them down an immaculate marble corridor. Glass doors with brilliant gold handles stood at the end. The woman moved in front, making room for them both to pass. On the other side of the doors was a small balcony complete with a table set for two.

Flowers hung in intricate displays, leaves spilling over the ledge. Terra looked down the sheer drop, able to see the plaza unfold before her. She was startled to discover that the water feature connected with the foliage and the ornamentation to create an image of a skull.

"Well, that's morbid," Terra muttered.

"That's Atlantica," Nora replied. "The owners can do what they want, and they do. The city and the law have no say in how someone may decorate their place. Private is private. Of course, you know that better than most."

Terra gave a small nod. Something akin to a gunshot sounded in the upper levels. Terra glanced up, narrowing her eyes at the other balconies. She was about to engage APRIL's scanner when Nora announced, "Take a seat. You don't need to worry about being on duty tonight. The evening is ours."

Terra frowned.

Nora motioned a hand at the empty seat. "Please."

Terra dropped into the chair. A clean white mug with a golden handle sat in place, black coffee steaming inside. "You knew my order." It wasn't a question. Terra wasn't surprised that this woman would be able to think three steps ahead of her.

There was something about Nora she couldn't put her finger on. A discomfort at feeling so exposed beneath the woman's gaze, yet also security in understanding that this woman was a force working for good.

Or, at least, she hoped.

Terra sipped her coffee. "That's damn good."

Nora grinned. "I'm glad it's to your liking."

"It's not poison, is it?"

Nora laughed, the sound rough, like a choking gas engine. "If I wanted you dead, I could've done that a long time ago."

Terra smiled, but something in the woman's voice made her think that was true.

"How would you have done it?" Terra asked.

Nora raised her eyebrows. "You want me to explain to you how I'd kill you?"

"Hypothetically, of course," Terra replied.

"Of course." Nora glanced down as the glass in front of her lit up. A rectangle of optics appearing on the table displaying the available menu of the restaurant. Terra's lit up too, although she chose to focus on Nora.

Nora scrolled through the items. "Well, there are many options."

"I meant my death, not the food," Terra interjected.

Nora glanced up. "Did you want me to answer or not?"

"Apologies." A chill prickled Terra's skin, although she was unsure whether that was from the breeze or the woman's gaze.

Nora adjusted in her seat. "There are a thousand ways to kill someone on this island, few of them very original. Of course, there's always the poison option. As you pointed out, I could've easily slipped something into your coffee to dispose of you. Then there's hiring an assassin, which is one of the messier ways to ensure someone's demise, given that there will be financial records tying the two together."

As she listed the possibilities, Terra couldn't help but marvel at her tone, as though she were simply reading the menu set out before her. As she spoke, she stabbed a stubby finger at the table, selecting her meal.

"Then you have to consider manipulation. It doesn't take much to turn friends against each other, make lovers turn to haters, and drive them to the point of murder. The human psyche is surprisingly fragile and malleable. I could've conditioned Imani to kill you if I chose." She exhaled a long sigh. "Then it's a case of getting someone onto private property to dispatch them outside the boundaries of the law."

Terra nodded, impressed. "A few nice options there, nothing too original."

Nora stabbed a finger on the table, selecting her final course. The screen showed a display of her options on a carousel, then faded to darkness. Nora leaned on the table. "Or, I could've chosen not to save you with that program inside your head."

Terra clenched her jaw. "You never said it was you."

Nora held her gaze. "Every hero needs someone to set their gears in motion. I've been watching you for a long time, Terra. I know you. I know your family, your history, your heart. When I caught wind of what had happened in that accident, I knew the time was nigh, and I knew that you'd be the one to handle it."

She sat back, eyes narrowed on Terra. "I was there, Terra. The day they installed that gear in your skull. I watched from the balcony, ensuring the doctors wouldn't let you bleed out on that table. I clasped my fingers and prayed for your recovery, knowing the possibilities that were at our fingertips if you could pull through.

"And you did." She smiled with a look of admiration. "Terra Kris, the ultimate supersoldier for the AJS." They held each other's gaze a moment longer before Nora nodded at Terra's menu screen. "Pick your meal. The staff won't bring mine out until you've ordered. I'm hungry."

Nora sat back and turned her attention to the view, the building snaking around the plaza like a giant horseshoe. Other guests sat on their balconies, raising glasses to the sky and enjoying the evening.

Terra wanted to ask more but knew how to play the game of conversation. She quickly scrolled through, choosing a Beef Wellington and a side of vegetables. When the confirmation screen showed her food, she attempted to pull Nora back into the moment. "You said you were there? Why? Why go through all of this trouble for me?"

Nora continued to stare out at the plaza. In the distance, the city howled and whined and sang, lights sparkling, car headlights snaking through the streets. "Because Atlantica is fucked."

Terra waited for her to continue.

"This place is a cesspool," Nora announced. "You know this. I know this. The fucking mayor knows this, but who's doing anything about it? No one. That's who."

Her brow set in a deep crease. "For years, I've been scouting for the best of the best from the AJS force. Those who could handle the force, but who also held onto their integrity like a life raft. Over the years, many have come close to fitting the bill, but they've all fallen at the final hurdle.

"You get to a certain status in the AJS, and crooks surround you, offering you more cash than you've ever seen in your life to turn a blind eye. I know. I've been there. I fell into that trap."

"You're a self-professed crook?" Terra asked.

"Was," Nora clarified. "I've made mistakes. We all have. The point is that this city is in major need of disruption if any change is going to occur."

Terra nodded. "I've known that for years."

"Yet, has anything happened?" Nora asked. "Has anything changed?"

Terra shook her head. The glass doors opened, and a team of servers entered, presenting perfectly curated meals on golden platters. They moved as if in a choreographed dance routine, the group stepping back into a perfect line, towels draped over their arms while a young woman with a Hollywood smile asked if there would be anything further they required.

Nora waved her away. The servers bowed, then left in single file.

Nora tucked into her meal as though she hadn't eaten in weeks. Gravy dribbled down her chin, and the sounds that came out of her mouth reminded Terra of pigs eating from a trough. It seemed strange how composed this woman could be, yet also how destructive. Terra prodded her meal with a fork, her stomach not yet demanding satisfaction. The questions were burning in her mind, and she wanted answers.

"I'm still struggling to understand." She tapped her temple. "How does all of this connect to the APRIL system up here?"

Nora looked up from her meal. She took a napkin and dabbed her face, cleaning the remnants of food away. "Believe it or not—"

"—not." Terra smirked.

Nora continued, "We put the APRIL program in place for good. The glasses have been deep in testing for many years to magnify the AJS support force. Several other investors and I birthed the program. We all came together in the name of justice for the city...or so I thought."

Nora sighed. "Early testing of the glasses showed the program as a success. With input from Deng Zenim's team over at Tynamo Inc, we were able to get a prototype off the ground. We fed the AJS database into the system and managed to get our first testers to use the equipment successfully.

"We celebrated. We clinked glasses and spoke of the positives that could come from this kind of technology. If officers didn't need partners out on the beat, we could double the AJS workforce."

Nora wrinkled her nose, eyes straying to the food she hadn't yet tackled. "But all good stories have their villains, and it didn't take long to realize that our little team of innovators had fallen subject to the city's poison. Late one evening, we met on a video conference to discuss the program and its next steps.

"One of us was missing from the call. Jim Elrod had been one of the most promising startup CEOs on the island, but it seemed that he'd gotten involved with some bad people, and someone found his body washed up on the riverbanks near this very spot."

Terra nodded, remembering the picture of the guy plastered across the front of the newspapers.

Nora shifted in her seat. A siren wailed in the distance. "That was the first hint that the group was falling down a dark path. The next came only a few weeks later when, at a charity fundraiser in the Upper East, I stumbled across another colleague from the project, Ludlow Kravitz.

"Kravitz had been drinking rather heavily, and I caught him running his mouth about the program to his friends. After pulling him aside and quieting him down, we got to talking. Turns out that Kravitz had been one of the highest donators to charity organizations on the island that year, a man whose total net worth towered over many, and here he was giving generous chunks of his wealth to the needy."

"Sounds like a great guy," Terra replied.

"You'd think." Nora scooped a mouthful of gravy-covered meat between her lips, then spoke as she chewed. "I certainly did. When the place began to empty, and as the cloud of liquor finally loosened his tongue, my hackles rose. There was a look in his eyes, a hunger that I only associated with crooks and assholes, and it seemed strange to see that in his gaze."

She swallowed, then drew another long breath. "I've always prided myself on judgment of character. Something was different here. It was only in the final throes of his slurred discussion that he let go, revealing a side of him that I'd not seen before.

"A darkness dwelled in his gaze, and he leaned closer, words barely audible as he unfolded his thoughts. Something as simple as, 'Just think. Soon they'll be eating out of the palms of our hands. Under our every want and whim.'"

Nora's shoulders softened, and she turned her gaze back to her food. "I didn't know what to take from that at first. I asked for more information, but none came. He fell asleep, lying there on the chair. I left, ordered someone to ensure he got home safely. After that day, things began to change."

"How?" Terra asked. "What happened?"

"Small things, at first," Nora informed her. "The investors grew more shifty. Their motivations moved from justice to income. Meetings became less frequent, and the program looked as though it would fall apart right at the moment when we were going to launch. I tried to speak to the other investors, but they closed down. There I sat, a silent powerhouse on one of the highest boards of the AJS, denied access to the very people supposed to be helping me with my cause."

"Sounds rough," Terra stated. "Unsurprising, though."

Nora nodded. Her plate was clean, and that seemed to upset her. "In short, they tried to push me out of the program—unsuccessfully, of course. At least contracts hold their sway in Atlantica, although there have been a few efforts to kill me along the way."

"So, this Ludlow…" Terra asked. "What's his position among this all? Is he still guiding the ship?"

"No. He left."

Terra raised an eyebrow. "He left?"

"Yep," Nora confirmed. "Took his leave and disappeared from the program. Stepped down without reason, providing only a statement confirming his resignation from the project."

Silence stretched between them. Terra's head hurt from trying to put the pieces together.

Nora read the discomfort in Terra's face. "It took me a while to stitch it together, too. In the beginning, him leaving was a blessing. The program rolled into testing phase. You were one of the first to trial the glasses, and you benefited greatly from their programming."

"It went wrong," Terra stated, understanding beginning to dawn. "Someone interfered. Took the program into their own hands."

Nora nodded. "The other officers have been fine with the program, working as they should, obedient soldiers to the AJS. But you...the one who's willing to break the mold and fight for *real* justice, not just *Atlantica's* form of what justice should be... you were a break in the chain. You exposed the truth."

"They tried to kill me," Terra stated flatly.

Nora's face hardened. "That's something we have in common."

She tugged down the collar of her top, revealing a severe rash of bullet scars just south of her shoulder. The skin was bright pink, puckered along its edges. For the first time, Terra noticed that she grimaced when she moved her arm. She waited for her to continue, but Nora was silent.

The servers returned to clear their plates. Nora thanked them, Terra offered a smile. The young woman informed them their menus would appear if they required them for desserts.

When they were gone, Terra spoke again. "This shit is big, isn't it?"

Nora nodded. "Ludlow has started a game he doesn't want to play with me. We must find him and bring him down before he can do more damage to the city."

Terra replied, "How do we do that? Where do we start?"

"That's the thing," Nora answered. "I don't know."

Terra frowned. "What do you mean?"

Nora glanced at the table. "I have no evidence to pin him down. Nothing. No clues, no tangible cues that point me in his direction. He's a ghost in the system, lost from all accountability and responsibility."

"How do you know it's him then?" Terra asked.

"Because I know," Nora replied. "Trust me."

"You have nothing to pin him?" Terra shook her head, wondering if this entire conversation was a complete waste of her time. "Zilch? Nada? Even I know you need some kind of evidence to track a man down and bring him to justice. That's *if* you're right."

"I'm right," Nora stated firmly.

Terra held her gaze, measuring the resolve behind her eyes. "Even if you're right, where do you propose to begin? I don't know if this needs stating, but I'm not heading off on some wild goose chase just for the sake of it. I'm no one's guinea pig."

Nora raised her eyebrows.

"The APRIL system is different." Terra deflated. "And something that I thank you for, even if it has caused me a shitload of problems since installing it."

"All of those problems have been triggered since Ludlow quit." Nora leaned back across the table. "Every problem, every murder attempt, everything has come since he left the group.

"What's more, only the original investors had access to the source code for the APRIL program, so it makes sense that he'd be the one to try and control you if you were running AWOL. You're the only threat to him. A renegade cop who's not afraid of stepping over the line. That would be his worst nightmare, don't you think?"

Terra considered this. "Say you're right. Say what you think you know is true. Where would we start?"

"To catch a criminal who doesn't play by the city's rules," Nora started, "you'll have to think like a justice officer who's unafraid of breaking the rules and playing their own game."

Terra's lips pressed together.

Nora reached into her pocket and drew a small business card. On the front was a logo that Terra didn't recognize. "I told you about The Executioners, Terra."

Terra nodded. "You did."

"Now I want you to go find one." Nora leveled her gaze at Terra, watching her as she flipped over the card and read the name on the other side.

"This is impossible."

"Nothing is impossible." Nora sat back, eyes narrowed.

Threat level: one hundred percent, APRIL's voice barked in Terra's head. **Protect Nora Asplin.**

Terra looked up from the business card, and her blood ran cold. A bright red dot showed on Nora's forehead.

CHAPTER THREE

"Nora! Get down!" Terra exclaimed as she stood quickly, arms fixed beneath the table, and flipped it into the air. The items on the table spilled onto the balcony floor. Glass smashed around them. The legs of the table rose higher as the table lifted.

A gunshot sounded, the bullet speeding toward them both. Terra watched Nora through the glass as if in slow motion. The other woman grabbed the golden placemat from the table and held it in front of her face. The bullet shattered the glass table, then *clinked* off the golden mat, falling impotently to the floor.

Terra swerved around the table, grabbing Nora by the collar. She spun, allowing APRIL to perform an initial scan of the surrounding balconies. Within the space of a second, APRIL had identified the person lying on the casino's roof. *Capture the information, APRIL.*

Affirmative, Terra.

Nora stumbled, trying to keep her balance. Terra pulled her with the hand that had the biotech, her metallic thumb gripping the material. Nora came after Terra, fumbling until they were out of the open. They headed inside the corridor where the servers stood, eyes wide, looking at them in shock and wonder.

Terra glanced back, assured that the gunperson couldn't get them from here. She turned to Nora, who simply shrugged. "Perks of the job."

"Getting fired at by assassins on rooftops?" Terra asked incredulously.

Nora chuckled, undeterred. "Not my first rodeo." She wandered past the servers and thanked them for their service. When she reached the woman at the elevator, she muttered something that Terra couldn't hear. The woman nodded and opened the elevator doors for them.

Terra moved inside and stood beside Nora. Her senses were still on edge. APRIL's scanner was doing its best to monitor the sniper as the doors slid closed and the metal cube began its descent. Terra noted that the woman hadn't joined them in the cabin this time.

The lights showed their progress, tracking the numbers on the panel as they channeled down toward the "1." When they neared, Terra took note of the fact that the elevator didn't slow.

The lights stopped, but the elevator continued its descent. She glanced at Nora, who stood stoically looking at the door. After another twenty seconds, the elevator stopped.

The silence was thick. Terra let a hand drop to her side, fingers brushing against her pistol. The doors slid open.

"Follow me," Nora instructed.

She walked fast. Terra was still surprised by the woman's speed. The corridor was all black marble, with nothing hanging on the walls and no defining features. A series of dull spotlights illuminated their way.

Nora shook her head. "Such a shame…"

"What?" Terra asked.

"I was looking forward to dessert." Nora sighed. "They do the most delicious strawberry panna cotta."

Terra couldn't help but grin. It felt nice to be with someone whose resolve wasn't easily shaken, even after publicly becoming the target of an unknown assassin.

"Who do you think that person was?" Nora asked. The corridor seemed to go on endlessly into the distance.

"I don't know," Terra replied.

"But you do," Nora returned, casting a knowing look at her.

Terra raised an eyebrow, for a moment almost forgetting the software built inside her head. *APRIL, assess the footage of the sniper.*

Assessing footage.

A small window appeared in Terra's vision, showing a recording of the dark figure on the rooftop. It moved in slow motion. Terra could only get a cursory glance as she fought to protect Nora. When the figure was in sight, APRIL zoomed closer, detailing a series of biometrics around the shooter.

Readouts of heart rate, body temperature, blood type, and more flashed and scrolled. A moment later, five names appeared around the gunperson's form. Terra noted them down, all of them men, none of them familiar.

"Like what you see?" Nora asked.

Terra processed the names, working them into her memory. "No standouts. Five possible matches. All men."

"I wish men would find other ways to hit on me," Nora quipped. "I guess I'll take what I can get. At least we're not looking at the Red Countess here."

Terra glanced down at the floor, careful not to give away her strange, if not strained alliance with Valentina Winters. It wouldn't help anybody if they knew that Terra had worked alongside the Red Countess on a couple of occasions now. She wondered if Nora knew of Valentina's interference with the APRIL system, how it had been the city's most notorious mercenary who had cut the ties to any interferers or onlookers.

"Why were they shooting at you?" Terra asked as the tunnel took a sharp right and the end came in sight.

"Could be many reasons. You think someone of stature and caliber in the city is protected at all costs? I'm not immune to the city. No one is. Rich, poor, whoever you are, you're all equally at threat."

"I don't even know what you do," Terra replied.

Nora grinned. "You don't need to. Just know that I'm an ally with influences at the AJS that are unseen but felt."

"Then why would you put yourself out in the open?" Terra asked. "If you're such an influence…if you're constantly under threat, why risk it?"

Nora stopped then. She turned to Terra and said something that caught her off-balance. "Because I have you."

Terra didn't know how to take that. It could've been a compliment. For Nora to feel safe in her company meant that she knew Terra could handle herself, no matter the situation. On the other hand, Terra's skin prickled at the idea of being simple body fodder, offered as a disposable tool to protect her.

Nora studied Terra. "Do you know how long it's been since I've been able to dine out in public?"

Terra cocked her head.

"Too long," Nora informed. "For years, I've been in hiding, doing my best to stay in the safe zones the city offers or linger out of sight. Tonight, I was able to enjoy a delicious meal on a balcony with a view over one of the most public places in the city. Well, as public as you can get while dining on private property. The point is, you made me feel safe. I knew I could trust you to do what was right when the moment came—*if* that moment came." She smirked.

Terra opened her mouth to ask a question, but Nora had walked ahead. Terra caught up. The tunnel opened into an underground parking lot. The floors were immaculate, the lights reflected off the smooth marble. High-end sports cars and pristine vintage vehicles littered the lot.

"What is this place?" Terra asked.

"All Atlantica's rich and powerful need a place to feel protect-ed." Nora strode over to a rich purple BMW with a custom, nano-hive black soft-top, the lights flashing as the doors unlocked. "This is a guarded parking facility. You pay a high premium for protection, but it's well worth it."

Terra raised a quizzical eyebrow. "Can't the guards be bought off too? Who's to say they're going to protect you if the money is right?"

Nora glanced her way. "You think like a true Atlantican. I knew we were right to trust in you." She climbed into the car, indicating that Terra should do the same.

The windows were thick, bulletproof glass. The console was state-of-the-art, with several dials and buttons that made no sense to Terra. Nora filled much of the front space, her mass spilling over to Terra and touching her sides. There was a smell of pine and leather in the air.

Nora thumbed a button. The car reversed by itself. "It's not only driverless cabs that can benefit from the self-drive tech." She smirked. "Sit back and enjoy the ride."

Terra remained quiet as the car silently and smoothly slipped out of the parking space. It carefully navigated its way to an entrance where several armed guards were standing. They nodded as Nora passed. The pair of them soon made it to street level some distance from Brutus' Palace.

As the city shrouded them and the car sped along the labyrinth of roads, Terra brought her attention back to the large woman beside her. Curiosity pounded in her head as she strug-gled to pull all the pieces together and understand her place in all of this. "You told me you felt safe. Why? I don't understand why me. Why do I have to go through all of this?"

Nora popped a stick of gum in her mouth and offered one to Terra, who politely declined. "Because you can. Because you've proven your heart is pure and that your priority is justice—*true* justice. Not the bullshit they rep on TV. It's a quality that we haven't seen in half a century, which is why you need to go and find the last living relic of a better time."

"The Executioner," Terra muttered.

Nora nodded. "Find him, and you might begin to understand your place in all of this." She motioned to the city. "The world shouldn't be like this. This place, this island, belongs to the damned, and it's in urgent need of rapture. As long as some injustice prevails, all justice suffers. You understand that, don't you?"

Terra nodded.

Nora continued. "You've been gifted with a power that you must use. That piece of silver in your head, it's your weapon. Forget the guns and the bludgeons and the other shit the AJS provides. *You* are the weapon, and now you need to be trained to believe."

The city slipped away behind them as they passed into the rural fields on the outskirts of the metropolis. Tall crops of corn swept by, the silver moonlight desperately trying to break the fog. The effect cast the world in a ghostly glow as Terra narrowed her eyes at the road flowing under the car.

"All I've ever wanted was a cleaner Atlantica," Terra mused. "From the moment I was able to formalize my first thoughts, I wanted justice. I was four when I first saw a man beat his wife in the street. I was seven when they tried to bully me for my lunch at school. All my life I've seen people suffer unnecessarily, their abusers walking the streets without any repercussions for their actions. I can't stand it."

Nora smiled. "You won't have to for long."

They passed a large lake on their left with several small rowboats docked at the shore. Terra gritted her teeth. "Where do I have to go? Where can I find this executioner?"

"That's a very good question," Nora replied with a coy smile.

"You have no idea, do you?"

"No. I've been searching for him for years. For all I know, he could be dead by now."

"Then how do you expect me to find him?"

Nora pointed at her head. "You have the power inside you."

Terra closed her eyes and drew a deep breath. It was odd, knowing that your head was filled with technology, considering that she felt no different from how she did before APRIL's installation. *APRIL, are you logging this information?*

Affirmative. However, I cannot search for an individual without any additional information. Please provide some basic intel, and I can narrow my search.

She opened her eyes and found Nora observing her. "What did APRIL say?"

"We need a name," Terra replied.

Nora nodded. "That's the only thing I do have."

Terra waited patiently.

"Ty," Nora offered at last. "Find me Ty Katakura."

CHAPTER FOUR

Terra stood at the bar, martini clutched in her hand.

Her nose wrinkled at the taste. The powerful perfume of the liquor and the burning feel of the drink slipping down her throat were awful. Still, something was satisfying in its intensity.

The bar was sparsely populated, only an extension of the guarded facility where she'd spent her days since being rescued from the rooftop of the manufacturing facility. A solitary barmaid served a man whose shoulder muscles bulged as large as his head. The tables were clean and white, the chairs were off-white, and the walls were cream.

How fucking clinical.

Music played at a steady volume, not so loud as to disturb the smattering of employees chatting and enjoying their after-work drinks. Terra felt uneasy, knowing that all of this was simply manufactured safety. Judging by what she knew about Nora, each staff member in this facility would have been thoroughly background-checked to ensure they were serving her purpose, but that didn't make Terra feel any more comfortable. Artificiality could make someone's mind warp, especially if artificial technology molded their minds—

"Whoa, who died?" Imani strolled up to join Terra at the bar. She had made a modest effort, wearing skin-tight leggings and a halter top in a shade of blue that brought out her eyes. She took Terra's glass and sniffed the contents. "Martini? Shaken or stirred?"

"Poured," Terra shot back, throwing a half-smile.

"A bit straight for a woman of your tastes, isn't it?" Imani asked. She held a finger up to the barmaid and ordered herself a grasshopper. "How's it sitting?"

"It's burning," Terra replied truthfully, feeling that hot sensation in the pit of her stomach. "But it's doing the trick."

"Helping you forget?" Imani asked.

"Not quite."

The barmaid returned with a bright green cocktail in a glass. Imani thanked her then sipped. "Mmm. Sour."

They stood together for a moment, casting their gazes around the room. The last time they'd been in a bar together seemed like a lifetime ago, back during a time when Terra had first worn the APRIL glasses. Despite the burden of slumming it in the outer city precinct, Terra's troubles had been half what they were now. She wasn't sure if she would be the target of an attack, which side she was truly playing for, or what the hell she had unearthed by handing Garcia over to the authorities. Now...

"We've dug up something big," Terra stated softly.

Imani nodded. "You have."

Terra glanced her way.

"It was all you, Terra," Imani offered. "As much as I wish I could take the credit, it's you who pulled the trigger—figuratively speaking. The things you've done to uncover this bullshit...and you made it happen. You brought Garcia to justice. You did what we planned, by yourself, taking no prisoners and making it happen."

Terra offered a weak grin. "It still doesn't feel like enough."

"Will it ever?"

Terra considered this. "No."

"Good." Imani smirked. "Then you're in the right business. Justice fighters can never be fully satisfied until the world is clean, and let's face it, that's an impossibility on the grandest scale."

"Then why do we do it?"

"To tip the scales," Imani stated. "It's a never-ending battle, but that doesn't mean we can't tip things in our favor and make it better for everyone involved."

Terra thought about this, eyes tracking a couple of drunken women in their mid-twenties twirling on the dance floor. "How did you get involved with Nora?"

Imani nodded. "You're starting to ask the right questions."

"Do I get an answer?"

Imani downed her drink, then winced. She ordered another. "Nora found me not long after the captain demoted you. A black car pulled up curbside and made me an offer I couldn't refuse. Despite my reservations, I couldn't hold back my intrigue, and I went with them, meeting Nora in an underground facility where she filled me in on her plight for justice."

"She told you about me? About my part in this grand game people seem to be playing?" Terra asked.

"No. She kept that from me until recently. I knew a larger game was afoot, but I didn't know your role. While you dominated the outer cities, I kept an eye on Garcia, doing what I could to provide intel to Nora and her team. It was only when your role became very clear through your pursuit of Garcia that they brought me into the fold."

Terra downed her martini. Imani gave an impressed nod. Imani ordered Terra another, despite her eye roll.

"Nora is good people, Terra," Imani stated when the drink made it back to Terra's hand. "We're in a position to make some real change in this city. Are you ready for it?"

Terra narrowed her eyes, thinking about all she had been

through since Garcia had demoted her to the outer cities. All the shit the city threw onto the front pages every day, all of the crap she had to deal with seeing, despite her best intentions to do good for the people of Atlantica. Her lips thinned as she gave a firm nod. "I am."

"Good." Imani set her drink down, then took Terra's from her hands. "That's the right answer."

She grabbed Terra's wrists and pulled her away from the bar. "What are you doing?" Terra asked.

Imani laughed. "What do you think I'm doing? I'm celebrating, you miserable bitch."

Terra, caught a little off-guard from Imani's sudden change in tone, found herself laughing back. "Excuse me? What have we got to celebrate?"

"The last night of true freedom," Imani replied. "Because from tomorrow morning, the moment that hangover kicks in, we're hitting the ground running, and there's no turning back. Take in tonight, let's have some fucking fun, and pretend like we're teenagers again. If not for you, then do it for me."

Imani's smile was contagious, bright white teeth beaming through her lips. Terra drew a deep breath, then shrugged. "I mean, I suppose I could. There's only one problem with your scenario though."

"What's that?" Imani asked as she reached the dance floor.

Terra tapped her head. "I don't get hangovers."

Realization dawned on Imani's face. "Double bitch."

Terra winked as they started to dance.

CHAPTER FIVE

Terra's headache lasted all of thirty seconds.

APRIL, stabilize biochemistry, please. She blinked, each flutter of her eyelashes pounding inside her head.

Stabilizing biochemistry, APRIL replied. A cooling sensation washed over Terra as she sat up in bed and blinked in the daylight. A soft smile grew on her face as a deep appreciation settled in, knowing that in her former life this hangover could have lasted hours, even days.

"I wonder how Imani is doing." Terra glanced around the walls. She engaged APRIL's scanner and made out the nondescript shapes of others in the building around her. She wondered which was Imani, if it was the shape curled up into a ball on her bed.

She rose from the bed then stretched. Outside, the world was hazy, the fog creeping over the canopy of trees and swaddling the building. At the end of the bed were Terra's clothes. She pulled them on, then headed downstairs.

There was a breakfast buffet waiting. Staying at this place was like staying in a hotel on vacation, which unsettled Terra. She wondered what was going on in the outside world, on the streets she used to patrol. She missed the bullpen, the stale scent of cigarettes and coffee. Somehow, despite it all, she missed Hewlett and Dunston.

A thought flashed across her mind. Now that they had caught Garcia, what had become of Gina and Spencer? She knew that Black had returned to her post, but had those two been taken into custody, too?

Shoveling down a bowl of granola and Greek yogurt, Terra readied herself for the day. She didn't know where to start with her search for this Katakura guy, but she knew the only way to begin was to get back into the thick of things. It was strange, though. There was an apprehensive knot in her stomach. She somehow knew that whatever she was about to do would cause an irreversible rift in Atlantica's fabric.

Her bike—her trusty old Ducati with its reliance on fossil fuels—was waiting for her outside. Familiarity warmed her heart as she straddled the seat and drew a long breath.

Footsteps sounded behind her. "You're leaving without saying goodbye?"

She glanced over her shoulder and laughed. Imani approached from the building. A pair of dark shades covered her eyes. She'd hunched her shoulders, and had one hand raised to shield against the additional light triggering her pounding headache.

"You look like shit," Terra offered.

Imani smirked. "Thanks. You look amazing."

"Thanks."

Imani brought her cup of coffee to her lips, wincing as the scalding drink burned her tongue. Attached to her side were her APRIL glasses.

"You taking those everywhere you go?" Terra asked.

Imani glanced down. "Perks of the job. They're useful for keeping an ear on what's going on in the city. Thanks to Nora, I can keep my job at HQ but take more time out to focus on 'higher priority objectives.'"

"Is that fancy talk for a promotion?" Terra asked.

"Kind of," Imani replied. "I'm not sure."

Terra chuckled, eyes narrowing up at the building where she imagined Nora to be. "What is it Nora does, anyway?"

Imani shrugged. "I wish I knew. She has pull inside the AJS, and that's all we need to know. As long as she can unlock certain doors for us, we're happy sailors." She sipped again. "Speaking of which, have you caught up with Black recently?"

Terra raised an eyebrow.

"Right," Imani replied. "You've been here." She tapped her temple. "Blame the hangover. I'm not on form today."

"Your fault," Terra stated.

Imani laughed. "You don't need to tell me." Her attention turned to the bike. "Are you still adamant on that as your choice of ride?"

Terra stroked the chrome exterior. "What's wrong with it?"

"People can hear you coming from a mile away, for one," Imani replied.

"Good." Terra smirked. "They should fear the approaching rumble of Terra Kris."

Imani shook her head. "Number two, it's a shitshow for the environment. We have better technology now, *cleaner* technology. The island is kind of famous for it."

Terra considered this. "There's something about the old world I like. It feels more grounded."

Imani moved closer, examining the bike. "You ever going to head out and see the wider world?"

Terra nodded. "One day. When my job is over."

"You can take a vacation, you know," Imani offered.

"I know. Rome and Paris and Nepal and Bangkok will all be waiting for me when I finish." She closed her eyes. "It'll be the road trip to end all road trips."

"Fair enough." Imani grimaced as she took another scorching mouthful of coffee. "In the meantime, where are you headed?"

Terra glanced at the road leading away from the building, the borders of the parking lot surrounded by electrified fencing, topped with barbed wire, the land outside dense with growing crops. "Into the city." She tapped her temple once more. "I have a scanner that's going to be pushed to its limits to find its target."

Terra roared through the streets, hunched over the bike, head low. The Ducati rumbled loudly, drawing disapproving glances from nearby and distant pedestrians.

The city swallowed her upon entry, great skyscrapers filling her peripheral vision. She loved this city, the architecture, the randomness of the designs, the atmosphere of multi-cultural belonging. It was because of this city that she yearned to travel and see the world. The buildings and people around her represented so many of its cultures. There was no set standard, no two buildings alike, and that, in her opinion, was a beautiful thing.

Cold air rushed through her hair. She flowed with the traffic, working her way closer to the center of the city, snaking beneath the suspended maglev train lines, past the inner city parks, around roundabouts with statues and decorations of fallen Atlantican legends.

APRIL, where's best to get this party started?

The nearest bar is two blocks east. Archie's was first established in 1999 and was one of seven bars built to celebrate the millennium, specializing in tequila—

I meant, where's the best place to scan and search for this Katakura guy? Terra interjected.

APRIL processed the request. On the sidewalk, a woman struggled to hold onto the eight leads filtering through her fingers as she walked several small to medium-sized dogs.

To boost the scanning range of the APRIL system, one must search for a transmission beacon powered by Atlanti-core technology. The nearest beacon of this kind is on top of the *Atlantica Gazette* building, four blocks north of your current location.

I'm currently heading south.

I'd suggest making a U-turn, APRIL replied dryly.

Terra looked around, checking the surrounding traffic. With a jerk of the handlebars, the bike skidded across the lanes, straightening in the alternate direction. She looked ahead to the towering glass construction on the edges of her vision and aimed dead ahead.

Massive block letters spelled *Atlantica Gazette* across the front of the building. Terra had a hate-hate relationship with the *Gazette*, her only dealings with Atlantica's primary news outlet being inquisitive journalists who tested the boundaries of the AJS caution tape. Too many times, she'd had microphones and Dicta-phones shoved into her face, forcing her to respond with the customary, "No comment."

Still, even with no official information to go on, the *Gazette* would always make its version of a story, amplifying a murder to scare citizens or destroying the few well-intentioned politicians in the city to protect their corporate board's agenda.

She pulled to a stop a short distance from the building and parked her bike at the curb. The sudden cut in noise was jarring. Terra strode over to the building and glanced up to the sky.

She couldn't see the top through the fog. The tower disappeared at its tenth floor, looking as though it would go on forever.

Are you sure about this? Terra asked APRIL.

Are you asking an artificial intelligence if they're sure about the inputted factual data in their system?

"You make a good point," Terra stated softly, eliciting a

concerned glance from a man in a three-piece suit strolling past. "How do I get up there?"

You could take the stairs, APRIL offered.

Terra narrowed her eyes. "Any alternatives?"

The elevator might suffice.

Terra sighed. "Fine. Let's do this."

She entered through the automatic glass doors into a squeaky clean foyer. There were several desks scattered around the entrance with staff dealing with different purposes. Terra strode straight toward the elevator, only pausing when a friendly voice called, "Can I help you, miss?"

Terra acknowledged the cheery man, his cherub face showcasing rosy red cheeks and gleaming white teeth.

Terra flashed her badge. "I'm with the Atlantica Justice System. I need access to your rooftop."

The man's cheery face didn't falter. "Is there a problem, officer?"

"I need to examine the transmission tower situated on top of the building," Terra replied. "It's in regard to a case I'm working on."

"Do you have a warrant?" the man replied, his smile still fixed to his face. The request was kind but well-trained. It wasn't unusual for Terra to meet this kind of resistance working with businesses. She was almost certain that standard training for most Atlantica-run operations involved ways to ensure that the AJS met with as much resistance as possible.

"I don't," Terra confessed. "However, the case isn't so much concerned with the *Gazette* as it is someone within the city. If you like, I'm happy for you or someone else to accompany me. I'm only requesting a brief visit and will certainly note your kindness and diligence with the Atlantica Justice System."

The man gave a firm nod. "Let me grab the access keys. I'll take you there myself."

Terra narrowed her eyes. "Just like that? You don't need to check with anyone first?"

The man chuckled, the sound warm and friendly. "Of course not. The *Atlantica Gazette* takes great pride in its recruitment process and ensures that all employees are trusted and respected for their choices."

Terra watched as the man reached into his lower drawer, a discomfort settling in her chest. It was like watching a brainwashed Stepford wife with a plastic grin.

He shuffled from out behind his desk, stomach grazing the edges of the polished wood. He barely blinked as he headed for the elevator and thumbed the button. They waited in silence until the cart arrived, then stepped inside.

Soft, easy-listening music played in the overhead speakers. Occasionally he glanced at Terra, offering a small nod and grinning. The elevator stopped in fits and starts along the way, letting some employees in and others out as it obediently carried its passengers ever skyward.

For the entire duration of the journey, the man smiled. His trained smile never shifted as the cart rose to twenty, then thirty, then forty floors. Terra glanced his way, wondering what could be going on in his head. Sometimes it was harder to get a person's true nature when all they showed was joy.

APRIL, scan for threats.

APRIL dutifully scanned the elevator, clocking a middle-aged woman with a severe bob and hooked nose, as well as the jolly man in the corner.

Threat level twelve percent. No immediate concerns.

Then why the twelve percent? Terra asked.

You're on private land in Atlantica. Twelve percent is the customary standard assigned with danger levels in these environments.

Sounds about right.

Terra examined the information surrounding the chubby

fellow. According to APRIL's data, his name was Warrington Ignito. She was surprised to find that he was in his forties. She would have pegged him for a man in his late twenties. As far as the system could tell, he had no outstanding convictions or any evidence of previous misdemeanors.

Terra gave an appreciative smile. It was rare to meet someone with a squeaky clean record in Atlantica. Still, that only made her more uncomfortable as the elevator emptied and the cart reached its inevitable end.

"Here we are," Warrington announced at last as the doors opened directly onto a set of grated metal stairs.

The stairs rose another level before stopping at a thick steel door. Warrington fumbled through a ring of keys, finally selecting the right one.

"No digital passes on this one?" Terra asked.

Warrington chuckled. "This building was erected decades ago. While most of the main occupied space has been updated over the years to meet the standards of the city, no one ever seemed to want to pay attention to the roof." He pushed the door open, and a gust of air greeted them both.

"I can see why," Terra stated.

The world around them was white. Great billows of blustering clouds swept around them, the dead spaces filled in by the hungry fog. She could see to the edge of the rooftop before her but couldn't see the other three edges. At her feet were cracked tiles and layers of dust and debris.

She slowly approached the edge of the building, cautious to keep Warrington's whereabouts in her mind. She looked out over the ledge and saw the glass and brickwork beneath her descend into a white pool of mist. There was something fantastical about it all, as though they were floating on an island in the middle of a snow-white sea. She wondered how long it would take for her to hit the ground if she were to jump.

Approximately twenty-three seconds, APRIL informed her.

Terra swallowed.

She turned back to find Warrington standing in the doorway, keeping a keen eye on her, keys in his hands.

"Like what you see?" Warrington asked.

She took a long breath. "It's breathtaking." She looked around. "Where's the tower?"

"Here," Warrington replied.

Terra narrowed her eyes, the hazy orb of the sun still bright in the sky, even if the fog was absorbing most of its heat. She glanced around, unable to make out the sight of any kind of tower that might be transmitting signals around them.

"Where am I looking?" Terra asked.

"In general?" Warrington replied, laughing at his own joke.

"Where's the tower?" Terra repeated.

"It's here." Warrington held his arms out. "The building *is* the tower."

"Oh," Terra replied. "I was looking for—"

"An ugly metallic contraption that looked like a miniature Eiffel Tower?" Warrington asked. "All of that went years ago. They installed the infrastructure for the tower in 2007. It's primarily gold wire, a series of transmitters based around the upper folds of the roof, and Atlanticore. Sophisticated stuff."

Terra raised her eyebrows. "Yet you couldn't upgrade the door?"

Warrington shrugged. "I just work here."

Terra strode around the rooftop. *APRIL, where's the best spot for you?*

Testing broadcast strength.

Terra heard a low-level hum in her head as a progress bar appeared in her vision. As she moved around the building, the bar pulsed higher and lower, indicating the hot and cold spots of the building. When she neared the southern-most corner, APRIL commanded her to stop.

Here. Scanning city. This may take a minute.

Terra fell to her knees as hundreds of images and details flashed before her eyes. She saw feeds from CCTV cameras. She heard the broadcasting of radio stations, she glimpsed images through people's webcams.

The onslaught was endless. It wasn't painful, but it was distressing as she struggled to focus on one thing at a time.

She closed her eyes, hoping that would rid her of the images, but still, they played behind her lids, scrolling and scanning as APRIL soaked up as much information as possible about the current state of the city.

Finally, as Terra felt nausea rise in her stomach, the images stopped.

She opened her eyes, unsure when she had rested on all fours. Her breath was labored. Sweat peppered her brow. "What the hell, APRIL?" Terra asked.

Apologies, Terra. Stabilizing biochemistry now.

The nausea dissipated in an instant, but it took a few moments for her breath to recover. Terra gently shook her head. "I hope that was all worth it—whatever that was."

APRIL confirmed it was. **While there are no solid records or data points for Ty Katakura, I located the most recently sent message regarding a character of his name.**

"What do you mean—" Before Terra could finish, a message popped up in her vision.

Agreed. On my way to Harper's House. Katakura assures me he'll be there.

"Who sent that?" Terra asked.

Harmony Erron, APRIL answered. **Relation to Katakura, unknown.**

"When was it sent?" Terra asked.

Three days ago.

"That leaves us with a cold trail," Terra replied. "Are you sure there's nothing else?

Last populated records stand from the 1990s. It appears

that, after that time, Katakura disappeared from all public records.

"Even in the city archives?" Terra asked.

City archives hold Katakura's name, date of birth, and birth location. The name has an old residence filed. However, security footage accessed in the broadcast shows no traces of Katakura remaining in that location.

Terra shook her head. "We're hunting ghosts."

Ha. Ha. Ha.

The laugh took Terra by surprise, each syllable perfectly monotonous. "What's so funny?"

You made a joke, APRIL stated.

"I didn't," Terra replied, confused. "How did I?"

According to his records, Katakura is ninety-three years of age. The joke is that, because he is old, he will soon be a ghost himself.

Terra raised an eyebrow. "They need to work on AI humor."

Did I get the intonation incorrect?

"Yes," Terra replied with a chuckle, processing what APRIL had told her. "Hold on. He's ninety-three?"

"Having fun talking to yourself?" Warrington asked from behind.

Terra turned quickly, momentarily forgetting he was there.

"Nearly done?" he asked. "Only, I have some work to be getting on with, and I think your favor has expired now."

Terra offered a warm smile. "Yes, thank you."

"Who were you talking to?" Warrington asked as they headed back to the stairs.

"Oh, you know…" Terra replied. "The voices inside my head."

For the first time since she'd met him, his smile faltered.

CHAPTER SIX

Terra dabbed at the corners of her mouth with the napkin and cleared off the last of the grease.

It felt good to be back in the city. Although her senses stayed heightened, always on the lookout for anyone who might be out to get her, she'd enjoyed a brief moment of distraction at the sandwich place as she tucked into a grilled cheese and ham panini.

She exited the diner and aimed for her bike. A man stood next to the Ducati, bent over and examining the paintwork.

"Can I help you?" Terra initiated the scan with APRIL.

Threat level thirty percent. Prior convictions across several felonies including arson, robbery, and grievous bodily harm.

"Thing of beauty, ain't she?" the man offered, straightening. He was attractive, with a flashy smile and a mystery behind his dark eyes. He wore a leather jacket and Terra noticed dirt beneath his fingernails. "She yours?"

"She is," Terra replied.

"Don't get them like this much no more," the man stated. "It was a better time. Much better time."

"Back when the world was in desperate need of cleaning up its act before the world imploded in a cloud of carbon dioxide?" Terra responded.

The man blinked stupidly, then held out a hand. "Karl Thompson."

Terra saw the legend in her vision detailing his name, "Roger Shellows."

Terra ignored his hand. He retracted it and shoved them back in his pockets. "As I was saying, a fine ride."

"It is," Terra replied. "She's not for sale."

The man held her gaze, the pair measuring each other up for a moment. He finally turned. "See you around."

Terra waited until the man had rounded the corner, eyes narrowed. When he was gone, she asked, *What was all of that about?*

APRIL replied, **Roger Shellows was placing a bomb beneath your seat**.

Terra took a step back, looking at the bike. There was no sign of tampering—at first. As she looked closer, she made out the small strokes of grubby fingers against the polished metalwork. APRIL enhanced the scan to reveal a small device planted beneath the leather.

What do I do? Terra tried to act natural as citizens walked behind her, oblivious.

Remove the seat so I can get a closer look.

Is that safe?

Affirmative.

Terra wasn't sure how APRIL knew, but she'd learned to trust the AI by now. She carefully lifted the leather cap of the seat, displaying a small hollow where she could normally store items. There it was, plain as daylight. A tiny makeshift bomb was fixed to the base by a series of strips of masking tape.

"Holy…" she breathed.

Analyzing detonation device, APRIL stated, and for a few heart-stopping moments, Terra simply stared and watched as the world wheeled by around her. For all she knew, the device could be on a timer, designed to go off at any moment. Movement, speed, or a remote detonator could trigger it. The longer she stood and stared at it, the more chance there was that she would find herself back in the hospital, her second explosion in as many months. Fire and white flashed before her eyes, the ghost of her last so-called "accident." She wondered if they could replace her entire brain with AI should she lose it all in another incident…

Analysis complete.

Terra waited. *Well?*

Detonation device is remote controlled. A small node—the grey bump on the right-hand side is the receiving device. Removal of the receiver will remove any immediate concerns for detonation.

APRIL's calm, centered, robotic voice was unnerving. It was as though it was telling Terra how to pluck a rose from its stem.

Terra reached for the receiver.

Careful, APRIL warned. **There's a grey wire. If separated from the main body of the device, it will also trigger the explosion. Deft hands, please.**

My hands are your hands, Terra stated. *Can't you help in some way?*

Terra reached forward, her hands steady, but the heat of the situation bringing out the sweat on her forehead. Chatter came from behind, pedestrians strolling past in conversation, some on their phones. Traffic hummed around her. She didn't want to raise the alarm, but she also became aware that if something went wrong, it wouldn't be only herself in danger.

Her fingertips brushed the little bump APRIL had detailed. Under the shadow of her hand, she noticed a tiny green blink of light. The metal of her thumb *clacked* on the casing.

Pinch, then rotate counterclockwise.

Terra obeyed, gaining friction, then twisting the piece of the device. It was stiff at first, then yielded beneath her grasp. After a couple of twists, it freed from the casing and pulled away to reveal a copper wire leading into the device.

Now cut the line.

With what? Terra asked.

Anything, APRIL replied.

Helpful.

Terra glanced around, unable to find anything nearby that was sharp. She glanced back at the device, craning her neck to see where the wires led. *Can't I just pull it free?*

You can try.

Terra sighed. *You understand that I can't read nuance in your voice, so if you're being sarcastic here, it's highly unappreciated.*

You asked a question. I gave you an answer.

You sound uncertain.

I thought you couldn't understand nuance?

Terra growled, exclaiming, "APRIL."

A woman crossing the road shot Terra an odd look, then gave her a wide berth as she passed behind her.

You can try pulling the wire, APRIL explained, **because I see no reason why withdrawing the cable should trigger the explosive device.**

A digital layout of the blueprint of the bomb appeared in Terra's vision. **Here, does this help?**

Actually, it does. Terra studied the picture, getting familiar with each piece of the puzzle and seeing what connected to what. Although she was certainly no Valentina Winters when it came to technology, she was logical by nature. She'd spent enough time on the force to gain a little understanding of homemade detonation devices and how they worked.

More confident than before, she yanked the wire. She closed her eyes, bracing for a possible impact, but was thankfully surprised to find that nothing happened.

Step one, complete.

Terra examined the piece of cable and receiver in her hand, then pocketed the item.

Okay, so what do I do with the rest of it? Terra asked.

APRIL ran a second scan. **My suggestion would be to get it somewhere safe for deconstruction. Wrap it up in something that will reduce the knocking and stresses as you re-mount your cycle. Then you should be fine for short distances.**

Why short distances? Terra asked.

Bombs are always unpredictable. The myriad factors which could lead to detonation of the device are incalculable.

Great, Terra thought as she wrapped the detonation device into the folds of her jacket, praying that it would be soft enough to keep her safe. She remounted her bike, then kicked the engine into life.

One more note, APRIL stated.

What? Terra signaled and turned into the traffic as she headed toward her next destination.

Your motorcycle fails the efficiency provision policy put into action in the city of Atlantica in 2019. The reduction of fossil fuels is not only beneficial for the planet but there are also more efficient methods of travel. Some which reduce noise pollution, as well as overall pollution, while also increasing the efficiency of...

Terra twisted the throttle, the noise drowning out APRIL's sentence. *But can the other vehicles do this?*

The bike lurched forward. The front wheel rose off the ground, wind careening past Terra's face. Adrenaline surged before being dampened by APRIL. Terra beamed from ear to ear.

Yes, APRIL stated at last. **Yes, the other vehicles can do that. Not the noise, but the wheelie.**

Terra rolled her eyes. *You know, for an artificial intelligence software bound with the biological matter inside my skull, you're not very fun.*

CHAPTER SEVEN

Terra slowed as she pulled up to the precinct.

The foot traffic was light, but several familiar faces stalked the building. Terra had always admired the electric blue uniform of the Atlantica Justice System. There was something powerful about the form-fitting suits and the electric blue design that gave her a feeling of authority. She missed it, being kitted out as one of the AJS, considering the last few weeks she'd had.

She parked the Ducati, then drew a deep breath. She dismounted, grabbed her jacket, and strolled across the clean brick pathway toward the entrance. The sun was beginning to set, and pinkish-orange streaked the sky behind the haze.

A couple of officers passed Terra as she hopped up the steps to the doorway. They gave a small nod of acknowledgment but avoided her gaze. It threw Terra back to her first days of school after taking down one of the apex bullies who had roamed the halls. Betty Dross, a seventh-grader with bad acne and an even worse attitude.

Terra had watched from afar as Betty had cornered yet another sixth-grader and scared the life out of him during lunch break. The boy was minding his own business and eating breadsticks with cheese spread by the library when Betty and her minion, Susan Bertrum, had loomed over him.

Terra studied the situation through narrowed eyes. She knew how these normally played out. With no teachers around to intervene, the voice in her gut that had guided her half her life told her what to do.

It was when Betty started socking it to the boy that Terra jumped in. Utilizing a hold she had learned recently in her martial arts class, she pinned Betty to the floor, wrist behind her back, strained to the point of nearly breaking. She had been concerned that Susan might join in to save her, and with Betty calling for Susan to help, it had been a real possibility. However, with Betty down, Susan had no cover to help her. Susan ran away, disappearing into the science block while Betty grumbled and ate asphalt.

A small crowd formed pretty quickly, as it so often did in school. By the time the teachers came, Betty was in floods of tears, her face scratched and reddened by the ground.

Terra received two weeks of detention. Betty got four.

When Terra arrived at school the next day to begin serving her punishment, there was a strange atmosphere around her. A mixture of respect and fear followed where she went. Kids ducked to avoid her while some patted her on the back.

This was very much like that moment. Terra had taken down a key officer, after all, bringing Garcia in for the injustices he had brought on the city. She had exposed corruption under a floodlight. There were many in the world who, even when presented with the facts, didn't like the change that brought in its wake.

Terra had proven herself.

Some didn't like that.

She strode through the halls, taking in the familiar scent of stale coffee, sweat, and cleaning products. She made her way toward the bullpen, past boards filled with flyers and notes from staff and local businesses. Terra looked through the glass at the desks, some computers abandoned, others with officers hard at work.

She saw her desk and was strangely glad to see that it was as she'd left it. Her photo of her parents stood next to another snap of Skooch. Her heart ached at the memory of her dog, and she hoped that her parents were taking good care of the fluffy ball of life.

As she turned along the perimeter of the bullpen, she heard two familiar voices behind her.

She glanced over her shoulder, catching Hewlett's eye. He turned toward her, but she didn't slow. Instead, she made straight for Black's office. She couldn't be bothered to deal with the pair today. She was sure that Hewlett and Dunston would have nothing of value to add to her day, and she had places to be.

Her hand gripped the small package in her pocket.

Black's door came into sight. She pulled her hand free and reached for the handle, then withdrew when the door opened from the other side. She stepped back as another familiar face came into view.

"Well, well," Tommy Vincenzo stated. He looked tired. There were dark smudges around his eyes, and he seemed to have aged over the last few weeks.

"Excuse me." Terra made a move to slide past him.

Tommy stood firmly in her way.

Terra sighed, then took a step back. "Can I help you?"

Tommy examined her closely, seemingly seeing her for the first time. A pregnant pause hung in the air, his eyes giving nothing away of his thoughts. Finally, he extended a hand to Terra. "Good work, Kris."

Terra shook it. "Thanks."

Tommy nodded. "You've always had that annoying quality about you."

Terra cocked her head. "What do you mean?"

"The quality of getting things done," Tommy replied. "No matter the cost."

"You say that like it's a bad thing."

"No." Tommy shook his head. "I mean, it's annoying as shit when you get partnered with you. I've always respected that. Taking down Garcia...man. Who saw that coming?"

"I did. That's the whole reason I'm here."

Tommy smirked. "So, what are you still doing here?"

Terra considered this. It was a question she'd been asking herself. What was she going to do when this was all over?

"I'm not here," Terra replied at last. "I came to see Black."

Tommy glanced over his shoulder. "All yours." He sidled away, stopping only a few feet from her. "Hey, Kris?"

Terra turned.

"You keep strong." Tommy turned and headed off down the hall.

Terra returned her attention to the doorway, then let herself into the reception.

She wasn't sure what to expect when she arrived. So much had changed over the last few weeks that it was impossible to see the road ahead. She was unsurprised to find Gina sitting at the reception desk, straightening some papers. What she was surprised to note was the surly aura that exuded from the woman.

Her dark eyes studied Terra.

"Gina," Terra acknowledged, remembering the small snippet of information Slim had given her before they last parted ways. According to Slim, Gina had been screwing Black's temporary replacement, which seemed highly out of character for the smiling receptionist.

"Terra," Gina replied dryly. "Do you have an appointment?"

Terra shook her head. "No. I do have a bomb." She pulled the detonator from her pocket and unfolded her jacket to reveal the rest of the small device.

Gina's expression dropped as Terra continued through, not waiting for permission before entering the corporal's office.

Leonie sat at her desk, face illuminated by the bright screen of the computer. She was still a little worse for wear, with the bruises and lacerations on her face from her encounter with Cross still healing. It would take some time, Terra knew, and some of those cuts would likely scar, but at least the corporal was alive.

"Back where you belong," Terra stated. Black hadn't turned to see who had entered the room.

Black sat back from the computer and rubbed her tired eyes. The main lights were off—as usual—and Terra wondered why Black preferred the gloom of a cavern over the bright artificial lights of the rest of the building. She grasped an empty coffee cup in her right hand and shook her head. "You ever find yourself struggling to get back into the zone? Like, you go on holiday for a few weeks, and when you come back, it's difficult to re-settle?"

Terra thought about this. She sat in the chair across the desk. "I've never been on a proper vacation. Maybe a couple of days here and there for bachelorette parties and family gatherings, but that's about all." She glanced at her feet. "Besides. I'm always doing what I love. Why take a vacation from your true purpose?"

Black chuckled. "What brings you to my dank corners of the world? I thought you were in hiding?"

Terra glanced at the door as if a terrorist might be about to kick it in and gun them both down. "About that..." She took the device and placed it on the table.

"What's that?" Black asked.

"A bomb," Terra replied casually.

For a moment, there was humor in Black's eyes until she tracked Terra's gaze and saw that she wasn't joking. "You're serious?"

Terra nodded.

Black thumbed the button for the intercom and requested

Gina enter. Gina appeared as a silhouette in the doorway. "Could you run this down to the disposal squad, posthaste?"

Gina gave a cautious huff, then took the bomb carefully in her hands.

"Don't worry, it's not likely to explode from heat," Terra commented.

Gina glared at her then left the room.

Terra shook her head. "You'll get no heat from that frigid bitch. Honestly, what's up with her?"

"I was going to ask you that question," Black replied.

"Why me?" Terra asked.

"Slim told me to," Black stated.

Terra smirked. "In short, I think she had a thing going with your temporary replacement."

"Spencer?" Black asked.

"Mmhmm," Terra replied.

"Eww." Black frowned.

"I know." Terra sat back and folded her arms. "How you doing, Corporal?"

Leonie pinched the bridge of her nose, then rubbed her eyes. She detailed the struggles of getting back into work, feeling like there was constantly someone out there watching her while she roamed around the office. Ever since her return, she didn't feel safe and trusted the higher-ups even less than before.

"Now we have this." She waved at the corner of the room and the pile of cardboard boxes precariously stacked atop one another.

The boxes were nondescript, with only a white packaging label on the side. Terra asked what was inside.

"Go take a look," Black suggested.

Terra wandered over. The top box was open, the lid flap standing at an angle. She brought the box down and examined inside, finding several smaller white boxes stacked neatly.

She sighed. "Really?"

Black nodded. Terra took out one of the boxes, recognizing the logo and the images on the side, which read APRIL.

"Glasses for the whole department," Black stated. "Despite the reservations of several officers, the program is being rolled out city-wide. Since your exposure of Garcia, central is looking to monitor the force more closely, ensuring that the AJS is working to its best capacity and multiplying our capabilities by allowing officers to go solo with the glasses on smaller cases."

"Fuck," Terra murmured, turning the box over in her hands.

She thought back to her first time receiving this package when she acted as a test run for the program. She wondered what the ramifications of this would mean. Did she now have more officers to watch out for if she needed to go rogue? Would this be good for the city by increasing the AJS's reach? So many questions...

"What're you thinking?" Black asked.

Terra shrugged. "I honestly don't know. This is Pandora's box. I know my experience with them wasn't great, but that doesn't mean officers couldn't benefit from the technology."

"I'm sensing a but," Black stated.

Terra thought a moment. "What happens if the technology gets into the wrong hands?"

She let the words linger. She'd been a victim of that herself. She was wary of the creators and investors of her software, and here they were deploying the glasses to the entire force.

Black gave an understanding nod. "The potential for good or bad is enormous. Unfortunately, my authority in these matters is limited. All I can do is keep an eye on what's going on and pray that we do good unto the city." She drew a long breath. "Speaking of...I have a mission for you."

Terra raised an eyebrow. "I didn't realize I was back on active duty."

"You're not." Black grinned. "Well, sort of. Since you're here, there is a matter that could do with your attention. Something I wouldn't ordinarily ask my officers on duty, but since you're currently treading that fine line and under the cautionary gaze of Miss Asplin…"

"You know Nora?" Terra asked.

Black placed a finger to her lips and nodded.

"What the hell does that woman do?" Terra asked.

Black chuckled. "I'd advise you don't walk that path. It's not one you want the answers to. Suffice to say that I'm aware of the protections she grants you. I need someone to go deeper than an officer usually can, if you understand my meaning."

Terra chewed her lip, knowing that she had a mission to complete but also drawn in by curiosity. "What have you got?"

"Something that could save a great number of lives," Black stated. "You in or out?"

Terra steeled her expression. "In."

"Good." Black smiled. "Welcome back, Officer Kris. Let's get you kitted up and ready for active duty."

CHAPTER EIGHT

Terra had never seen the angled storm shelter door at the back of the building.

Hidden by a thick cluster of bushes, Black led Terra around the back and sidled toward the entrance.

"What are you showing me?" Terra asked.

"You'll see." Black crouched and unlocked the doors with an eight-digit code. Something *hissed* inside, and one of the doors hinged open on a set of hydraulics.

"Follow me." Black headed down a set of stairs and into the darkness.

Terra did. When she was clear of the doors, they closed behind her, a small *beep* indicating that the locks were clicking back into place. Several LED lights came on as they descended a metallic staircase. Black led confidently ahead, the sound of their footsteps crashing around them. Terra had been down several secret bunkers in her lifetime, but she never expected to see one beneath the lowly precinct she'd been at for several months now.

Black stopped at a thick, steel door. She thumbed another eight-digit code, then stood still for the retina scan. Once it verified her, the door nudged open and allowed them entry.

Terra tilted her head as a sound reached her that seemed impossible. She couldn't make out why it would be down here, behind all of these barriers. Another few yaps made Terra pause as something small and yellow sprinted toward her.

The dog leaped into Terra's arms. She gasped, clutching Skooch around her middle and bringing her to her chest. Skooch eagerly lapped Terra's cheeks, eyes, and lips. She laughed, closing her eyes against the sudden attack. "Skooch, calm down. Yes. Yes, it's mama. Hi."

She crouched, placing the dog on the floor. Skooch skittered around her, jumping up and attempting to cover her face with affection again. Another set of sounds caught her attention, and as she looked up into the doorway, tears came to her eyes.

Marie and Michael Kris stood in the doorway, with Michael's arm around his wife's waist. Terra beamed, then ran over to them both. The three embraced as she allowed a few hot tears to dampen her father's chest.

"How you doing, sweetie?" Michael's voice was like sweet toffee to her ears.

Terra didn't reply. She hadn't realized how much she had missed her family until this moment, thanks to the craziness of the last few weeks. She squeezed them until she felt she'd finished, then took a step back.

Marie offered a warm smile. "Your father asked you a question, hon."

Terra chuckled. Skooch leaped at her ankles. She scooped her up. "I'm better now. What are you doing here?"

Michael cocked a thumb over his shoulder. "Black brought us in when all the fuss kicked off with your buddy, Garcia. AJS thought it best that we be removed from harm's way, considering the crowds you've got yourself mixed up with." He shook his head, the smile not fading from his face. "I always knew you'd end up kicking the wrong hornet's nest."

Marie elbowed him gently in the side. "The *right* nest, dear.

The bigger the nest, the more worthwhile the cause. What's the point in dealing with the lower-level stuff when you can shake the whole system, eh?" She winked at Terra.

Terra chuckled. "Right, Mom."

"Well, don't just stand there," Marie stated. "Come inside. We've not had company in some time. It's great to see another friendly face."

They ushered Terra inside the bunker, closing the thick door behind them. Skooch rushed inside, sprinting around the room excitedly.

The place had everything they'd need to survive for some time. There were small rooms sketched out in the large space with no dividing walls except for a bedroom and a bathroom. A large fridge hummed in the kitchenette. There was an area with a pool table, a ping-pong table, and a large TV fixed to the wall. While there was no aerial to connect to the outside world, there was a stack of Blu-Rays of films Terra hadn't watched since she was a kid.

"They take care of us," Marie explained.

Terra shook her head in disbelief. "I don't understand. What is all this? How are you down here?"

"Simple," Michael replied. "One of the perks of working for the AJS all these years. Your friend, Miss Roberts, sorted out a hiatus for me, so I'm technically on a 'paid sabbatical.' As for your mother…"

"I've accrued plenty of holiday time over my years," Marie took over. "Even so, I'm not far off retirement, so what does it matter in the end? I can pick up my pension if I need to. The lives of my family are more important to me than all the money in the world."

Terra felt a wave of appreciation wash over her. "I love you guys."

"We love you." Marie threw a cheeky grin at Michael.

"As much as I hate to break up the family reunion," Black

announced from a door at the back of the room. "We do have some business to pay attention to."

Terra reluctantly excused herself and crossed to Black. Leonie held the door open for her, then thanked Michael and Marie.

Michael announced, "I thought you were finally going to show *us* what that door leads to?"

"Not in your lifetime." Black grinned.

She closed the door behind them, shutting out Michael, Marie, and Skooch. Black studied Terra. "Emotional return?"

"I wasn't expecting that," Terra replied softly. "I'm sorry, give me a minute to compose myself." Her face felt warm with cheeks flushed red from the reunion.

"We needed to keep them safe," Black commented. "After all that went down out there with Garcia, we knew the main ammunition anyone coming after you would have would be your family. They're here, and they're safe. It was a struggle getting them here in the first place, despite what they say, but at least they're out of harm's reach."

"I don't get it," Terra replied. "What is this place? How did I not know about it? I knew we had safe houses, but one directly under the AJS precinct? Are you kidding me?"

"It's new," Black admitted. "Truth is that this was mostly an abandoned storm shelter which we occasionally used to store old stock. Asplin sorted us out with state-of-the-art facilities and created something of a treasury for your path ahead."

Terra frowned. "Hold on. How did Asplin know I'd come here?"

"She's a great read of character. She *knows* things. Don't ask me how."

"Seriously," Terra exclaimed, "what the hell does that woman do?"

Black laughed, then swept by her, ignoring the question. She jangled a set of keys as she approached a door painted black. She slotted the key inside the lock, then turned it before craning her head forward for another retina scan.

"I hope you have backups," Terra replied. "If you die, what happens to this facility?"

"Don't worry, your retinal information is in the system," Black replied. "Failing that, your APRIL has a built-in frequency system that can unlock it."

Terra unconsciously touched her head.

"I'm kidding," Black replied. "Man, you are shaken."

"Wouldn't you be?" Terra shot back.

"If that rattled you, wait until you see what we have in store for you." Black shoved the door open. Lights burst into full brilliance, illuminating what appeared to be a large walk-in wardrobe. Only its contents weren't limited to clothing.

"You're kidding me…" Terra breathed.

She glanced around at the array of items. Contrasting against a bright white wall was an AJS uniform in all its electric blue glory. Hanging beside it was a series of dark metal plates she'd never seen before. A thin chest plate showed a triangular panel in the center that almost looked like a screen of some kind. Dark boots, a utility belt that wasn't standard issue, and a thigh strap for additional weapons completed that selection.

On the adjacent wall was a series of firearms. Everything from pistols to assault rifles to what looked like a rocket launcher and a sniper rifle hung on display. Terra shook her head in disbelief. "This isn't your standard welcome packet, is it?"

Black stood beside her. "This is your new uniform, Officer Kris. AJS tactical division, a brand new arm set up for you and you alone. Asplin wanted you kitted with the best and sourced the finest items to help you on your quest." She scoffed. "I'll be honest. I'm pretty jealous."

Terra glanced at her. "You're not serious?"

"Not really," Black replied. "Those days are behind me, I think.

I'm much keener to run the control panels and instruct my officers to do what they need to in the field."

She pointed at the AJS uniform. "The uniform looks standard but is fitted with the latest-grade nano-hive technology to protect you from gunfire. Each visible hexagon has a hundred more hexagons inside with technology to inflate and buffer against bullet wounds and stab attempts. There's also a string of internal wiring and hardware that will sync with your APRIL AI unit and provide a clearer overview of your vitals and body readings so you stay protected in the field."

"Holy shit," Terra marveled.

"There's more." Black brought Terra closer to the black plates that were hanging near the uniform. "That chest plate is also a centralized computer. It links to your AI and will allow a boost in protective reactionary speed while you're on the field. APRIL will synchronize seamlessly with the hardware—I'm told."

Terra reached out and took the plate off the wall. She brushed her fingers over the cold metallic surface, eyes sparkling.

"Try it on," Black instructed.

Terra brought the plate over her head, sliding her arms through the straps. She positioned the plate in place, then stared down at the black screen.

She waited for something to happen.

"How do you get it started?"

"Ask APRIL," Black replied.

Terra raised an eyebrow.

Black nodded at the plate, waiting.

Terra thought, *APRIL, activate scan.*

Vibrations coursed through Terra's chest. The screen illuminated, displaying a digital image of a diamond that dissolved into a series of spotlights before reforming. The diamond spun, then faded as the words "APRIL systems" appeared on the front.

It took a second for Terra to realize what the vibrations were. When she understood that APRIL's reply wasn't coming from her head but projected from the chest plate instead, she stepped back and stared in wonder.

"Activating scan," APRIL announced.

Hearing APRIL's voice out loud was strange. Ever since she had first used the technology, the replies had been inside her head. Now, she glanced over at Black, who looked at her in fascination.

"Scan complete," APRIL declared. "No immediate threats in the vicinity. One ally. Corporal Leonie Black."

"Well, at least it can tell that I'm not a threat," Black replied.

That took Terra aback. She looked around at the walls, taking stock of all the toys on offer. "Are you sure this is all for me?"

"Who else would it be for?" Black asked without humor or irony. She moved in front of Terra. "You've been given a gift here. You have a shot to do everything the founders originally built the AJS for. All of this is yours to utilize and ensure that we're invoking justice—real justice—on this island."

Terra thought about this, then gave an affirming nod. She looked up at the uniform, suddenly excited to dress head-to-toe in the electric blues she had grown up admiring and had worn proudly every waking day of her adult life. She allowed her disbelief to sift away as she embraced what was before her, spurred on by the belief of her family and friends and the equipment provided.

She remembered a quote she had once read in a book. *Be the change you want to see in the world.*

"Okay." She took the uniform off the wall. "Let's do this."

CHAPTER NINE

Terra waited with her parents until the cover of darkness.

Marie warmed up three TV dinners in the microwave, then presented the family with their steaming plates. At first, Terra was cautious, concerned about the processed foods that waited behind the rising waves of heat, but after a few mouthfuls, she greedily ate the whole lot.

They spoke of old times, Michael and Terra comparing notes about their time in the AJS, Marie rolling her eyes as she sat on the fringes of their conversation. Skooch slept by Terra's feet, curled up and exhausted after her exuberant bursts of welcome. Leonie left them to it, returning to her duties on the surface.

As evening fell, they took their places on the couches and sipped coffees. Soft music played from an old-fashioned stereo in the corner, the silver CD spinning rapidly behind a glass case.

Terra rested her head back against the thick couch cushions and exhaled a long breath into the air. In her peripheral vision, Marie studied her through concerned eyes—the same look she'd been giving Terra most of the evening.

"I'm going to be okay, Mom," Terra informed her, breaking the silence that had fallen over the trio.

Marie chewed her lip. "I know." She didn't sound so sure.

Michael leaned forward, resting his elbows on his knees. "She's a big girl, Marie. You have to trust her."

"Oh, I do," Marie replied. "Wholeheartedly. It's this city I don't trust. It's those people. Even Black…" She lowered her head. "How can you be sure that you're working for the right people?"

Terra's lip curled into a warm smile. "Because I've seen these people in action. Leonie, Imani, Slim, they've all proven themselves. Whenever I've been in trouble or shit hit the fan, they've been there. You can't prove your intentions with words, only with your actions. They've proven themselves again and again."

Michael let out a soft snort.

"What's so funny?" Marie asked.

"You taught her that," he replied.

Marie chuckled, then lowered her head. "I want you to be careful."

"I couldn't be more protected." Terra tapped her forehead. "State-of-the-art, remember?"

Marie narrowed her eyes, studying Terra's head as though she could see through the skin and skull. "Yeah. State-of-the-art." She drew a deep breath, then wiped away a tear that had formed in the corner of her eye. She reached forward and slid a box out from under the table. The large letters on the front read, "Scrabble." "Who's up for a quick game? For old time's sake?"

Terra glanced at Michael, the pair laughing.

"Sure, Mom." Terra sat forward, disturbing Skooch when she moved her feet.

The game lasted an hour and ended with the sudden *beeping* of an alarm clock. Terra glanced at the time. "That's my cue."

She rose from the couch and stretched. Michael and Marie remained quiet as Terra crossed to the back room and unlocked the door with the code Black had given her. Fifteen minutes later, she returned kitted out and armed.

Marie made the sign of the cross over her chest. Michael shook his head. "Since when did you get religious?"

Marie nodded at Terra. "That's a bit excessive, don't you think?"

Terra stood straight, feeling more powerful than she ever had in her life. The uniform fit perfectly, tucking into every contour and crease of her body. The blue rippled, catching the light and accentuating her curves.

Across her chest, the black paneling was so dark it seemed to suck the light into itself like a black hole. In her hands was the AR-15. The assault rifle was painted in the same metallic black as her chest plate, with a few accents of electric blue. It had a scope on top, plus a small additional barrel attached. Terra had yet to determine the second barrel's purpose.

"I don't know what I'm going to find out there," Terra replied. "I'm a one-person justice force, now."

Marie made the sign again. Michael gently pushed her hands away. "You can do this. We both believe in you."

Marie nodded but remained silent.

Terra gave an affirmative nod. "Okay, APRIL. Activate chest panel."

The panel on the chest plate lit up with that same diamond motif. This time, the image remained. APRIL's voice appeared from hidden speakers. "APRIL program activated. Are you informed on your current mission, Terra?"

Marie's eyes widened a touch. Michael grinned.

"Pretty cool, huh?" Terra noted.

"I'll say," Michael replied.

Terra crossed to her parents. She leaned down and gave them each a kiss and a hug. As Marie held her and squeezed, an alert came from APRIL's speaker. "Marie Kris. Threat level fifteen percent."

Terra smirked and leaned back. "Mom? Are you trying to kill me?"

Marie put a hand to her chest. "I have no idea what she's talking about."

"It," Terra corrected. "APRIL is a program, not a gendered entity."

"Still…" Marie replied.

"APRIL," Terra asked. "What are you basing your threat diagnosis on?"

"Embrace from Marie Kris held for longer than the national standard, with additional pressure employed around the throat and chest. Fifteen percent chance of escalation leading to asphyxiation or suffocation."

Terra burst into laughter, joining her father. Marie looked between them, confused. "I'm not sure I understand."

"You hugged her too hard," Michael replied.

Terra grinned. "Don't worry, Mom. I know you'd never kill me."

A second alarm rang behind her. Terra went to the exit. "At least, I hope you won't." She winked at Marie, then blew Michael a kiss as she left the bunker.

Terra climbed the stairs and paused before the storm shelter door. "APRIL, scan for immediate threats."

APRIL's scan returned a negative signal, indicating that no one was waiting for her outside the door. She emerged into a crisp, cool evening. A light film of rain fell, dampening the ground around her. She closed the doors behind her, ensured they locked in place, then skirted the building, remaining vigilant for anyone who might see where she was coming from and be able to trace her appearance to the bunker.

She rounded a side building and came out into the street lights that lined the walkway to the AJS precinct. She straightened her spine, lifted her chin, and confidently walked toward her bike. She passed a smattering of officers who all gave her strange looks as she emerged, clearly confused over whether to admire Terra's new look and equipment or question where it had all come from.

As she neared the parking lot, she glanced back. Hewlett and Dunston stood in the AJS precinct entrance, jaws almost to the floor. A smug satisfaction warmed Terra.

She crossed to her bike, only sensing the approaching figure when APRIL announced, "Jenna Newman approaching, nine o clock."

Terra jumped, glancing down at the chest plate with disdain before turning to greet the woman. "Hey, Slim."

Slim smirked, eyes fixated on Terra's chest plate. "That's probably not the most tactically stealthy way to operate." She chuckled. "Still, it's nice to finally hear the voice of the AI who's been guiding you around."

Terra nodded, then noticed the APRIL glasses on Slim's face. They were stylish, with little indication of the power of the technology inside, only slightly different than the ones Terra had tested in the first place.

"So you don't hear that voice in your head?" Terra asked.

"Oh, I do," Slim replied. "Sounds somewhat different out loud."

"You don't sound too pleased at having to wear those things."

"Would you be?" Slim asked, the humor clear in her voice at the irony of what she had just said. She glanced at the Ducati. "Where you headed?"

"Out," Terra replied. "Got a couple of jobs to attend to."

"Funny," Slim mused. "I thought that after all the help I gave you before, you'd be more open with what you're working on."

Terra raised an eyebrow.

"Of course, I'm kidding," Slim stated. She looked Terra up and down. "That's some pretty equipment. Maybe one day I'll rise through the ranks and get kitted like you."

Terra's smile slipped. "I wouldn't wish any of this on my worst enemy."

She let the silence hang between them until Slim blinked and tapped her finger to her ear. "I have to go. There's a new update on the Miller case over on Broad Street."

Terra nodded. "APRIL, bring up the Miller updates. Keyword: Broad Street."

A ream of images and videos flickered through Terra's vision, showing a man who looked more like a bullfrog than a human. Images showed piles of dead bodies found in abandoned spaces through the city, with case files and geographic locations of several leads. Terra could also have sworn that, for a moment, she could see herself in the barrage of images.

APRIL, go back. Identify Terra Kris in media compilation.

The footage moved to a live video feed, showing Terra from Slim's point of view. As Slim blinked, Terra disappeared, then reappeared.

"Something wrong?" Slim asked.

Terra shook her head, absorbing this new information. Did she also have access to the rest of the APRIL glasses? And, if that was the case, did any of them have access to her?

"I have to go," Slim announced. She thumbed a key fob in her pocket, and the headlights of a nearby cruiser flashed. "You take care."

"You, too." Terra watched Slim disappear into the vehicle, then head into the city.

She mounted her Ducati, the ghost of the detonation device still lingering in her mind. She looked out at the city, twisted the throttle, then sped away from the precinct.

CHAPTER TEN

Samina Openheimer swanned into the indoor auditorium, her long emerald gown fanning behind her. The shoulderless dress glimmered in the spotlights that littered the ceiling like stars in the night sky.

Around her, rows of velvet seats all curved in elegant rows, their focal point the theatrical stage laid out before them. The large curtains matched the seating, the walls decorated in perfect statues and carvings of nymphs and cherubs and goblins.

She smelled the excitement in the air. A gentle chatter tittered. There were two large balconies, one higher than the other, angled to look down at the stage from on high.

Samina emerged into the royalty box, the tittering chatter falling to a dead stop. Her thick brown curls hung over one shoulder, and her ruby red lipstick accentuated plump lips. She felt the eyes of every warm-blooded man and woman in the theater studying her, scanning the royalty that was Samina.

Not that she was true royalty. Samina wished for the monarchy's powers, but as far as Atlantica underground royalty went, she was queen.

She sat, the silence hanging for an unnaturally long time. A man took the seat beside her, his thick, Hell's Angels goatee ill-fitting for a man accompanying a woman of her nature and class. He wore a powder-blue suit and had pulled his rat tail back tightly to sit in the center of his shoulder blades.

The lights dimmed.

The show began.

Music belted out from the orchestral pit, the brass instruments dominating the room. A single man stepped into the spotlight, dressed in a three-piece suit. His crimson red shoes reminded Samina of the ruby slippers worn by Dorothy in the tales. He began his monologue, announcing the show's narrative as the music rose even louder, and the rest of the cast appeared on stage, dressed in smiles and florals.

Then something changed.

At the height of the number, as the chorus joined in and the music rose to its crescendo, the first shot fired. It happened in the darkness, the bullet tearing out from somewhere in the shadows. Someone screamed. Another shouted. A moment later, the audience was on its feet, looking around in fear.

The cast continued, uncertain but as professional as ever. The shouts rose. Another shot rang out.

A man appeared on the stage with an assault rifle held ready as he aimed at each of the cast in turn. "On your knees! Hands up!"

The cast obeyed instantly, minus one brave soul who charged at the unknown man. Without hesitation, the man shot, catching the actor center mass. He stopped mid-run, then collapsed to his knees. He was dead before he hit the floor.

The man swept the rifle around the rest of the cast. "Any more brave shit, and you'll be next. Got that? We don't need heroes here."

As if on cue, the house lights rose. Samina turned to the man beside her, and her face turned a ghostly shade of white.

Blood pooled from his chest. The white of his shirt was stained crimson. His head lolled back in his chair, eyes empty and lifeless.

Samina let out a blood-curdling scream. Below her, those who had run for the doors now paused under the glaring eyes of the guards standing sentinel at each exit.

The man on stage turned his attention to Samina in the royalty box with a hungry, keen look in his eye. "Madame Samina Openheimer. Pleased to make your acquaintance."

Samina trembled in her seat, doing her utmost to recompose herself as the man turned his gun toward her. "I think we need to have a conversation, don't you?"

Someone in the auditorium coughed. Another groaned. One by one, the audience members collapsed onto their chairs, each somehow hit by an invisible force as they went down like tiles on a Guess Who board.

"What's going on?" Samina murmured.

The man answered with a cocky grin on his face. "You think we'd take over this joint without having some kind of insurance policy?" He motioned at the dead man before him. "You saw what happened to this brave fellow here. The best way to secure a place is to eradicate the chances of any interference." He nodded at a guard who stood off-stage and raised a cup filled with beer.

Samina understood instantly. More audience members fell, awkwardly sprawled over each other and the backs of seats.

"Long live the queen," the man on stage murmured.

Terra sped through the city, guided by APRIL's GPS to find her destination while avoiding the busier roads and pathways.

Her skin bristled with life, an electric current running through her body that charged her up and made her see the city in its full glory. Colors were brighter. Images were sharper. The Ducati's roar was astounding.

She curved around the streets, closing in on the little tag that appeared on APRIL's digital map. As she pulled up to the curb, an announcement rang from her chest plate. "Arrived at your destination."

Terra glanced down at the panel. A small image of a thumbs-up appeared on the screen. "You know, APRIL, if we're going to remain covert with this, you're going to have to decide better when to use your indoor voice and outdoor voice."

God, I sound just like my parents.

Affirmative, APRIL announced. **Updating instructional information to scan for threats and assess the level against the audio information received by host.**

"Host?" Terra asked.

A man glanced up from his view of the sidewalk and scowled.

Yes. Host.

"I'd prefer 'friend,'" Terra stated softly.

Adjusted 'host' to 'friend.' Confirmed.

Ew. I've just made friends with a robot. I never saw that one coming.

Terra looked around the nearby buildings, gaining her bearings. She was in the middle of a densely populated residential area, with towering apartment buildings all around her. The structures disappeared into the fog. Several illuminated windows gave the impression that the buildings had eyes.

The city was quieter than usual, only a steady stream of residents making their way back to their apartment. On the corner was a 7-Eleven.

"Where is this place?" Terra asked.

Last biological readout was from thirty-fifth.

A video appeared, showing a man emerging from a transit van with another group of figures clad in black in tow. They walked down a set of stairs into an apartment building, each of them armed to the teeth with weapons.

"There's a lot of them," Terra stated. "Have you got my back for this one?"

Affirmative.

"What about the private versus public rule?" Terra asked.

An exemption is stated on the profile of this case, notarized by Nora Asplin, who accepts all responsibilities of the mission.

"Well, there you go." A wave of excitement fluttered through Terra.

She narrowed in on the apartment building, then took a stand outside. She instructed APRIL to perform a scan, then marveled at the number of people surrounding her who glowed in vibrant oranges and reds. They appeared like fiery constellations, showing the true life and vibrancy of the city.

She turned her attention to the building before her. She cocked an eyebrow, staring at the enormous fire that burned in her vision, larger than any pyre she had seen. It took her a second to realize that this was no pyre but a gathering of hundreds of people in a small space tucked away inside the building.

"What is this place?" Terra asked.

The property belongs to Alexandria Raven, a theater mogul most commonly known for her work on such productions as *Who's Earnest, Anyway, Tiles Upon Tiles*, and *Runaway With Me*. The Raven Theater was an investment undertaken in 2016 as an underground alternative to mainstream Broadway shows.

"A theater inside the apartment block?" Terra gave an approving nod. "That's one way to make a bit of coin." She narrowed her eyes as she fancied she heard the sound of a gunshot, only slightly muted by the building. "I guess that's where our guy is?"

You've got it, friend.

Terra rolled her eyes. "Come on. Let's get inside."

She stopped at the door and pressed her ear against the wood.

There was no one on the other side. A digital panel beside her showed a series of buttons to activate the intercom of the residents inside. "APRIL, can you override?"

Attempting to override security systems. A *beep* sounded. A light turned green. **Confirmed.**

"How do you do this?" Terra asked.

Ask me no questions and I'll tell you no lies.

"Are you quoting Bing Crosby?" Terra asked.

Affirmative.

Terra gave a small snort of derision. *This from an AI that doesn't understand the nuances of human language...*

She nudged the door open and entered the apartment block lobby. The place was strangely quiet, with no one behind the reception counter. A doorway to the left led to a small room filled with mailboxes and a set of stairs that zigzagged to the upper levels. Ahead of her was a painted red door with "The Raven Theater" printed in gold lettering.

Terra made her way toward it, only stopping when she drew in line with the reception counter. Something caught her eye, and as she craned her neck to see over the desk, she saw two figures lying on the floor.

She moved closer. The man and the woman were, according to APRIL, in their late twenties. With a few minor convictions to their names, nothing was outstanding about them. Although the fact they were asleep on the floor was a definite concern.

"What happened to them?" Terra asked, skirting the desk to get closer to them. She scanned them for bullet or stab wounds but found nothing of note. The twin computer screens showed an animated screensaver message.

She spotted the two cups on the desk.

"Poison?" Terra asked.

APRIL answered, **It's a definite possibility. We'll need to run an analysis.**

"We don't have time to get this to a lab," Terra replied.

Something vibrated in her chest. A mechanical noise sounded. Terra looked down to see a thin tray slide out of the chest plate, directly to the left of the screen. **Place a sample on this, please.**

A tiny strip of paper that made Terra think of litmus paper she'd played with at school to test the alkaline and acidic values of liquids protruded from the tray.

Terra took the tiny slip of paper and dipped it into the lipstick-stained mug. Once it absorbed enough of the dregs, she put the strip in the tray.

The tray slid closed.

Analyzing sample.

Terra watched with fascination as the screen displayed a series of codes, showcasing the chemicals found inside the liquid. Quantities and other statistical information she didn't understand scrolled by. An hourglass timer at the side of the panel flipped over onto itself to show the scan was in progress.

Finally, APRIL announced, **Diazepam detected.**

"Diazepam?" Terra asked.

Known more commonly as Valium. Diazepam is a benzodiazepine that binds to GABA receptors in the brain and initiates sleepiness. Effects can include sedation, loss of muscle coordination, and dizziness.

"I know about Valium." Terra turned her attention to the two staff members. "Sleep well, kiddos. We'll make sure you wake up to less chaos than you'll sleep through."

She turned her attention to the large orange mass on the other side of the walls as a scream pierced the air. "APRIL, get me in there. Preferably undetected and as quiet as possible."

Terra's vision filled with virtual blueprints of the building that moved and tracked her like a cart on a rollercoaster ride. The projected image showed her traveling through the door, up a set of stairs, and into an area that appeared to be where the crew controlled the lighting rig.

Assessing route, APRIL stated, then followed with, **Confirmed. Directing now.**

Terra spotted two orange blobs in the shape of people in her target room. She only hoped that she would be able to suppress them before they noticed she was there.

CHAPTER ELEVEN

Terra waited outside the door to the upstairs booth.

APRIL scanned for her, kicking back information on two females crouched in the small room. Terra detected little threat from the pair.

She gently tried the door handle and found the door locked. Through the scan, she spotted the two women look at each other, then toward the door. One of them raised a shape that looked like a gun.

This is going to be fun...

Terra took a lock pick from her pocket and worked at the door. She was quick, with APRIL's technology able to help her see through the mechanism and work the right components. When she nudged the door open, she remained where she stood, muttering, "Stay calm. I'm not here to hurt you."

She picked up the sound of a hammer cocking back.

"I'm going to open the door slowly," Terra whispered, able to now make out the disturbed shouts of someone coming from inside the theatre. "Don't shoot."

She leaned through the gap in the doorframe, meeting the relieved faces of the two women crouched beneath the desk.

"You came quickly," the woman with the gun announced.

"You called the AJS?" Terra asked.

The second woman showed a concerned look. "They said they wouldn't come. *Couldn't* come. That this is a private matter."

Terra gave a small nod. "That's true. Luckily, you have me." She stepped fully into the room and slowly closed the door. The two women exchanged a look as Terra's assault rifle came into full view. "Nothing to worry about," Terra soothed. "Just fill me in on what's going on here."

She crouched and made her way toward the glass panel above the control desk. Below her, a large crowd of people were slumped over chairs, laid on the floor, or dumped at odd angles around the auditorium. On stage, several actors had their hands in the air. One man in a thick black combat vest pointed a gun at a woman in the balcony on the right.

The woman looked positively regal, a flowing emerald dress juxtaposed against the pale white of her skin. Her lips shone a bright red, even from this distance. The man beside her was unconscious like the others.

Not unconscious, dead, Terra thought as she spotted the blossom of red covering his chest.

She turned her attention back to the man on center stage. *APRIL, analyze.*

APRIL zoomed in for Terra, also magnifying the man's sound. Data appeared around his figure, showing Terra that she had found her target, the man Corporal Black had asked her to find.

Her heart rate increased as a smirk appeared on her face. She thought back to the thousands of times when she had to wait and watch on the outskirts, standing outside the buildings where criminals were getting away with whatever the fuck they liked. So many times she had heard gunshots but was unable to do anything.

But now…

Now she had permission, as well as resources.

That was a powerful combination.

"Remain perfectly still," the man identified by April as Rob Custer informed the woman.

Terra read the scan, taking in her information, too. Samina Openheimer. According to her data, Samina ran in questionable circuits but had come out with a clean record. It wasn't unusual for the rich to be clean on paper, given that most of the smart ones got other people to do their dirty work for them.

Rob continued, keen eyes fixed on the beautiful woman. "One of my attendants will come and collect you. There'll be no harm. There'll be no fuss, as long as you listen to what we ask of you."

Several other guards were roaming around the unconscious crowd, fishing into pockets and bags and collecting wallets, jewelry, phones, and anything else of value. Terra couldn't help but notice the number of knocked-over drinks spilling the remains of their contents onto the thick carpet. Only a couple of audience members sat upright, petrified to stillness.

They tried to drug them all.

"What are you going to do with me?" Samina's words were as shaky as her breath.

Rob smirked. "You'll be fine, princess. I have a buyer who's very interested in having a conversation with you, is all. Come with us without fuss, and you'll arrive in one piece." He added, "He didn't specify if he wanted you dead or alive, so I'm erring on the side of caution at the moment."

Terra's blood boiled. She examined her immediate environment, looking for a way down to the main area. There were several guards there, each with weapons that would cause her a lot of problems.

A man appeared behind Samina.

Someone in the crowd stood and fired at Rob.

The shot went wide by an inch, hitting the curtain at the back of the stage and causing it to ripple.

Someone screamed.

Someone fired.

The man cried out as bullets from three different guards tore into him. Poorly aimed fire hit a few unconscious people around him, blood spraying as they silently bucked.

Terra growled, blood boiling despite APRIL's attempts to calm her. She brought the rifle up to eye level and lined up her shot on Rob, ready to take him out. She knew that toppling the head domino would normally bring the rest of the problem to its knees. However, as she lined up the sights, she noticed something interesting.

Not only did a red dot take the center of the cross-hair, but it looked as though the viewfinder was projecting a digital image. She centered Rob perfectly in the scope, but as she did, the weapon *hummed* in her hands. Mechanisms whirred inside, the sight filling with information on how far away Rob was. The barrel of the rifle rotated, swapping with one thinner and sleeker. Only when it locked into place and the message **Sniper Mode Engaged** appeared did Terra understand.

"Holy shit," she breathed.

The sight zoomed in, the weapon working with her movements to balance itself out. She had no idea what was in this technology, but she certainly wasn't complaining. All she had to do was pull the trigger.

"And breathe…" Terra told herself as her finger tightened.

The sound of scuffling came from behind, and the next thing she knew a loud report sounded in her eardrum. She lowered her weapon as glass smashed and chaos unfolded. The woman beside her pointed the revolver at the man on stage and took her shot.

The woman screamed.

Terra spun, taking the woman by the arm and dragging her to the floor as gunfire rained in their direction. The second woman whimpered as tears streamed down her face. Terra's annoyance mixed with her immediate need to help as she roared at the first woman, "Stay the fuck down. That's an order."

The woman looked set to argue but remained still.

Terra moved back toward the door and readied herself. She remained low enough to stay away from gunfire as her gaze locked onto something above her. "APRIL?"

Yes, Terra.

"Make sure you've got my back. Things are about to get messy." Before APRIL could warn Terra to stop, Terra ran toward the broken window. She jumped in the air, leaping over the control desk, one arm out before her.

Gunfire tracked her movements. Bullets ricocheted off the metal grid where the lights and wires snaked toward the stage. Terra grabbed a cable, almost an inch thick and covered in dense plastic, and swung high above the auditorium. The conduit moved with her as her fingers coiled over it and her weight bore down, stretching to its full length and aiding her as she descended toward the upper stalls.

With her other hand, she blindly aimed down at her attackers on the upper balcony. The rifle adjusted in her hand, the barrels switching to allow an explosive burst of fire at the guard stationed near the exit.

Drywall erupted around him as a line of fire worked its way closer. She caught him in the chest, and he went down.

Two more were behind her. Her feet neared the backs of the chairs. She landed on her toes, then sprang off and onto the floor. The surface was slanted, attempting to throw her off balance. Terra used this to her advantage by rolling away from immediate attack.

She came up in a crouch with one knee on the floor, brought the rifle to bear, and shot the guard across the way. The other woman went down as a bullet caught her in the center of her thigh. Terra remained low, the sight still to her eye as she moved her focus to the final guard in the upper stalls, pulling the trigger and catching his midriff as he tried to leap behind the seats.

Terra closed in on the woman and slapped a set of magnetized cuffs on her wrists. They drew themselves together, causing her to grimace as her bodily position adjusted and her thigh spiked with pain.

Terra had no time to slow down. Bullets fired up at the balcony. She peeked as far as she dared and saw that Samina was gone, as was Rob.

Fuck.

Terra used APRIL's scan to track the threats below her. She picked up the shapes of four guards, all barraging the balcony with gunfire. She moved out of their immediate target area, then popped up over the balcony.

Her movements were swift, switching from one target to the next. First one went down, then two, then three. The final guard tried to flee but only made it as far as the side aisle when she caught him in the center of the back.

"How many more, APRIL?" Terra asked.

Three remain in the immediate vicinity. On the balcony directly below you.

Terra scanned and found them. She moved on the upper balcony until she stood directly over one of the orange shapes, then cracked her neck. "Let's see how far I can push your system." She fired her rifle at the floor.

She shot in a circle around her feet, the floor weakening until it bowed beneath her. The next thing she knew, she dropped through it and fell fifteen feet. A chunk of detritus stuck to her feet. She landed directly on top of the guard, who grunted before falling between rows of seats. Terra rolled, again using the balcony's gradient to dispel some of the impact.

Someone fired. The bullet caught the back of her leg. The hexagonal material flared with light, pushing the slug away, but Terra still grunted. Pain radiated and the area would likely bruise, but at least it didn't penetrate the material.

Terra returned fire, taking the woman down in an instant.

The final guard had ducked through the back door and was sprinting down the stairwell toward the exit.

Always good to leave one alive to tell the tale, Terra thought.

You've left three alive, APRIL replied.

Terra turned back to the theater. She vaulted over the balcony, using a thick coil of rope that might have been there for some acrobatic effect during the production, and lowered herself to the main floor.

The theater was quiet. Without the guards standing by, there were only the gentle snores of the drugged-out crowd. She turned to the balcony where Samina and her—partner? Husband?—had sat and spotted the forms of three figures running toward the back.

Terra sprinted toward the stage. The actors tracked her cautiously, not one of them tempted to break the quiet. Terra's footsteps echoed around the large space as she ducked into one of the side wings and the backstage area.

The place looked deserted, but Terra saw the shuddering shapes of backstage staff hiding in the dressing rooms and any cupboards or offices they could find. Guided by APRIL's tracker, Terra worked toward the loading bay, eventually barging through a fire exit to emerge into a concrete parking lot.

A flash of emerald caught her attention. Rob was forcing Samina into the back of a Rolls Royce with a missing license plate. Terra raised her weapon. "Freeze! AJS."

The command only caused further hurry. He and a guard bundled Samina into the vehicle. Terra shot, catching the guard in the chest as the door slammed shut and the car drove off.

Shit. Terra ran after the vehicle. The guard remained in the center of the lot, blood pooling around his chest, while Rob sat in the passenger seat beside Samina, the driver taking them far away from this place.

Terra ran faster than she had in her life, aided by APRIL's strange concoction of biochemicals. The car swept out onto the main road, then sped off to the right. Terra chased it as far as she could, knocking into civilians who watched her with cautious eyes, fixing their gaze on her bright blue uniform and assault rifle. Some gave her a wide berth. Others were too slow, and Terra shoved them aside, much to their chagrin.

The car soon vanished in the distance.

"No," Terra muttered firmly, switching direction and turning right. "APRIL, keep track of that vehicle. Use the local CCTV footage and watch its every move. We need to get Samina back."

Affirmative, friend.

Terra didn't have time to argue.

She rounded the front of the building and located her Ducati. She straddled the seat, then kicked the bike into life. With a swift twist of the accelerator and a U-turn in the center of the road, she sped off after the car.

Despite the late hour, the streets were annoyingly busy. The traffic made it difficult for Terra to weave between the gaps safely. She made steady progress, following the arrows APRIL presented in her vision as they closed in on the Rolls Royce. A string of numbers indicated the remaining distance between her and her target, and it was encouraging to see the gap close, even if it wasn't happening as quickly as she'd hoped.

She narrowed her gaze, focus fixed only on the job at hand. The city whirred by her, lights streaking in her peripheral vision.

The Rolls worked its way toward the edge of the city. The commercial districts and the well-maintained megastores melted into the lower-grade buildings as they entered the suburbs. Terra closed in, wind whipping back her hair. She was close. So damn close.

Terra, look out! APRIL cried, the sudden alarm sounding in her head and sending a jolt of pain through her. She looked up at the top of a nearby building and caught a wink of something metallic. Something flared, and the projectile streaked toward her.

Terra jumped sideways, leaping off the Ducati. The bike slammed to the ground and skidded on its side, leaving a long trail of paintwork. Terra rolled several times before hitting the side of a parked car, narrowly avoiding a Mercedes that had been speeding by.

The projectile landed next to the Ducati and exploded on impact. Asphalt tore from the ground as a small crater developed, sending debris in all directions. Fragments of pavement, rock, and dust streaked toward Terra, who shielded her eyes with the crook of her arm.

Car alarms sounded. Civilians shouted. Flames crackled.

Terra looked through the thick smoke and found the orange blob at the top of the building, thanks to APRIL's enhancements. Without another thought, she adjusted her rifle and looked through the scope. The barrel switched to sniper mode, and Terra fired.

The bullet *hissed* from the chamber. A moment later, the orange blob shuddered, fell off the twenty-story building, then collided with the ground in a sick *thud*. More screams rang out.

Terra gritted her teeth and frowned. She got to her feet, then worked her way toward the Ducati. Dirt stained her uniform, but she and it were still intact. She hadn't sustained any lacerations or cuts.

She moved through the smoke toward the crater. A small set of flames flickered, beginning to fade under the steady drizzle of rain that started to fall.

Terra growled as she stared at the mess of components littered around her. The bike was totaled. Pieces of the engine had scattered across the road, one wheel was missing, and only the broken frame remained. She thought back to the man who had tried to plant a bomb in her seat. Anger rose within her. What did people have against Terra having nice things?

Someone tried to ask her a question, something that sounded like, "What *was* that," but spoken through ten-inch glass. Terra ignored the civilian. Instead, she went directly toward the place where the man had fallen.

Cars screeched to a stop. She spotted the figure in a set of bushes nearby. The closer she got, the more grotesque the picture that unfolded before her.

Terra stopped a foot short of the mess. While some of the body was intact, much of it was missing. The shot had caught the man in the stomach, and now all that remained was a hole. As for his legs and arms, they had buckled upon impact and now stood at strange angles.

His face, though…that was mostly undamaged.

Terra stared at what remained of Roger Shellows.

"Son of a bitch," Terra muttered. A sense of satisfaction for bringing this fucker to justice mixed with that strange guilt that never seemed to go away, no matter how many dead bodies she came across. She examined what remained of his pockets and took out his wallet and a few scrap pieces of paraphernalia he had on his person, then turned back to the street.

Several faces stared her way. Terra ignored them, looking in the direction that APRIL had been leading her before. "How far are they?"

APRIL brought up the information. **One block. A small safe house, by the looks of things.**

Terra's jaw clenched as she gave one last glance at her Ducati. "They won't be safe for long."

CHAPTER TWELVE

Samina grunted behind the gag. The thick rag stuffed inside her mouth and tied around her head was difficult to breathe through.

"What the fuck was that?" the man who had kidnapped her bellowed at a short man with apish arms and a sour expression. "What the fuck happened back there?"

The apish man shrugged. Beside him, the driver who had ferried her across the city to this rundown building scratched the back of his neck. "No idea. AJS ain't supposed to enter private property."

The man paced the room, his pistol shaking in his white-knuckle grip. "Motherfucker. I'll have someone's head for this. That should've been an easy take back there. Didn't need to have half the fucking casualties. Do you know how many men I lost back there?"

Ape shook his head, stoic and silent.

The man growled. In a fit of rage, he picked up a half-empty bottle that had been resting on a nearby table and hurled it against the wall. Liquid sprayed into the air, and the room filled with the scent of liquor.

There was a knock at the door. A woman's head appeared, her

long hair combed back tight to her scalp. Her lips were thin and barely visible. "Coast is clear, boss."

The man gave a satisfied nod. "Keep an eye out on all sides. I don't trust that bitch—whoever she was." He shook his head again, turning his attention to the driver. "AJS aren't supposed to enter private property."

He spoke in the same tone as if repeating the point would make the whole situation fall into clarity.

"I know," the driver repeated. "Surely there's someone in City Hall we can contact to get her sanctioned? There must have been camera footage, too?"

The man nodded, then grumbled again. "We can't contact City Hall. We've kidnapped a bitch."

Samina glanced down as he turned his gaze onto her. He stopped talking, taking a minute to process the situation as if remembering what his prize was. He stalked closer to her, his shadow falling across her in the dimness of the room. He stank of stale cigarettes. "You better be worth all this trouble, darling."

Samina tried to speak, the cloth catching her words. She stopped when a blinding pain sprang from her temple. Her world went black for a second before slowly coming back through a thick fog. It took her a moment to recognize the pain of the pistol striking her across her face. Warmth rushed to the wound.

"Boss," Ape cautioned. "They need her in good condition."

The man glared at her, taking a few deep breaths. "You're right." He nodded. "You're right." He took a step back. "Put her somewhere safe until we hear back from the buyer. They're not going to be happy we've had to switch locations at the last fucking minute."

Ape nodded and left the room. The driver sat back, resting against the side counter. "What do you want us to do in the meantime?"

The man turned his way. "Bring in backup. Put them on

patrol. I don't trust that bitch as far as I can throw her. I have a horrible feeling we're not rid of her yet."

The driver nodded, then exited the room.

Samina quivered. Despite the heat emanating from her fear, a chill had set into her bones. She kept her gaze on the man as he sat on the table and thought. She muttered something through the gag.

The man looked up, impatience clear on his face. "Problem?"

Samina shook her head. She only wished she knew who this man was. If she could work out his identity, then when...*if*...she escaped, she could set her team on him.

For now, all she could do was bide her time.

It wasn't long before more guards came to usher her out of the room and into one cast in total darkness.

Terra zeroed in on the warehouse.

She hugged the sides of the buildings across the road, aware of the guards piling up and hiding in her targeted facility. A few made no effort to hide their sentinel duties, their silhouettes clear through the glass, but several extra bodies piled up out of sight, appearing only as orange blobs in Terra's vision.

"Justice before mercy," Terra muttered, unsure why she felt the need to say it but echoing Imani's words.

She moved through the alleyways, snaking closer to the building. When she was on the same side of the street, she entered an apartment block three buildings up from the safehouse.

She climbed the stairs to a fire escape that led to the roof. Only one or two residents spotted her running past, and they quickly ducked out of view, clearly with something to hide from the AJS officer.

The rooftop was flat and square with a small lip around its edge. Terra worked her way to the side of the building and looked down. The buildings descended like enormous stairs. The one nearest was four stories shorter, the one after that appeared to be three levels lower, and the safehouse was below that.

Terra examined the edge of the building, then lowered herself onto the nearest ledge. APRIL paved the way for her, scanning the best footholds and handholds until she was near enough to the next roof to turn and consider the jump.

The gap was six feet across. If Terra fell, she'd have an uncomfortable landing ahead of her. She drew a deep breath, steeling herself to spring onto the gravel-strewn rooftop.

The distance is achievable, APRIL reassured her, bringing up a series of diagrams showing jump trajectory and landing position. **Even at fifty percent energy expenditure, you'd land on the edge of the building. At full capacity, you would land here.**

Terra saw the impact spot, and it still didn't fill her with confidence. While she knew APRIL was likely right, the idea of the jump wasn't the most comfortable thing she'd experienced.

"Okay...here we go." Terra glanced down at her feet, allowing her body to sway from the building's side. As she slowly moved away, she twisted, then pushed off the ledge she stood on, freeing herself from safety and soaring across the gap.

APRIL was right. Terra landed in the exact spot the AI had predicted. Still, that didn't take away the images in her head of her foot slipping and her body clumsily flopping down like a rag doll through the gap. She landed, knees flexing to absorb the impact, then tumbled to further decrease it and her momentum. Her shoulder scraped against the gravel, but the uniform protected her from the worst of it. The rifle, which she'd slung over her back, clattered and moved to an awkward angle, but as she stood, she adjusted it once more.

"One down, two more to go." Terra drew a recovering breath, then stalked to the edge of the rooftop.

Hold, APRIL warned.

Terra paused as APRIL scanned ahead. **Guards looking up this way. Wait for their positions to change.**

Terra waited. Five minutes passed. The city hummed. She grew impatient, knowing that each second that passed would open up the possibilities for their targets to get more backup.

Finally, she muttered, "I'm moving forward."

APRIL didn't argue, for which Terra was thankful.

She stayed low, crouch-walking to the edge of the building. It was dark where she was, but there was no telling what kind of technology the guards had on their side. She lowered to her stomach and crawled the last few feet.

She narrowed her eyes, focusing on the orange shapes standing out among the darkness. "APRIL, zoom in."

APRIL did. She saw the tops of their heads, messy crops of hair, and foreheads of the figures standing on the building. They were all female, scanning and keeping their wits about them. Terra chewed her lip, bringing her rifle up to her sight. She could pick them all out from here, but would that arouse further suspicion? Did it matter? Where should she draw the line?

"It would be amazing if this rifle had tranquilizers," Terra noted, half-expecting the weapon to oblige and give her the required bullets, but nothing happened. "Damn, thought that might work."

You need to get closer, APRIL stated.

Terra obliged. "Fine. How do you propose I get down there?"

Stay low, APRIL replied.

Terra rolled her eyes. "Why didn't I think of that?"

APRIL started answering.

"Enough, APRIL. That was sarcasm." Terra turned slowly and lowered herself off the second roof.

Noted.

The descent wasn't as far, but no less tricky. Terra navigated to the spot suggested by APRIL, then launched onto the final roof. She was aware of the noises she made on her landing and was thankful for the hum of an engine down below that cloaked her disturbance.

She stayed lower than before, working her way to the edge until she was practically over the guards. She lay down flat against the building and finally sized up her targets.

The three women had rifles and pistols of varying grades. Their armor was shoddy, with only thin Kevlar vests covering their vitals, according to APRIL's enhanced scan. A few guards had explosives strapped to their hips, which APRIL analyzed as smoke and stun grenades.

"Plot out my route," Terra whispered.

APRIL took a few moments to assess the situation. As it did, it illuminated several other targets in the building below them. Three floors down, Terra made out a figure sitting in a chair by themselves while everyone else was walking around near the windows or pacing several rooms.

That has to be her. Terra's lips thinned.

Agreed, APRIL replied.

A moment later, a series of instructions lit up in Terra's vision. Terra examined the notes, a grin appearing on her face. "You're a genius. You know that?"

APRIL replied, **It's the way I'm programmed.**

Terra looked down at the first of her targets, adrenaline once again beginning to surge through her.

CHAPTER THIRTEEN

The first the guards knew of Terra was the clattering of a projectile nearby.

Three heads turned toward the noise before the large rock stopped moving.

"What was that?" one of the guards helpfully asked.

"I don't know. It's dark. Check it out," another commanded.

Terra watched as two of the figures moved toward the source. One went faster than the other. The third—the nearest of the guards—remained where she stood, watching with curiosity.

It was almost impossible for them to see in the darkness. The first guard shone a flashlight, a cone of white illuminating the rooftop. While they scanned for the rock, Terra swept around the lip of the roof and started her descent.

She moved rapidly, following APRIL's directions. Soon she was low enough to be out of sight of the three above her. Across the gap was a fire escape, and Terra leaned toward it. She made a small hop, catching the metal bar with her hands. She swung a little, waiting until her momentum had stilled before moving closer to the stairs, cautious of making too much noise as she did.

Feet firmly on the fire escape, she slowly advanced up,

watching the figures on the roof above her. They tensed, aware that something was amiss now that they'd identified the rock. Terra climbed until she was a foot below the next lip, still out of sight.

She tucked her hand into her utility belt and took another rock. She launched it high, watching it arc toward the center of the rooftop. As it clattered, one of the guards exclaimed, "Okay, prep up, bitches. Someone's nearby."

Yet, they all still turned to the center, which gave Terra enough time to climb onto the roof and lunge for the nearest guard.

The guard turned for her, bringing her rifle high, finger tensing on the trigger. Terra was too quick, managing a swift punch to the cheek that knocked her head back. In one swift motion, Terra hooked an arm around the guard and twisted her, holding her in front of her like a hostage.

The other two guards pointed their weapons at Terra. "Let her go."

Terra grinned. "You'll have to ask nicely."

The guard on her left shot, her pistol thankfully fitted with a silencer. Terra twisted, the bullet scraping her hostage's shoulder. She reached toward her captive's waist and tugged the smoke grenade free.

"Sorry, ladies," Terra stated. "Looks like this isn't going to be a good day for you."

She flicked the pin off and threw the grenade behind them. The two guards fired, but Terra dropped to her knees, dragging her hostage down with her. She squeezed the woman's throat, bringing her into the foggy realm of unconsciousness before breaking and running into the smoke.

The two other guards ran for the doorway leading from the rooftop. Terra beat them both to the door, able to see better than both of them combined since APRIL's tools aided her. The first to arrive mistook Terra for her comrade until Terra grabbed the woman's hair and smashed her face into the door. The woman gasped and fell to the roof unconscious.

The final woman heard the scuffle and shot blindly into the fog. Her rifle was loud, filling the air with explosive reports. Terra spun and aimed a shot at her hands, then took out her shins. The woman crashed to the roof, lost in the dense smoke.

Terra moved on, conscious that she couldn't stop now that the guns had fired and had no doubt raised the alarm.

The door slammed open, Terra momentarily forgetting her strength. She sprinted down the stairs, keeping the orange blobs of other figures in her peripheral vision to track the best direction. Three were approaching from far down the hall to the right. Terra turned left before they came into sight, working toward another set of stairs at the far side of the building.

Before she could get to the end, one of the figures spotted her. "Intruder!" he shouted.

Terra spun, facing her enemies. Shots fired toward her, and Terra quickly ducked into a side door. She leaned out cautiously, firing back, taking down two of the enemy with ease.

The final one ducked out of the way. Terra noted the stirring of people below her and gritted her teeth. She had to get to Samina before they moved her again.

Terra looked out from her doorway, the entrance to the stairs a short distance away. She dove from the room, crossing into the doorway as a volley of bullets fired in her direction. "APRIL, amplify audio of that man."

APRIL did. Terra heard her attacker muttering into some kind of communication device. "She's here. Raise the alarm."

"Seems pointless," Terra muttered. "Looks like they already have."

She ran down the stairs, keeping her eyes fixed ahead as she spotted several figures on the next floor working their way toward the staircase.

Terra clenched her jaw, flexing her fingers on her rifle. "Enough of this shit. Let's let mama take her babies home."

Samina sat in the darkness.

Shapes danced in her vision, in all the colors she'd ever experienced. They hadn't bothered to blindfold her—why would they? They had kept the gag on her, though. It was rubbing against her lips and chafing the flesh.

She hummed softly to herself, a song she'd heard years ago when her mother used to sing to her. She couldn't believe the night she was having. One moment she'd been sitting with her chaperone, preparing to watch some theater, and now she was here, alone, about to be sold to someone, by the sounds of things.

Sold to do what?

She didn't want to think about it. Samina had spent her entire life in Atlantica, and she knew the horrors that lurked in its dark corners. Trafficking was a real issue, but it was one that Samina never thought would apply to her. That kind of criminal activity affected others, not the uncrowned queen of the city.

A silent tear rolled down her cheek. If only she could reach the cell phone in her dress' concealed pocket and dial Travis. That would make things a hell of a lot easier. In the commotion of the kidnapping and that cop's appearance, there had been a lot her kidnappers had forgotten to do.

She tugged against the ropes around her wrists. She was sure she was bleeding from the struggle, but it was impossible to tell in the dark.

She hummed.

Something sounded above her, the unmistakable report of a firearm. She shuddered. It could be someone coming to rescue her. Or, for all she knew, it could be an enemy of the people who had kidnapped her.

Why me?

The shapes danced in the darkness, telling the story for her as more reports sounded and the intensity grew. She'd heard more than her fair share of gunfights in this city, but never did she think that she'd be the target of their conflict.

Samina lowered her head, closed her eyes, and cried.

***

Rob's lips curled as he glanced up toward the ceiling.

He had his troop around him now, and that helped him feel safe. Still, the gunshots were getting closer, and that wasn't a good sign. They should have gotten her by now. One well-placed shot to the head, and she'd be gone forever. A problem no more.

They hunkered together, guarding the room where they'd stored Samina. They'd left her gagged so she would remain quiet, hidden in the area protected by a series of digital and physical locks. There wasn't even a visible door to the space, only a flat, smooth surface that could easily be mistaken for a wall for those who didn't know the situation.

More gunshots.

"You. Go," Rob muttered, commanding Boyce out of the room. He was one of his more reliable henchmen, standing nearly seven feet tall and with the sharpshooter skills of an assassin.

Someone cried out in pain. Rob tried to determine where she was, how far away, how many floors stood between this pain in his ass and himself.

He glared at the ceiling. *Don't think I'm not prepared to kill you myself, bitch. Don't push me to that edge.*

***

Terra looked around the corner. Half a dozen enemies sprinted toward her. She ducked back around the wall, using APRIL's scans to determine how close they were.

They stopped thirty feet from where she stood. Something *clicked*, and a moment later, a small item appeared in her sight.

APRIL had warned her about the device, and with a quick maneuver, Terra emerged around the corner. She booted the explosive before it touched the ground, sending it sailing back toward the group.

It exploded a few feet from their heads. Light strobed, and sound burst into the hallway. They groaned, clutching their ears and screwing their eyes closed.

Terra aimed her rifle and sent a spray of bullets into the hallway. She aimed at their legs, determined to cause as few real casualties as possible, although a couple of shots targeted the hands of those who were recovering and trying to shoot back.

Before anyone could register what had happened, Terra ran toward them. Most of them were doubled over, crouching, or lying down and clutching their wounds. Terra leaped over them, allowing her grenade to drop into the group. After a loud shout and a sudden scramble to clear the area, a second smoke grenade went off, filling the hall with smoke.

One more floor, Terra. Caution, they're ready for you.

Terra found the next set of stairs leading down into the floor she was after. She slowed as she made her way to the first step. A large figure was headed toward her, standing considerably taller than those she had worked past.

She lined up her weapon. The figure lingered out of her sight, but not out of APRIL's.

"I'll give you one chance to leave this place," a deep, baritone voice declared. "That's all you get."

"I'll give you one chance to get the fuck out of my way," Terra countered.

"I can't do that."

"Neither can I."

A moment of quiet passed between them. Terra could faintly hear the sounds of those in the hallway as they groaned and attended to their wounds.

"I'm afraid we're at an impasse, then." The voice aimed a gun that looked larger than the rifles the other enemies had.

"I'm afraid we are—" Terra started.

Before she could finish her sentence, the man fired.

A small explosive launched from the barrel of his weapon into the ceiling at the bottom of the steps. The building ruptured around her, wood and sheetrock raining down and blocking the bottom of the staircase. Terra hopped backward, moving away as the chaos continued up the stairs. She dashed back into the corridor, narrowly avoiding the floor caving in beneath her, working her way into the safety of a nearby room that was undamaged by the sudden projectile.

"Holy fuck," she grunted, listening to the sound of the mayhem outside as more of the building buckled in on itself. "They're going to extreme lengths to protect one woman."

It's not just one woman, APRIL stated.

Terra cocked her head, "Yes, it is."

No, APRIL continued. **You're an officer of the Atlantica Justice System fighting for justice inside a private residence. You're fundamentally shaking the unspoken agreement between criminal activity and law enforcement.**

Your presence in this place strikes fear into the heart of the ones committing the wrongdoing. If they can't perform illegal activities in private residences, as Atlantica promises, then where are they safe?

Terra thought about this for a moment. "You know, for a robot, you're pretty smart."

I'm not a robot. I'm an—

"I know, I know," Terra interjected. "An artificial intelligence. I'm still getting used to that."

Terra examined the room around her while the dust started to settle outside. Raised voices came from down the hallway, more of Rob's men running to his rescue. She initiated a scan and spied the hotspot of people hanging around in the room one floor below her, not far from where she stood.

"Two can play this game." Terra crossed to a thick walnut desk placed near the wall. She moved behind it, then kicked it over with her boot. The desk toppled. Terra tucked behind it, then unclipped a detonation device from her belt.

She tossed it to the far side of the room, then covered her ears and shrank behind the desk, bracing the heavy object with her feet. "Here goes nothing." She thumbed the detonator, and the device exploded.

Splinters of wood flew around her, smacking into the walls. The force of the explosion pushed the desk against her, but she bent her knees and absorbed the impact. Shouts rose from below. A water pipe burst and sprayed into the air.

Terra waited a moment, then got to her feet. She examined the roughly twelve-foot hole she'd made in the floor. She cautiously approached the edge, testing the surface around her in case it crumbled under her weight.

The room below was a kitchen of sorts. Dust and debris littered the countertops. A kettle had fallen over, and the refrigerator door hung open.

Terra lowered herself through the hole and onto the countertop. She turned, then hopped onto the floor, debris crunching beneath her feet.

A woman coughed in the corner of the room, clearly thrown backward by the explosion. There was a cut on her forehead, and a bead of blood trickled toward her eye.

She stared at Terra for a moment.

Terra stared back.

APRIL, threat level, please.

Threat level: twenty percent. No firearms or weapons on her person.

Why twenty percent, then?

The kitchen is full of potential weapons. Knives, hot items, hazardous substances.

Terra held the woman's gaze, assessing her mettle. After a calm moment, she ignored the woman and walked toward the door. Terra liked to think she had a good read on people, and if APRIL's threat level read on her was low, she would take that as gospel.

She pulled the door handle, and the whole door fell out of the frame. Taking a side step, she allowed it to slap against the floor. She glanced back at the woman, offered a half-shrug, and exited the room.

CHAPTER FOURTEEN

According to APRIL's blueprint, the doorway led into a hallway on the other side of the building from the explosions. Terra stalked the hallway, which appeared silent and unoccupied all around her. APRIL's scan showed most enemies on the other side of the building, with many piled up around the door leading into the room where Rob and his crew had clustered.

"It's going to be a bitch to get in that way." Terra eyed the hazards and studied the lay of the land before her. The hallway carpet muffled her footsteps. Several abstract oil paintings decorated the walls.

Then we'll use an alternative.

"Where, though?" Terra asked. Her gaze locked onto the orange figure of a woman sitting alone in a room. *That* has *to be her.*

If you can't get through a door, make a door, APRIL advised.

Terra considered this. "I like your thinking."

She moved down the hallway toward the lone figure, one hand dragging against the smooth wall as she did, the other keeping her rifle tight to her side.

Movement flashed to her right. Someone stood in a room by

themselves. They neared their door, then eased it open. A single eye appeared in the crack.

Terra responded quickly, knowing that any alert to her whereabouts could mean death. She kicked the door before they had a chance to close it, sending the figure crashing into the wall behind the door.

Terra kept the pressure on the wood, pressing the woman against the wall, preventing her from using her hands or feet to defend herself.

"Please…" the woman choked.

Terra moved toward the woman, closing the door behind her. She aimed the rifle with one hand at her chest, holding the firearm at hip height.

"What do you want?" the woman asked.

Terra held her gaze, the gloom of the room making it difficult to define the woman's features. Still, APRIL's scan identified her.

Louise McLoughlin, twenty-three years old. Outstanding convictions include firearms smuggling and extortion of political figures.

Terra absorbed this information. Those were nothing unusual in Atlantica, and she had to keep her eye on the prize—saving a woman's life.

Terra didn't answer. Instead, she turned the woman around and pressed her face against the wall. With one swift movement, she handcuffed the woman's wrists.

"Hey, what the hell?" The woman groaned.

Terra leaned close, her lips next to the woman's ear. "Play the game nicely, and there won't be any issues. I can't have you wandering around and alerting your boss to my whereabouts, so what I can do is incapacitate you until I finish my job. You'll stay here like a good little girl while I rescue the woman your boss is attempting to kidnap. Then when I leave, you'll be free."

"How?" the woman asked. "How is that possible?"

"These cuffs link with a frequency that remains strong as long as I'm nearby," Terra explained. "The moment I'm out of the vicinity, they'll unclasp, and you'll be free. Got that?"

The woman nodded.

"Are you going to do anything stupid?" Terra took a moment to press her gun barrel into the woman's back.

"No," the woman replied.

"Good." Terra stepped away, then left the room.

You lied to that woman, APRIL declared as Terra sped up and worked her way toward the place where she believed Samina was.

"I did."

Why? APRIL asked.

"If she believes she'll be safe, she won't cause any problems. It'll only be in thirty minutes or so she'll realize that it was all bullshit."

She stopped at the place where the figure glowed on the other side of the wall. "Sometimes you have to lie to protect the masses. She's dangerous left unleashed. If she gets wind that she's under threat, she'll cause many more problems than she will locked in cuffs." She sighed. "Besides, it's not my job to go around killing everyone."

Noted, APRIL replied.

Terra stood facing the wall. At least ten feet separated her and the figure sitting on the chair. She examined the smooth surface, rubbing with the flat of her palm, then extended a fist and knocked against the surface.

She was gentle at first, the thick wall absorbing much of the noise. She tested high and low, looking for any possible points of penetration. At one point, she thought she heard a change in tone, but upon second inspection, it was the same.

"If only I could see inside," Terra muttered.

Scanning now. The wall morphed before her as a series of sonar frequencies bounced and registered with the AI in her head. The image changed into a strange shade of blue, with certain parts in a dense royal and a couple of spots in a lighter cyan.

The longer she stood there, and the more frequencies that came back, the clearer the picture appeared as wires, pipes, and structural beams came into view like an old-fashioned TV finding its image through the static.

"Holy..." Terra muttered. "Is there anything you can't do?"

I could provide a list if you like?

Terra chuckled, imagining the string of information that APRIL would undoubtedly subject her to at her request. "That won't be necessary."

Her eyes focused on a point of lighter blue where there was a gap between intersections of pipes and wires. She reached into her utility belt and drew out a black steel combat knife. She touched the blade against the wall, marking a small X in the location she wanted to strike, then reared back.

She punctured the wall easily, the metal slipping through the drywall with little resistance. Sawing the blade through the wall, she created a large enough hole for her head to fit through.

She reached through and found another layer of sheetrock, which she attacked in the same manner. Chunks of the white stuff fell away, revealing a room filled with inky darkness. Dust filtered before her, and the moment she stopped sawing, she heard the soft sobs of someone inside.

"Samina?" Terra whispered.

She stepped back, allowing a soft glow of light to pass into the room. She could just about make out the top of a woman's head, the hair unkempt and disturbed. Terra listened for a reply and heard the muffled tones of words filtered through a gag.

"Hold on tight," Terra murmured. "We're coming." *We?* she thought momentarily.

Impatience growing at the rate with which she could enter the room, Terra gripped a chunk of the wall in her hand and pulled hard. She focused most of the grip on the metal of her thumb, avoiding grazes or skin getting damaged by brute force. After a moment she was able to get the heel of her boot against the wall, further expanding the hole she'd made.

The network of pipes and wires was a problem, but Terra figured she still might be able to make it through. An idea was forming, and for this to work, she'd have to move fast.

She looked around her feet and found a length of throw rug covered in dust and dirt. She rolled it into a log and passed it through the hole, listening for the confirmed *thud* on the other side of the wall as it fell to the floor.

Next, she assessed the hole, figuring that if she twisted and climbed through, she'd just about make it in. The only remaining problems were, first, would the pipes support her weight if she used them to lever herself in? Second, if they were for hot water, she would risk burning her hands.

Terra glanced back at the room where she'd left the woman in cuffs. She ran to her, then stole a blanket from the couch in the room. She returned to the hole and used the blanket to protect her hands as she tested the pipes.

They groaned but remained firmly in place. She slowly placed her weight on the pipes, lifting herself off the floor, until one buckled and fell free of its clamps.

Shit, Terra thought. She tossed the blanket to the side, then took a few steps back. "Here goes nothing."

She ran at the hole and dove through, arms out in front of her as if she was about to enter a swimming pool. She slipped into the darkness, then used her hands to find the floor. She rolled over one shoulder, coming to an abrupt stop as she hit the wall on the other side of the room.

"Fuck..." she complained.

Samina gasped, turning to face her. Terra rose to her feet and dusted herself down. "Don't worry. I'm here to get you out." Terra tried to do something to soothe the woman and erase the fear that had sparked in her eyes.

Someone spoke on the other side of the wall. "What was that?"

Terra worked quickly, knowing she only had a few moments to make this happen. She grabbed the rug she'd rolled up and pressed it against the hole, returning the room to total darkness. She used her knife to stab into the sheetrock and hang the cloth up, then dashed to the other side of the room to wait behind the door.

Footsteps approached. The handle jerked. The door opened a few inches, a triangle of light widening as a head poked through. Terra couldn't tell who it was but knew it was a man as they spoke. "You causing problems?"

Samina shook her head desperately. The man's breathing deepened. "Shame… All of this to sell you. Wonder if I'll have time to play with you myself…"

A voice called, "Well?"

"Nothing." The man closed the door behind him. "She's safe."

The room returned to black. Terra engaged APRIL's night vision and crossed to Samina. She leaned close to her ear and whispered, "Don't worry. You're going to be okay. I'm from the Atlantica Justice System, here to get you out."

A voice came through the wall. "We can't find her. She's gone."

"I'm going to remove your gag," Terra stated. "If you scream, you'll endanger us both, understand?"

Samina nodded.

"Good." Terra loosened the cloth tied around Samina's mouth. "Are you okay?"

"No," Samina managed, her words shaky. "No, I'm not. I don't know what the fuck's happening, I don't know where I am, and I've seen people die today."

Terra gave her a pitying look Samina couldn't see. "I know this is rough, but I promise you, stay with me, and I'll get you out of here."

"How is this possible?" Samina asked. "Cops can't…"

"No, they can't," Terra replied. "I'm not your typical AJS officer. Trust me on this one. Do you want out or not?"

"I do," Samina confirmed. "Please."

"Good," Terra replied firmly. She worked at the bonds around Samina's wrists. They loosened enough for her to shift in her seat. APRIL's night vision mode showed Samina rubbing her wrists.

"Thank you," Samina stated.

"Don't thank me yet. We still have to get you out, first."

"You can do that? How?"

Terra turned to the door, one hand reaching toward her utility belt. "With my new docket of toys."

***

Rob was twitchy.

The sounds outside the room had been colossal. He hadn't expected his grunt to blow the fucking building down, but it wasn't the worst strategy. At least that way they could take down the rogue cop. If not, at least they'd waylaid her.

Now he was surrounded, yet he still didn't feel safe. The room was cast in pregnant silence as they listened for any further attack. The entryway had at least half a dozen guards, and the room had another half dozen armed to the teeth.

They would be fine.

Then why was he so nervous?

Toby returned from Samina's room, closing the door behind him and ensuring that the creases were covered and the entry hidden once more. He was sure he'd heard something in there, but now it was gone.

"Coast is clear," Toby declared.

Rob turned his attention back to the door, not sure if he felt safe or felt like a coward. His lips peeled back into a snarl. If that girl came anywhere near him, he'd tear out her fucking throat.

Or at least that's what he told himself, moments before the world filled with sound and smoke.

———

Terra kicked the door, smoke grenade leaving her hand as it arced to the center of the room.

There were people everywhere, and she used APRIL to scan and monitor them all as they turned toward the sound of the disturbance, guns sweeping toward her.

The smoke grenade exploded, the room instantly filling with a dense cloud. Terra jumped to the side the moment it detonated. She was barely in time as a spray of bullets peppered the doorway and lost themselves in the dark of the hidden room.

"Idiots! Don't shoot there! You'll kill our hostage," a voice called. "Get her out of here!"

Terra ignored the voice, focusing on the nearest of the brutes. She could see him in almost crystal clarity, a green and orange blob of heat that she sped toward and knocked out with one clean punch to the nose. Not too far away from him, another ran toward the place where Terra had entered the room. She kicked out a leg, tripped them up, then followed with a swift kick to the head.

"Over there!" a voice called.

Bullets turned toward her. A few of the orange figures sped toward the room where they'd left Samina. Terra dodged with a quick side-step, navigating around the chairs and various pieces of furniture. She picked up a decorative glass orb from a side table and launched it at the figure on the far side of the room. A moment later, the sound of breaking glass followed a grunt.

Someone charged toward her. Terra braced herself as a figure appeared through the smoke and grabbed around her waist. She was shoved back into the wall, the air expelling from her lungs. She elbowed the top of the woman's head, then tried to kick up a knee. The woman held firm, calling the attention of the others to shoot where her voice was.

Terra worked her arms under the woman's shoulders and loosened her grip. She brought her up into a type of bear-hug, then spun her around. The woman faced the onslaught of bullets as Terra ducked behind her, using her for a protective cushion.

The woman went limp in her hands.

The two figures who had run for the dark room were now on the floor, unconscious. Terra spotted Samina's figure behind the door, ready with the chair in her hands to take out anyone else who got near her.

Terra smiled.

She shoved the woman away from her as she skirted the edge of the room. A man who she recognized as the same shape as Rob was in the center of the room, spinning wildly around with a semi-automatic rifle in his hands. Terra waited until he turned his back, then jumped at him.

She landed on his back, hands snaking around his body and grabbing the rifle. A spray of bullets erupted, their destination uncontrolled as Terra picked off the remaining few who were still in the room. She wasn't oblivious to the group outside the door who all readied themselves, their weapons aimed at the exit.

Rob spluttered as Terra brought the rifle to his throat, using it as a brace to hold her steady while she cut off his breath. "Samina, now!"

Samina rushed toward her, keeping close to Terra. Terra pressed sharply until Rob's breath began to fade. He weakened in her grip, and Samina grabbed the rifle from his hands before slapping on a pair of handcuffs.

Terra hopped off, helping Rob stay upright. His head lolled, eyes struggling to stay open. Terra lifted him into a fireman's carry.

"You're going to have to help us get out of here now," Terra told Samina. The smoke had begun to clear, but they still didn't have a direct line of sight to the doorway. Terra studied the thermal images of the crowd waiting for her. It was going to be a tough escape to take more of them on.

"Anything," Samina replied, holding the gun uncertainly in her hands. "Just tell me what to do."

Terra turned back toward the darkened room. "Only one way out. We're not waiting on the element of surprise anymore."

"What're you—" Samina started.

Terra took the final grenade from her belt and pulled the pin. She lobbed it into the room, aiming to get as close to the wall as possible. She counted to three as one of the waiting grunts outside reached for the door handle, the others with the weapons ready to fire.

The bomb exploded. The wall crumbled. Terra moved toward the darkened room, finding the way ahead full of problems. The floor had loosened and now angled toward the floor below. Electricity sparked from the wires, and a spray of water erupted into the air.

The door kicked in behind them. "Go!" Terra bellowed.

Samina went first, running into the room and falling on her ass. The floor worked like a strange slide, and though it wasn't elegant, Samina stumbled into the hallway below.

Terra swiftly followed, dropping Rob as both of them tumbled down the slope. Gunfire erupted behind them. Terra grunted, then regained her footing. She picked up Rob and once again threw him over her shoulders.

"There has to be a quicker way out of here." Terra engaged APRIL's blueprint readings as arrows appeared in her vision.

She took a sharp left, heading into a room that appeared untouched for some time. A couch, TV, and en suite bathroom took the space, but it was to the window that APRIL directed them.

"Shoot the glass," Terra commanded.

Samina complied. The light revealed the torn and dirty hem

of her flowing emerald dress. The glass shattered. Terra ushered Samina out first, then clambered out behind her. They emerged onto a fire escape and sprinted down toward ground level.

Voices called behind them. Bullets ricocheted off the metal. They doggedly continued, finally making it to the ground. "Almost there!" Terra called.

Samina and Terra ran beside each other. Terra couldn't believe she was keeping pace with Samina with Rob on her back.

Or is Samina slow, and she's only just keeping pace with you?

When they entered the main street, they met a thick crowd of people. Some were staring up at the building, curiosity drawing them to the multiple sounds of explosions inside. Some walked by, giving Terra and Samina strange looks as their dirt-streaked forms entered the public domain.

Terra took a left and speed-walked along the sidewalk. Samina followed closely. They didn't turn back. Terra knew that whoever was in that building would be stupid to shoot an officer once they were back in the public domain.

The hypocritical law worked both ways, bitches.

CHAPTER FIFTEEN

The great thing about driverless cabs was the lack of conversation and judgment.

Terra sat in the back, an unconscious Rob next to her, head lolling as the cab guided them through the city. Samina sat in the front, quiet and pale. There was a stale scent in the air, and Terra couldn't work out which one of them it came from.

The cab pulled up to the precinct, pausing at the front of the long, paved walk. It was still dark out, the way to the front doors lit by a set of street lights. Only a couple of officers were in sight. Terra touched the transaction pad with her phone and dragged Rob out with her, picking him up once more to throw over her shoulder.

"You, too," she instructed Samina.

Samina looked doubtfully at the precinct, then nodded. Terra understood her hesitancy. Guilty or innocent, there was something apprehension-inducing for civilians entering the headquarters of justice in the city. Terra knew that Samina had convictions, but this wasn't about that. This was about figuring out what had happened that night.

Her fellow officers gave Terra a wide berth as she beelined for

Black's office. Slim looked up from her desk with a grin of appreciation, offering a saluting nod as she passed. Hewlett and Dunston followed Samina with their eyes the entire journey, making it clear exactly what was on their minds.

Terra ignored Gina on the way in, much to her chagrin.

She threw Rob into a chair in Black's office, then stood beside him. She invited Samina to sit. She did, although still with a level of caution.

"Rob Custer," Terra declared. "Your target. Caught in the act of kidnapping Samina Openheimer."

Samina gave her a sideways glance. "How do you know my full name?"

They ignored her. Black leaned back in her chair with a satisfied smile. "Good work, Kris. I assume you created quite the ruckus along the way?"

"Not intentionally. I walked into the middle of a sting. It was lucky I got there when I did."

"Where were they?" Black asked.

"The Raven Theater."

Black grimaced. "Intriguing."

"I'd advise a clean-up squad, but the whole incident occurred in private boundaries," Terra explained. "There'll be plenty of media attention, no doubt, given the number of theater patrons drugged into sleep."

"Little we can do to address that. I'll inform Nora in advance of their arrival unless she's picked this up on the grapevine."

"There were actors, too," Terra outlined. "Quite a few witnesses to my presence."

"You'll be fine," Black soothed. "You're doing your job. Let Nora do hers. If there are ways for criminals to get away with their shit, there are plenty of ways for us to get away with this."

Terra gave her a doubtful look. "Seriously, what does Nora—"

"Are you okay?" Black interjected, turning her attention to Samina.

Samina nodded, looking unassured. "I think so. No... Not really."

She explained to Black the circumstances of her night. They confirmed many of Terra's details while highlighting the additional nugget of information that Custer planned to sell Samina to the highest bidder. She cried somewhere in the middle of her story, lamenting the loss of her close personal friend, as well as her fear of what might spring from this.

"If one person is trying to buy me," Samina stated, "that must mean there are more out there with ill intentions."

"That's likely." Black didn't try to sugarcoat the situation. "If you want my recommendation, stick to public spaces for a while. Or, in those instances where you go home to your residence, let the AJS in. Hire security. Do whatever you must to feel comfortable and out of harm's way. This city is no place for an underground princess to inhabit."

Samina cocked her head. "How do you—"

"It's my job to know things." Black reached into her drawer and withdrew a pair of APRIL glasses. She put them on, then proceeded to list a long line of personal details about Samina and her history on record.

Samina flushed, placing a hand on her chest.

"Tell your friends," Black continued. "The AJS is now armed with a hive mind of AI designed to help us recognize, restrict, and redress criminal activity in this city. Any secret, anything you wish to hide, we know it. It's all in here."

Custer groggily opened his eyes, grunting as he tried to focus on the room.

"I hope you heard that, Custer," Black stated firmly. "You and all your shit bag friends are reaching the end of their reign. You want to keep doing what you're doing, hide in the private spaces, although even they won't keep you safe for long."

Custer coughed, then strained against his cuffs. Terra turned and placed her boot on his chest. She leaned in close to his face, enjoying the fear in his eyes. "I'd learn to stay put if I were you. You're going to spend a *long* time in jail, so get used to staring at the same four walls for extended periods."

Custer opened his mouth to reply, but Terra struck him before he could. His head snapped left, eyes closing as he fell into unconsciousness once more.

Terra turned to Black, who had her eyebrow raised.

Black asked, "Was that necessary?"

Terra shrugged. "You tell me." She glanced out Black's window as the traffic rolled past in the city outside. "Some fucker destroyed my bike."

Black nodded. "I know."

"How?"

Black removed the APRIL glasses. "I was watching you. Caught it on CCTV."

"So you saw the man fall to his death?" Terra asked.

Black gave a small laugh. "I'd say he was dead before he hit the ground, wouldn't you?"

Terra let the memory pass through her mind, the anger, the irritation…

Black rose from her chair, picking up a few of her effects before heading to the door. "We'll get you sorted, Kris. Don't worry. As for you, Samina, I'd like to get one of our team to ask you a few more questions for our records if that's okay?"

Samina considered this. "Do I have a choice?"

"Always."

Samina chewed her lip. "Fine."

"Good." Black leaned out the door. "Gina, can you call Newman in here please to assist Mr. Custer to his holding cell?"

Gina didn't answer but reached for the phone.

Black motioned to Terra and Samina to exit her room. "Shall we?"

Terra sat in the locker room, resting her back against the cool steel of the lockers.

At this time of the night, the locker room was nearly always empty. Officers were out on the beat, mid-duty, and it would be some time before the morning changeover brought several bodies in here.

She glanced around the room, feeling more out of place than she ever had before, thanks to her upgraded uniform, mind, and weapons.

When had she asked for all this?

The ghosts of her memories floated in front of her, showing officers ribbing each other as they stripped off their uniforms and put on their day clothes. Those coming into work were fresh-faced and ready for duty, some of the guys playfully whipping each other with clothing as if they never quite grew out of their high school football shenanigans.

The world had grown bigger for Terra. Part of her wished for those times to return, but she knew now that she was on the verge of a greater change. That each hard-fought day would bring her a step closer to her dream of finally turning this city around.

"Daydreaming?" Slim appeared in the doorway beside her.

"Remembering. It feels like forever since I've been here."

"It's been a few weeks." Slim took a seat across from Terra.

"I know." Terra smiled. "I'm not what I once was."

"You're a robot."

Terra spotted the glasses on her face. "You're halfway there."

"They're good, aren't they?" Slim replied. "Put aside all the haunting fears that external forces are controlling you, and you could start to get used to them. In the two days since I got mine, I've doubled my arrests and closed a bunch of loops on ink circles that have been outstanding for months."

"Sounds like great work. Of course. You're one of the good ones."

"Even Hewlett and Dunston are getting theirs," Slim continued. "Not that the pair enjoy their separation. They're itching to get back together, but Black won't allow it. Says that the glasses need to be used to their full potential, or else what's the point?"

Terra rested her head against the lockers. "Things are changing."

"They always do. That's the beauty of it."

Terra nodded. "Shouldn't you be out on your next mission? Don't let me get in the way of progress. You have records to smash, promotions to seek."

Slim smirked. "I thought you'd need a friendly ear. I can't imagine what it's like inside that head."

"Oily."

They both laughed.

"Seriously," Slim stated. "I'm here if you want to talk, okay? Everyone needs downtime. Ever since your crash, all you've done is run at a hundred miles per hour. A little fun, a little rest could help give you some perspective."

"You sound like Imani."

"She's a good one. You know she has your best interests at heart."

"I'll see if she wants to go dancing." Terra grinned, making it clear she wasn't serious.

"No," Slim replied sharply.

Terra raised an eyebrow. "No?"

"No cops," Slim stated. "Haven't you got any friends who aren't working for the AJS? What about that detective guy?"

"Dick?"

Slim winked. "If you need it."

Terra scoffed. "I'm all right, thanks. I'd rather dive headfirst into a pile of broken glass."

"Surely you have someone?" An LED flashed on Slim's glasses. Her gaze turned inward, her back straightening as she read the message that appeared. "Okay, good talk. I have to go."

She crossed to the locker room door, then paused. "Seriously, I know you feel you can't. But try. Not everyone in Atlantica is out to get you."

She left Terra deep in her thoughts. Terra scrolled through her phonebook, looking at the list of names and numbers she had for her contacts. "Officer" or a variation thereof prefixed nearly every name. Those who weren't were family, and she wanted to keep them out of this.

She continued scrolling, one name standing out on the screen. She supposed it wouldn't hurt to give her a call, to catch up and find out how she was doing.

What was a couple of hours of downtime, anyway?

Terra slid her phone into her pocket after tapping the red button to end the call.

She strolled through the AJS precinct, making her way to the front door. Once again, Hewlett and Dunston stalked on the far side of the bullpen, looking as though they had some news or comments to share with Terra.

Terra sped up. She passed through reception, then into the cool night air.

She automatically aimed for the parking lot, momentarily forgetting that her Ducati wouldn't be waiting for her. A bubble of annoyance burst in her stomach. There were few material things she cherished in her life, but that bike had been one of them.

Black appeared beside her. "Don't look so glum, chum."

"Chum?" Terra wondered when Black had gotten so buddy-buddy with her. Perhaps it was after Terra saved her life from Cross.

"I know you're down about your bike getting destroyed," Black stated, "but let's look at the positives, shall we? We can finally get you onto an AJS-issue bike that doesn't draw the attention of everyone around when you arrive on the scene."

Terra sighed. "Not being funny, but I'd rather the rumble of thunder beneath my ass than the burning of rubber on asphalt. Those things are dolly-trolleys, powered by glowing blue rocks."

Black shook her head, a smile on her face. "Well, how about you ride this dolly-trolley back to HQ and ask Nora for a tune-up?"

Terra pinched the bridge of her nose and drew a deep breath. "Fine. Anything beats playing passenger in another driverless cab."

Terra straddled the blue and black motorbike and revved the engine. There was no roar to meet her, only a faint *hum* as the glowing Atlanticore drew power to the engine. "Vroom, vroom," she muttered, throwing a salute to Black before silently speeding along the streets and into the city proper.

CHAPTER SIXTEEN

"Seems you've had a busy evening," Imani stated as Terra parked outside of Nora's facility and glanced down at her bike.

She wasn't sure if she'd cut the engine. The silent bike showed no sign of change when she twisted the key. Terra's brow creased in confusion.

"Sweet ride," Imani commented. "Sorry about the Ducati."

Terra glanced up. "You know about that?"

"We have eyes and ears to the ground at all times. If it's in public, it's in our eyesight." She waved Terra on. "Come on, follow me."

Terra dismounted her bike and followed Imani. "Shouldn't *you* be doing some kind of work now? Why does it feel like I'm the one out there doing all the grunt work?"

Imani smirked. "Because you're the chosen one, Kris. My job is to ensure that you have all that you need to do your job. Not only that, but I also have to maintain pretenses at my old job to ensure that I don't arouse suspicions about my new job."

Terra cocked an eyebrow.

Imani laughed. "I'm happy to trade places if you like?"

Terra shook her head. "I'll pass."

"Good. Nice outfit, by the way. Looking badass." Imani led her through the reception, then along to a side door that Terra hadn't been through before. Along a small hallway, they met another door. Imani opened it with a digital signature, then they both emerged in a hidden parking lot.

Dozens of replicas of the bike Terra had dismounted filled the lot. "When Black mentioned a tune-up, I didn't think she meant a brand-new version of the bike I just left behind."

"You really hate them, don't you?" Imani asked.

Terra nodded. "They're boring. They have no character. There's no badassery. It's like riding a pushbike. At least with a fossil fuel engine, you get the growl, the roar, the rumble. It's like the damn thing is alive, and you have to fight and control the velociraptor to ride it."

Imani stopped and smirked. "It's a bike, not a dinosaur."

"It's a toy," Terra replied. "The Ducati was a *machine*."

They stopped by a motorbike that was gleaming under the bright white spotlights. Though its edges were a little sharper, its body more polished, the blacks even deeper and darker than Terra's assigned vehicle, she couldn't spot the real difference.

"This is your tune-up," Imani offered.

Terra circled the vehicle, rubbing her chin. There was something strange about it, but she couldn't put her finger on it. In the center of the motorbike's body, a small cage showed the pulsing blue glow of the Atlanticore.

"I don't get it," Terra offered at last. "What's the upgrade?"

"Give it a try," Imani encouraged.

Terra straddled the bike. It was more comfortable than the last. As the bike rocked a little, a couple of components crumbled away and hit the floor.

"It's in worse shape than the other one," Terra stated.

"Is it?" Imani replied. She crossed over to the wall, where a pressure blower was idly standing. She asked Terra to dismount, and when she did, she attacked the bike with a thin, continual stream of powerful air.

Components blew away, small pieces of thin paint and plastic took to the air, and the blower chipped away until a sleek, modern-looking motorcycle was left standing where the old model had been.

"Protective skin," Imani explained. "The factory has only produced a few dozen of these bikes, so buyers have requested cloaks and disguises for when they're transported. The old casing structure is just thin plastic, designed to be stripped away when the bike is ready to ride." She patted the seat. "Meet your new transportation."

Terra leaned in close, mouth hanging open. The bike was streamlined, slick, with considerably fewer parts than the old bikes. There were gaps and spaces where spokes used to hold the wheels together. She raised the bike up onto its back wheel, surprised by how light it was, then spun the front wheel.

The wheel spun without slowing, a frictionless mechanism ensuring that the wheel could continue to spin for eternity.

"Maglev?" Terra asked.

"Yep," Imani replied. "Frictionless, magnetic levitation technology. It's silent—which I know you hate—but it's fast. Not only that but it's built of the finest components found on the island, custom alloys and bespoke metals which will keep the bike sturdy without compromising weight."

"Damn," Terra replied. "It doesn't look half-bad, too."

"It's the latest design," Imani replied, motioning to the other bikes. "All of these bikes are the same, ready to be used by the team when our goal is inevitably met."

"Goal?" Terra asked.

"Well, Nora's goal," Imani replied. "To free Atlantica from crime."

"Damn…" Terra repeated. "A whole fleet of these sweeping through the city would put any criminal on the back foot. How fast do they go?"

"They'll hit zero to sixty in less than a second," Imani warned, "so watch that accelerator as you go, or hold on tight. At their top, they can hit speeds of almost three hundred miles per hour."

Terra stared at Imani. "I'm sorry?"

"You're forgiven." Imani winked.

Terra ran a hand over the cool metal, not quite believing what she was seeing. "Is it safe?"

Imani considered this. "As safe as can be. I mean, nothing is foolproof. As long as you ride it responsibly, it'll be fine." She grinned.

"Define 'responsibly.'"

Imani laughed. "Don't worry, it's built with all the latest safety measures. Bulletproof casing, self-aligning systems to ensure that you never fully topple off the bike. If you collide with something, a full three-sixty airbag will deploy, cocooning you in less than one second so that you can bounce to safety."

Terra gave an impressed nod. "You guys thought of everything."

"I had nothing to do with this," Imani replied. "This is all…"

"I know, I know," Terra interjected. "Nora's doing. Jeesh, at some point, I might actually find out what that woman does."

Imani smirked. "You'll be the first. She holds her cards very close to her chest."

"Clearly," Terra replied. She mounted the bike. "Can I take it for a spin?"

"Of course," Imani replied. "Just head toward that wall, and the mechanism inside the bike will trigger the door to open."

"Sweet." Terra twisted the accelerator, expecting to hear the roar of the engine. When silence met her, she looked disheartened.

"Don't worry," Imani soothed. "What this bike lacks in decibels, it makes up for with speed and adrenaline."

Terra nodded, then headed forward. The bike lurched, jumping in speed. Terra eased off the throttle, pulling the bike back a little as she left Imani laughing behind her. She closed in on the far side of the parking lot, where a midnight black garage door stood. As she neared the door, it rolled up, giving Terra entry into the night once more.

Terra played with the bike, testing small turns and slaloming along the asphalt. It was light and responsive, each micro touch delivering what used to take some effort with the Ducati. As she neared the edge of the compound, she lined the bike up with the straight road leading off into the fields and toward the city.

She stopped, placing her feet on the ground on either side of the bike. Guards watched closely from behind as Terra muttered, "Hi ho, Silver. Away!"

The bike tore ahead, Terra having to increase her grip to stay mounted. Wind rushed past her, the fields disappearing either side in a blur as the bike zipped along, a silent predator in the night.

Terra laughed, the sound snatched by the wind. Bugs flew into her face as she attempted to hold steady, letting the bike's technology do what it did best.

She slowed as she reached a turn, the bike slowing with such suddenness that Terra wondered how she didn't skid. She laughed again, trying to catch her breath as she rolled into the turn.

"That was insane," Terra muttered.

She glanced either way, then merged onto the road and followed APRIL's directions in her vision. Now that she was on a more trafficked road, she was more cautious, though that didn't stop her overtaking cars as though they didn't exist.

She made the journey to the city in record time, the silence a strange friend as the buildings took the skyline all around and she made for her final stop of the evening. She hoped this one wouldn't take that long since tiredness had begun to creep into her bones.

Eyes followed Terra as she passed, eager-eyed observers spotting the silent black bike cutting through the city traffic. Despite the late hour, Terra still had to work to close in on her destination, swerving through queues until she finally rounded the corner before pulling to a stop curbside.

Terra was cautious leaving the bike by the curb. "What if someone steals it?"

According to the recent data in my information banks, the AJS Sniper V226 has anti-theft technology, which requires biological signatures to start the engines.

"What does that mean?" Terra asked.

There is a digital thumbprint reader embedded in your key, APRIL explained. **It's not enough to twist the key in the ignition. One must also identify biologically as a paired rider of the machine.**

Terra ran a thumb across the flat black panel on the key. "Good call."

She turned to face the building across the road and dug her hands into her pockets. Her rifle still hung over her shoulder, although she wished she'd topped up the items for her utility belt before leaving the AJS precinct.

"Harper's House" occupied the bottom floor of a five-story building that looked as though the architect had lifted it straight from an old London city. Thick, dark beams crossed over a white facade, with lead-lined windows decorating its front.

A white light sign spelled the words, "Harper's House," although one of the lightbulbs had blown and instead showed, "Harper's Hose."

Terra studied the property, scanning its contents. It looked quiet inside, a small gaggle of people sitting in the gloomy interior and sipping their drinks.

"Ty Katakura..." Terra muttered. "Let's find out if you're home..."

CHAPTER SEVENTEEN

The room was gloomy, hazed with a thick blanket of smoke.

It didn't take Terra long to work out where the smoke was coming from when she spotted the table of gentlemen playing poker over in the far corner where a large fireplace housed a raging blaze.

Most eyes turned to Terra as she entered. She couldn't have felt more like a sore thumb with her vibrant blue AJS uniform sparkling in the firelight. She assessed all of the current patrons, determined no immediate threats, then crossed to the bar.

"Hope we ain't after trouble," a sour-faced man with a bright red, swollen nose grunted. He carried three steins in one hand, caring little for the amber drops that spilled down the glass and dampened the floor. "This is a private business. Ain't no AJS can do shit in here, you understand? My boys and girls are polite, patient, and respectful. You want to cause a ruckus; I'm well within my rights to tell you to fuck off."

"That won't be necessary." Terra raised a hand to appease him. "I'm not here to cause any trouble. I'm here to find someone."

The barman narrowed his eyes. "One doesn't necessarily exclude the other."

Terra grinned, leaning her elbows on the bar. "You said it yourself—private property. I can't do shit. You think I'd risk my job like that?"

The man eyed her suspiciously for a moment. His gaze darted to two men in the shadow of the overhanging balcony on the second floor. "What can I get ya?"

Terra ordered water in the absence of any coffee, juice, or hot drink. It seemed this place drew a lot of its inspiration from Victorian England, right down to the warped timber and the clientele that inhabited it. Most seemed not to have heard of luxury fashion brands or even soap for that matter. Men with scruffy beards or women with dank, greasy hair hanging low over their faces filled the place.

Terra cleared her throat, the thick smoke irritating her airways.

The barman grinned. "Don't be complaining, now. You want fresh air? You go outside."

"I'm good." Terra quickly drank her water. The cool liquid soothed her throat, but the sting was migrating to her eyes.

She sat at the bar and studied the crowd, looking for anyone who she believed could fit the title of Ty Katakura. *APRIL, scan, please.*

Of course.

The patrons' information appeared in her vision as tiny digital labels with their names and personal information. Terra slyly worked her way around the room but couldn't find anyone by the name of Ty.

There was another name that you mentioned, Terra thought. *What was the name of the person who sent the message?*

Harmony Erron, APRIL replied. **She is absent from this location.**

*Great…*Terra thought. *What a waste of time.*

"You know you're awful pretty to be sitting in a place like this alone," the barman grunted from nearby. Terra turned to find him resting on the counter on the other side of the bar, twisting a cloth in a glass that looked as if he hadn't washed it in the last five years. "Don't get a lot of your type in Harper's. Heard cops have their own bars."

Terra grimaced. "That's an urban legend. Chances are you've seen more AJS in your place than you know. Only, they wouldn't be dressed in uniform as I am."

"Why are you then?"

Terra smirked. "Because I'm dangerous."

The man's cool demeanor faltered for a moment. "Lots of dangerous folk in this city. Rogue cops are the least of our problems." He nodded out the door. "Just across the road is one of Atlantica's most notorious crack dens. Every day we hear guns and screams and fights. Ain't nothing your type does about that."

He pointed to the right. "Three buildings up is where they store whole rooms of bodies that thugs in this place are trying to discreetly get rid of without tipping off authorities or risking bringing them out in the public eye. Mostly they chuck them in the incinerator down below, but don't half leave an awful stink on a Tuesday morn."

He looked above him. "Three floors up, ten deaths in five years. Most of them domestic fights. Stabbings. Middle of the night. Ain't shit I could do about it. Happened on my watch, but I was none the wiser. Where were you cops when I called for your help?"

Terra sipped her water. "Outside listening, most likely."

"Couldn't come," the barman replied. "Left me in here with a killer." He pointed at a scar on his cheek. "Could've died. Almost took my sight." He scoffed. "Fucking Atlantica Justice System. Biggest waste of resources I ever seen."

A man with thick, muscular arms in a denim button-up vest took the stool beside Terra. "Is this slag off the AJS business? I'm in for that. Fuckers couldn't help my wife when the Groundhogs snatched her."

"The gang?" Terra asked.

The man nodded. His beetle-black eyes glimmered with sadness and anger in their depths. His teeth were yellowed, some missing as he turned to Terra and gave her a judgmental eye. "You know them."

"Of course," Terra replied. "We know a large number of the gangs that operate in this city."

"Don't do nothing about them, though. Do ya?" the barman stated. Terra could tell it wasn't a question.

"What do you expect us to do?" Terra replied. "It's your city you should be pissed at. Not me. Not the AJS. We can only operate within the boundaries of what the law gives us, so if we can't come in and help you, you need to lobby the city. Shake it up. Revolt."

The man exhaled, his lips wobbling and sending a fine mist of saliva over the bar. "Just like y'all. Blame it on someone else. It's the AJS's job to keep us safe."

"Believe me. We want to." Terra lowered her eyes to the bar. She sipped her water, a strange metallic tang hitting her taste-buds. "What happened to your wife?"

"Got her back." The man made it clear he wasn't going to divulge any more information.

The barman drew a deep breath, scrutinizing Terra with his glare. There was movement in the upper balcony.

APRIL, scan.

APRIL detected two bodies in the upper balcony, peering down at the trio. Terra side-eyed the area, trying to get a clearer picture of them. When APRIL detected the shape of a pistol, Terra jumped back off her seat and aimed her rifle at the balcony.

"You take that shot, and I'm going to have to dissolve you into red mist," Terra warned.

The two in the balcony made a run for it, knocking over tables and chairs as they dashed away. Terra made a break for the stairs. Then APRIL warned, **Terra. Watch your six.**

Terra reached the bottom of the stairs as something whizzed past her ear. She didn't have time to see where the projectile went or who it was from. She leaped the stairs two at a time, making it halfway when something bounced off the leg of her uniform.

She turned her attention, swinging the rifle around at her attacker. She expected the barman or the denim vest to have their firearms loaded, but they simply stood idly by and watched the action.

Terra. There.

APRIL drew Terra's attention to the dark corner at the far end of the bar where a skinny woman sat by herself. She had one leg crossed over the other, a half-finished pint resting in one hand. Her other elbow leaned on the table, lazily pointing the gun at Terra. She shot before Terra could take in the information, a bullet streaming right at her.

The bullet clipped the side of Terra's throat. She gasped, one hand automatically reaching for the point of entry. She expected to find blood but instead found the small dart embedded in her skin.

"Son of a…" Terra managed before drowsiness started to fog her vision. Her knees buckled. She took a step forward, then had to cling to the banister for support.

"APRIL, help…" Terra muttered, spotting the barman and the woman striding toward her.

Attempting to reject toxin, APRIL replied.

Terra felt a strong sense of cool wash through her as APRIL experimented with her biochemistry, looking for the solution to stave off the toxins. After another moment, it became clear that wasn't going to work as Terra tumbled forward, rolling down the stairs. She lay sprawled on the sticky wood as the barman and the woman loomed over her.

The woman crouched, lifting a single finger over her lips as Terra's breathing deepened and all she knew faded to black.

CHAPTER EIGHTEEN

The world smelled of petrol and gunpowder.

Terra's nose wrinkled, the strange scents intermingling and causing her to cough. She brought a fist to her mouth or thought she did, realizing when no hand came that she was bound to whatever hard surface she was lying on.

Someone walked around nearby.

They tutted. The sound of small items dropping into glass jars *clinked* around the room. "It's a sad state of affairs when you consider it…"

Terra tried to raise her head, but a leather strap held her forehead still.

"Atlantica," the voice continued, croaky yet oddly melodic. "The city of advances, or promise, of future…yet it can't handle its own business." The person tutted again. "An island with so much promise, so much to gain, and so much to give… Yet here we are. A law enforcement team that can't solve the very cases they're employed to solve."

Terra remained silent, staring up at the stone ceiling. She could feel APRIL working its magic on her system, releasing her from the grogginess of waking.

"Not even a century..." The person in the room moved further away, their voice echoing around the chamber. "Atlantica isn't even one hundred years old, and it's seen enough to last a thousand lifetimes. Was this what we were all meant to become? Is this the sad state of affairs that the founders dreamed?"

The person chuckled. Another *clink* in the jar. "Maybe..."

The footsteps drew closer. Terra closed her eyes, trying not to draw attention to the fact she had awoken. If she remained quiet, perhaps she'd glean some information from this person, find out exactly what was going on, maybe figure out a chance to escape.

She felt the shadow of the presence loom over her, could hear the shallow breathing, followed by a soft scent of sour strawberries.

"Hmm." The person grunted. "Maybe one day..."

The footsteps faded away. The person opened then closed the door. The room fell into silence.

After a few minutes, Terra strained again, trying to raise her head. She glanced around using her peripheral vision, unable to see where she was or what the person had been putting into the glass. Moss stained the stone above her. The air had a cool chill as though Terra was in a dungeon of some kind.

"APRIL," Terra whispered. "Analyze. Where the hell are we?"

APRIL ran the scan. **Unable to determine location. Triangulation failed. Signal blocked.**

"Blocked?" Terra gasped.

I'd advise you to keep your voice down, APRIL stated.

Terra hadn't been aware that she was speaking out loud. *Good point. APRIL, what's going on? What's the threat level?*

Unable to identify threat level, APRIL repeated. **Captor not in range. Unable to explore surroundings without optic stimulation.**

You mean you can't see because I can't? Terra asked.

Affirmative.

Shit. Terra drew a steadying breath, feeling something rough against her chest. *Is that what I think it is?*

I am unsure as to what you are referring.

The chest plate, Terra replied. *Am I still wearing the AJS chest plate?*

Something vibrated on Terra's chest. A glow of blue flared before her as APRIL's voice entered the room. "Affirmative."

Shut up, Terra shot back. The blue glow faded. *You're the one who was telling me to be quiet.*

You asked the question, APRIL replied.

Terra bit back her retort, her senses on fire as she listened for anyone who might have heard APRIL's outburst.

She heard only silence.

APRIL, what do we do?

It seems that your options are limited, APRIL replied. **According to the sensors in your suit, leather straps bind your ankles, wrists, and neck to a surface that is brittle, dense, and reads at a temperature of fifty-seven degrees. Your chest plate is active and undamaged, though there are no functions built within that could help you break your ties. Your Chimera firearm is exactly nine feet and seven inches from your body and is also in full working order.**

Terra frowned. *I'm sorry... What?*

Repeating information, APRIL stated. **It seems that your options are limited. According to the sensors in your suit...**

APRIL, stop. Terra clenched her jaw. *There are sensors in the suit that can detect restraints?*

Affirmative. The sensors can help detect materials and substances you contact, enabling you to protect yourself better in the field.

And the gun? Terra asked.

Is nine feet and seven inches away, APRIL replied.

I meant, how do you know? Terra replied bluntly. *How is that possible?*

The APRIL technology utilizes a series of transmitters and receivers. The Chimera firearm is detectable within this room and is sending intelligence updates to your chest plate, thus further updating the information I can receive inside your head.

*Holy...*Terra thought. *So, how do we get the gun?* Before APRIL could reply, Terra added, *Wait. What's a chimera?*

An image of a mythical being appeared in Terra's vision. It had the head of a lion, the head of a goat in the center of its spine, and a snake for a tail.

The Chimera, according to Greek mythology, was a monstrous fire-breathing hybrid creature of Lycia in Asia Minor, composed of the parts of more than one animal.

Terra grunted as her body tensed. "Why do you have to take everything so literally?"

She closed her eyes, annoyed at her outburst. She listened, but again met with only silence.

What's the chimera firearm? Terra added.

Your firearm is the Chimera, APRIL replied, **Likely named due to its hybrid ability to switch functionality and work intelligently with the APRIL systems.**

An idea came to Terra. *Can you call it here? Can you draw it toward me? Like, does it have wheels, or maybe a magnetic connection, or...*

Unfortunately not, APRIL replied. **If you want your weapon, you'll have to escape your bonds.**

How do you propose we do that? Terra asked.

I will force a surge of adrenaline through your body, APRIL informed her. **Once you're in a state of 'fight or flight,' attempt to break the bonds. Many reports have attributed adrenal maximization for assisting humans with great feats of strength, including lifting cars and large chunks of debris in earthquakes.**

Worth a shot, Terra replied.

Initiating adrenaline.

Terra's skin felt tight as the adrenaline coursed through her. Her heart beat double speed, eyes widening as she felt a sudden burst of raw energy.

Attempt escape now, APRIL commanded.

Weird, taking orders from a cyborg, Terra thought as she got to work. She strained against the bonds, feeling the muscles cord in her neck, wrists, and ankles. The leather straps stretched, but only marginally. She heard them creaking, protesting her sudden outburst. She pushed and pulled, twisted and jerked, hoping for the straps to loosen enough that she could escape.

The sound of some kind of mechanism joined the chorus. Terra paused for a moment and felt the leather grow tighter around her limbs. She fought against the sudden increase in pressure, but it made no difference. She was bound tighter than ever.

"Shit," Terra muttered, slightly breathless. "What was that?"

Unable to identify, APRIL replied. **Initiating recuperation initiative.**

What's the recuperation initiative? Terra asked.

After a sudden burst of adrenaline, the body needs a chance to recover, APRIL replied. **Inducing forceful rest protocol.**

Terra opened her mouth to reply, but before she had a chance, sleep washed over her. She slept soundly, her dreams filled with her home bedroom, and a sideboard decorated in landmarks from across the globe. She wasn't sure how long she was out, but as she was climbing the stairs to the viewing platform of the Eiffel Tower, the sound of a chair scraping on stone invaded her dreams.

The Eiffel Tower fell away. Terra opened her eyes to find only stone in front of her. She listened intently, confused for a moment as to whether what she had heard had been in reality or in her dreams.

A man's breathing filled the room with deep, labored breaths.

A ribbon of smoke curled away from someone she couldn't see, drifting up toward the ceiling where it dispersed and created a carpet of fog reminiscent of the world outside.

Terra remained still, not bothering to close her eyes. There was no point. Whoever was there had seen her.

The pair sat in silence for a long time, Terra feeling exposed and vulnerable in the gaze of the unknown man. After at least ten minutes of tense silence, the chair scraped along the floor. Footsteps accompanied the sound of something hard tapping on the ground.

The door opened.

The door closed.

The man was gone.

Terra coughed a little, left with the aftermath of the smoke. She lay back, watched the grey fog dance on the ceiling, and waited.

What else was there to do?

CHAPTER NINETEEN

When Terra woke up, there was someone in the room with her again.

She looked around for the smoke, but whoever it was hadn't bothered to light a cigarette this time. For the first time in a long while, her head was beginning to thump.

APRIL, you're slacking.

I can only do so much, APRIL replied. **While I can maintain the equilibrium of particular nerve centers to ensure that you're well, there are basic components of your biology that cannot benefit from my interception.**

In English, please? Terra asked.

You need water.

Terra noticed how parched her throat was. She tried to cough, but she only received pain. Whoever was in the room with her was silent apart from the minor shuffling sounds that came from them adjusting in their chair.

"I don't suppose you fancy offering me some liquids at some point, do you?" Terra asked.

Silence met her for a few moments. The person rose from their chair, finally coming into sight in her peripheral vision.

They had a short crop of grey hair that looked like a five-year-old had cut it. They crossed the room, rattling whatever those cursed items were in those jars, then stood over her.

It was a woman. The lines on her face were heavy, her features showing traces of Asian descent. Terra couldn't accurately estimate her age, but the woman was old. She wore a thin cotton robe far too large for the skinny arms that protruded from the sleeves.

She raised a wooden cup above Terra, then let the water pour onto her face. She was gentle and accurate, but with her body strapped in position, a portion of the water splashed up Terra's nose and made her splutter as she tried to breathe.

With great calm, the woman stopped pouring, waited for Terra to recover, then continued.

Terra drank greedily, only now realizing how thirsty she had become. There was no natural light source in this room, so she could only guess how long she'd been down here.

The woman paused again, eyes boring into Terra's. Terra offered a soft, "Thank you, that's enough," before the woman gave a curt nod and returned the cup to the side.

She returned to Terra's side, watching her intently in silence. Terra studied her in return, trying to figure out the power play and the dynamic here. This woman didn't seem a threat, but that was precisely the worst thing she could assume. Everyone was an enemy until you knew otherwise, even if they weren't immediately hurting you.

"Are you going to hurt me?" Terra asked at last, trying her luck with the woman.

The woman shook her head.

"Why am I here?" Terra prodded.

The woman drew a deep breath but declined to answer.

"Who are you?" Terra continued, undeterred.

The woman leaned closer, bringing her face inches from Terra's. She smelled of something sweet that she couldn't put her finger on. Small, thin whiskers protruded from her upper lip and cheeks, poking out from the thick crevices that lined her face.

She studied Terra for a moment, gazing intently at her eyes as if trying to read Terra's mind. When she appeared satisfied, she stood straight and nodded. "You are safe." The woman's voice was thin and cracked. Terra could imagine her voicing an animated frog in a Disney flick.

Terra scoffed.

The woman fixed her with an edged glance.

"I'm sorry," Terra replied. "We're in Atlantica. I struggle to believe that those three words ever mean anything."

The woman moved out of Terra's sight. Once more, that infernal clinking occurred as something hard was dropped into a glass.

"What the hell is that?" Terra asked.

"Vindication," the woman replied, providing no further context.

Terra rolled her eyes. This woman was impossible.

"Can you at least tell me why I'm here?" Terra asked. "I mean, what's the worst that could happen? You've got me strapped to a table, no way to escape… You have some kind of mechanism that tightens my bonds if I do try and get out. What have you got to lose?"

"Atlantica." The woman's reply caught Terra off-guard.

She returned to Terra's view, blocking out some of the dim light anchored to the ceiling above. The effect cast a soft halo around her head. "You come to seek something that has been lost in this city for some time," she continued softly.

"A thing which could alter the very center of the known world. It is not a thing we take lightly. It is a noble quest and something that we may even benefit by helping each other. But you have to understand, we've been in this position before, and things have not ended well."

Terra frowned, the headache beginning to ease as her body

accepted the hydration. "You're talking in riddles."

The woman nodded. "So figure it out." She slammed her hand on something that Terra couldn't see, although she felt its effects as the bond around her forehead loosened enough that Terra could finally lift her head.

Terra shook her head, freeing the leather completely. The woman stared stoically at her. "So many questions. Can you seek the answers?"

She wandered over to where Terra's gun was leaning against a thick wooden bench. Atop the bench were dozens of glass jars of varying sizes and shapes, each filled with brass bullet casings. The woman reached out, and for a blood-chilling moment, Terra thought she was going to take her gun. Instead, she dropped another casing into the jar, then turned for the door.

The door was gleaming steel, with a series of panels and locks by the handle. The woman opened the door, then paused. "I wish you the best of luck."

Terra raised an eyebrow. "Luck? What are you—"

The woman left without another word. She closed the door behind her. The sound of locks moving into place and the confirming *beep* of the digital panel engaging filled the room.

Terra strained against her restraints, her neck cording once more, glad to be free of at least one bond. "Come on, APRIL. Help me out, here."

As a cool sensation ran through her, there came the sound of flesh hitting something outside the room. The bonds around her wrists and ankles freed themselves, fading from sight. Terra froze for a moment, unsure of what happened. "Was that you?"

Negative, APRIL replied. **An external entity activated the system.**

Terra cautiously sat up. She rubbed the soreness from her wrists and stretched her body as she scanned the room and tried to work out what the hell was going on.

The place was quiet. She eased her legs off the table, then

stood. She tested each limb, ensuring that she'd shaken off the numbness and discomfort of her temporary bed.

"There are so many jars," Terra stated. "What do you think they're all for?"

Hard to determine, APRIL replied. **I can scan and analyze each casing to determine its origin or which firearm it might have initially launched from.**

"Don't worry about it," Terra replied. "That won't be necessary."

She picked up her rifle and looped it over her shoulder. She then crossed to the steel door and examined the various locks and chambers secured in place. "That's a lot of security for little old me."

They must be fearful, APRIL replied.

"Yeah…" Terra traced a finger over the digital pad, feeling its cool surface. "But *this* scared? They didn't seem all that frightened when I was lying on the table. Perhaps now they're worried they've set the tigress free." She shook her head. "Then why do it? None of this makes any sense."

She turned back to the room. The only objects that could be of any use were the jars. There must have been over a hundred of them, each filled with at least forty or fifty casings. "What are they for?" she repeated. Before APRIL could respond, she cut across with, "I don't actually need the answer from you."

She wandered over to them. They were all open-topped. She gingerly put her hand inside and scooped up a handful of casings. She let them fall from her fingers, noting the larger sizes and the oddness of seeing flat-capped ends where a bullet would normally be. "Strange…"

As they slipped through her fingers, there was a minor change in weight from one of them. It was too late to figure out which one, so she scooped and let them fall again.

"APRIL, can you detect weight and matter through my artificial thumb?" Terra asked. She remembered how APRIL had been able to emulate a fingerprint by manipulating the surface of the metallic digit, then grinned. "You probably can."

Negative, APRIL replied. **No infrastructure is built within the thumb to detect fluctuations in weight.**

Terra's face soured. "Okay, then. Activate scan. Find the anomaly."

The edges of the brass forms illuminated in Terra's vision. A tally counter appeared, clocking the number in the jar. Terra was surprised to see that the count reached over eighty.

Anomaly found, APRIL replied at last, one of the casings highlighted in red in her vision.

Terra carefully located it and plucked it from the pile. She shook it, feeling and hearing something inside moving around. She turned the flat end to face her, then picked at it. It resisted her efforts.

"There's something inside," Terra stated. "How do I get to it?"

APRIL didn't come back with any suggestions. Terra reached for her utility belt, where her combat knife was still secured in place. "Jesus, they are trusting. What's with this place?"

She picked at the cap with the knife, working it free. She managed to pry it off, sending it back into the pile. She tipped the casing and out slid a small, slender key.

Terra raised an eyebrow, glancing back at the door. Then she noticed the small series of holes around the outer frame. There must have been at least forty of them for her to find the keys to. "Damn. This is going to take some time." She looked down as her stomach rumbled. "I guess there aren't any sweets or food in these jars to sate my hunger, either."

Would you like me to perform a scan now, Terra?

"Yes, I would like you to perform a scan," Terra replied sharply. "Find me those keys so we can get the fuck out of here."

APRIL highlighted the hundreds of casings in the room. Arrows appeared, helping Terra to locate the ones that stood out as the anomalies in each jar.

For the next twenty minutes, she dug through and sometimes emptied jars while she added to her collection on the table. As she worked her way through the containers, she noted that she was withdrawing more brass than there were holes in the door. "They've got to be kidding…"

After another five minutes, Terra had eighty casings in front of her. She examined the room, ensuring that no cameras or devices were monitoring her—there weren't—then set to work picking off the caps of each.

In sixty-five, there were more of those small, slender keys. The remaining fifteen, the largest with the widest necks, held a mixture of dried raisins and tiny chopped walnut pieces.

I think they heard your plea for food, APRIL stated.

Terra held a walnut piece in front of her doubtfully. "Can you qualify these? Are they good to eat?"

From my limited scanning capabilities, they seem to be okay. Greater chemical analysis requires more bandwidth than I can currently access.

"Way to fill me with confidence." Terra sniffed the nut, then tossed it into her mouth. It was a little soft but otherwise seemed okay.

She greedily ate the rest, hoping that if anything did go awry, APRIL would be able to counter it internally. She then examined the keys and got to work on the door.

It was a chore going through each of the locks in turn, testing each key. She developed a good system, and the process sped up as she neared the last ten locks. A number of the keys were rusted and looked as though they might break inside the mechanism. Terra was cautious to ensure they didn't.

Finally, she slid the last key in place.

"Here we go," she muttered, turning each of them to hear a satisfying *clicking* as they unlocked their mechanisms. She tried the door handle, but the door wouldn't budge.

She looked at the remaining devices holding the door in place. "Damn, I hoped they were mock locks."

She crouched to the digital panel and traced her thumb along the surface again. A line of green LEDs illuminated in a path behind where she touched.

"APRIL, did you manage to get an ID check on that woman?" Terra asked.

Negative, APRIL replied. **Functionality and access to database impaired due to indirect access to frequencies and signals.**

Terra chewed her lip. Her gaze fell on the empty shells. "Are there fingerprints on those casings?"

She moved closer, allowing APRIL to scan. **Affirmative. Five individual readings of fingerprint traces. Scanning closely. Pulling images. Recreating fingerprints in offline database.**

In Terra's vision, several windows opened with five individual sets of fingerprints. She returned to the digital panel and pressed her thumb to its surface.

Her thumb vibrated, the metal creating the fingertip shifting to emulate each fingerprint in turn. After the third attempt, a green LED lit, and a *beep* sounded to confirm the mechanism opening.

Terra tried the handle.

The door opened.

"Man, that was easier than I thought it would be," Terra whispered, leaning around the doorframe and staring ahead at the dark, dungeon-like hallway.

It wouldn't have been for someone without the APRIL capabilities. They could have ended up stuck in that room for days or even weeks.

"You have a point." Terra narrowed her eyes to try and determine what lay ahead of her. She pulled her gun around her body, then readied it in her hands. "Whoever is behind this knows much more about me than they should."

CHAPTER TWENTY

A chill wind blew through the hallway.

Terra couldn't figure out where it was coming from. Even with APRIL's thermal vision and night vision scans, they couldn't tell.

She stalked the hallway, unable to stop the loud echoes of her feet on the stone. There were no doors, but intermittently, they'd pass a series of walkways springing off in either direction. Terra took her best guess, following wherever her gut led until finally, they hit a dead end.

"Are we in a labyrinth?" Terra asked.

APRIL cast a deeper scan but was unable to return a verified result. **The stone is lead-lined. My signals are getting blocked.**

"They've thought of everything." Terra turned back and retraced her steps, this time taking an alternate turn.

There was no easy way to tell where she was heading. Every direction looked the same. If APRIL hadn't been keeping track of their twists and turns, plotting a map in her head, Terra would certainly have gotten lost by this point.

Perhaps she still was.

Movement came from up ahead. Terra froze, bringing the rifle to her eye line.

She watched the darkness, waiting for further movement. All was still.

I don't like this, Terra thought.

Understandable, APRIL replied.

Terra crept onward, gun still readied. If anything were to appear from the darkness ahead, she would be ready. So far, APRIL couldn't detect a thing.

They took a left, then a right, then two more lefts. Again, there were only stone walls, ceilings, and floors. Terra wondered how the woman had navigated through here, whether there must be a secret entrance or exit or something she didn't know about.

She took a right, jerking into alertness as something orange flashed in her sight.

Immediate threat ahead, APRIL called as a gun fired. Stone chipped away from the wall beside her. The report bounced around the chamber. Another orange blob joined the first in the darkness.

Terra shot at the figure, her aim true. The figure dropped to the ground. The second appeared from the darkness, an attacker clad entirely in black. They raised their weapon and shot at Terra. She strafed to the right barely in time and fired back. The figure went down.

The echoes of the report lingered for a moment. Terra kept her guard up, moving closer to the enemy she'd downed.

They lay on their front. She nudged them with her toe, forcing them onto their backs. Closed eyes were all she could see through the slit in their black mask.

"Who are these people? What do they want?" Terra asked.

Unable to determine, APRIL replied.

Terra moved closer. APRIL brought up a list of this person's vitals. They were still alive, but their breathing had slowed rapidly. She cocked her head, confusion setting in as another shot fired from down the hall.

The bullet caught Terra in the ribs. She grunted, one hand moving toward the site of the wound. The AJS uniform was unbroken, but the bruising would no doubt spring up soon enough. Another shot had her leaping back against the wall. She spun, aimed at the attacker, and fired.

Her shot missed. The attacker ducked around the corner.

Terra ran for them, adrenaline fueling her, along with a desperate need to get to the end of this strange game and find out who was behind it all. She shot several more times at the corner, hoping to catch the attacker. As they came into sight, Terra saw half a dozen more waiting for her.

She clenched her jaw, then fired.

The first figure went down easily enough. The next charged at her, but Terra shot them in the stomach before they made much ground. With a rapid burst of bullets, Terra knocked the weapons out of the hands of two more.

The others closed in. Two black-clad enemies came at her, no firearms in their hands but ready for a fight. One kicked at Terra, who blocked it with a sweep of her thigh. The second caught her in the cheek with their fist, knocking Terra's head sideways and dizzying her. She blocked the second punch and twisted the attacker's wrist.

The first attacker followed with another kick that caught Terra in the chest. Terra fell back against the wall, fighting to keep her balance.

Duck, Terra. Gunfire imminent.

Thanks, Terra thought as she pulled a figure toward her and used them as a human shield. A volley of bullets sprayed their chest. Terra felt them jerk and buck in her hands. When there was a brief break in the gunfire, she shoved their body toward the other combatant, then made a break for it.

She swung the rifle back over her shoulder, then fired from

the hip. She took down the other two gunmen, then spun and fired at the remaining attacker while she was still running.

The attacker called after her, Terra's shot missing by a few inches. Terra continued ahead, determined to find the way out and put distance between anyone else she came across.

The hope was short-lived. More of the enemy popped out ahead of her. She couldn't figure out where they were coming from. There were no visible doors or windows. It was as though they had designated stations in the tunnel and waited for her.

One figure launched at her, jumping into the air and presenting the bottom of their boot.

Terra blocked the kick with her rifle and twisted. The attacker slid off to the side but quickly adjusted. They rose to their feet as two more came at Terra.

Terra ducked under a series of blows, retaliating with punches and kicks. She scrapped with the pair, occasionally twisting to avoid the attacks from the back. A fist caught her chin and knocked her back.

She fell into the enemy behind her but scooped her foot up to kick them in the crotch. The enemy folded. Terra hopped over their body to put some distance between the two ahead of her.

Do I have to push ahead? Terra asked.

APRIL gave the same reason she knew to be true. **The odds are likely that the more enemies you encounter, the closer you are to your goal.**

"Fuck..." Terra muttered. She brought her rifle around and opened fire.

The impacts threw the two in front backward, where they slammed into the floor and lay still. Those behind tried to avoid the gunfire but were too slow. Terra yelled, teeth bared, advancing on the group as she let rip with her rifle, tired of the bullshit and ready to see the world again.

She wouldn't fall to this group of attackers. She would rise from the ashes and follow her destiny. It was her time, and her time was now.

They fell away like dominos, toppling out of her way and lying still on the ground. Terra marched through them, pulling the trigger until there was no more movement. She stepped over bodies and closed in on the end of the corridor where, for a moment, she was almost certain she'd found another dead end.

Some of the fallen groaned behind her. Terra would call medical attention for the survivors soon. She looked carefully at the brickwork and discovered an arch in the shape of a door.

She felt around for a handle but found nothing. She slipped her fingers into the crevice but couldn't get purchase to open the damn thing.

Whirling around, she looked down at the enemy closest to her. APRIL scanned and detected a round nodule attached to their belt.

Terra worked it free, then held it up to the door, wondering if there was some kind of detectable magnet, or perhaps a slot where the nodule fitted. It was a long shot, but she had limited options.

A *crack* sounded as the door opened an inch.

Terra tossed the nodule to the side, unsure what had happened, and slid through the doorway.

A set of stairs greeted her. Terra closed the door behind her and scaled them, her footsteps louder than ever on the metallic staircase.

"Another door?" Terra complained. She needn't have, as one gentle nudge pushed it open.

White light blinded Terra. She brought an arm up to shield herself against the sudden barrage. The pain returned to her head, and she felt APRIL working to dissolve it.

Her ears tuned into strange sounds, *ordinary* sounds. People were walking around nearby. There was a general murmur of chatter. Somewhere, someone was *clinking* plates. The air smelled of cooked meats that made Terra's mouth water.

Terra's eyes adjusted to the light, able to discern the bright spotlights pointed at the door. Beyond them, the silhouettes of several people wandered by. Terra walked forward, moving out of the direct line of light until she was finally behind them.

"What in the name of Sam Hill?" Terra asked.

She was in a market of sorts. Still in the stone dungeon-like building, as evidenced by the high ceiling built of carved stone. She glanced around at the many stalls and long wooden benches that lined the long underground corridor. There were cloth canopies of varying colors, a pop-up bar nearby serving drinks of all kinds, and several sketchy-looking figures that Terra had never seen before in her life.

"This way, please," a voice commanded.

Terra glanced to her right and found the strange woman beside her. She was at least a foot shorter than Terra. Her focus remained fixed on the way ahead. She took Terra's wrist and guided her forward, directing her through a throng of civilian foot traffic.

"What was—" Terra started.

"Not now," the woman replied sharply. She led Terra past a stall selling back alley clothing brands and off-brand sunglasses. They passed another one selling firearms and questionable blades and knives. Somewhere far behind she heard a gunshot, although no one seemed to bat an eyelid at the sound.

The woman's grip was strong on her wrist. Terra wanted her to let go, but at the same time, she was immensely curious about where she was leading her. Civilians gave her strange looks, eyeing her AJS uniform.

Terra tightened the grip on her gun.

They took a side turn down a narrow alley where the market stalls thinned. Soon they came to a doorway between two competing stores selling what seemed to be artificial Atlanticore.

They entered. The woman closed the door, and the hubbub from outside cut off almost instantly.

"Wait here," the woman commanded.

Terra didn't argue. Curiosity got the better of her.

They were in a small room, the stone on the walls smooth here, rather than the rough-hewn rock she'd put up with in the depth of the labyrinth.

This is something to put in my Dear Diary, Terra remarked.

Noted, APRIL replied.

The woman shuffled over to a small partition in the wall and disappeared. Terra heard her mutter something to someone and was about to ask APRIL to amplify when the woman returned. "He'll see you now."

Terra frowned as her skin prickled with anticipation. "Who? Who will see me now?"

The woman ignored Terra, instead taking a step back and bowing as Terra passed toward the partition. Terra entered, finding a large extension to the room. There was a large television mounted to the wall, an old-fashioned sofa against the other wall, and in the far corner, a large, wide-wing armchair. Sitting in it was a man who couldn't have been far away from one hundred years old. His complexion was pale, but his arms still showed much of the bulk they must have once had when he was considerably younger.

He held an oxygen mask, which he pressed to his mouth. He took a long, hissing breath, then exhaled, his eyes never leaving Terra's or blinking.

Eventually, he lowered the mask to his lap. "I believe you've been looking for me, Miss Kris."

CHAPTER TWENTY-ONE

"Ty?" Terra asked uncertainly. "Ty Katakura?"

The ancient man coughed, a chunk of phlegm loosening in his throat.

Terra took a step forward. The woman beside her bristled.

"Let her be," the old man replied. He nodded. "Yes. I am Ty."

"How do you know who I am?" Terra challenged. The air was thick with tension, a slight smell of incense reaching her nostrils.

"It's my job to know," Ty replied. He brought the mask back to his mouth, then drew a long breath. When he finished, he set the mask in a dock to the side of the seat. He slowly reached down and picked up a cane, which he rested between his feet and leaned on. "You're skinnier than I thought you'd be."

"Sorry to disappoint," Terra shot back. "Still managed to hand your guys their asses, didn't I?"

Ty's nostrils flared. She noticed a thin wispy beard, almost lost against the pale color of his cheeks.

"Sorry," Terra continued. "Did you not want me to take them out? Was that not the point of your little obstacle course down there?" She took another step forward. "If you want to try and kill me, you have to try much, much harder than that. I don't know who the fuck you think you are, but I'm not like the girls you've met before now."

A faint grin appeared on Ty's lips. He glanced at the woman. "She's a fiery one."

"You bet your fucking ass I am." Terra swung the rifle into view and aimed it at the man. "Enough games. Tell me what the fuck is going on here and why Nora Asplin wants to find you so badly."

Ty took a painfully long time to answer. Instead, he rose to his feet, shakily leaning on his cane for support. Terra was surprised by how tall the man was, how straight he could stand, despite his advanced age. Although he leaned on the cane, it looked as though he could have walked okay without it. "Come with me," he instructed.

Terra growled. "Haven't I followed you guys enough tonight? I want answers. I want to know why you were trying to kill me."

"Oh, come on," Ty replied. "You're smarter than that, aren't you?"

He walked ahead to a door that Terra hadn't noticed in the corner of the room. The woman ran ahead of them all, opening the door for Ty. He thanked her and passed inside, taking a seat on a large leather chair positioned in front of a series of monitors. "Please, take a seat."

Terra obliged, looking up at the screens. Most of them were dark, the outer edges showing the stone walls and ceilings and floors from the labyrinth she had passed through. One monitor showed the bench Terra had been strapped to, the door left open.

"Where are they?" Terra asked, noticing something strange almost instantly. "Where are all the fallen?"

Ty switched the screens around, showing more and more empty hallways. "They're gone."

"I can see that," Terra replied. "What did you do with them? You cleaned them up?"

"Relax," Ty stated. He pressed another button, and an image

flashed up of a large room filled with men and women in their twenties and thirties. A stack of black clothing was in a central bin, and most of the individuals walked around in just their underwear.

A few sat clutching ribs. Others laughed and chided their colleagues.

Terra's face creased in confusion. "Is that…"

"Your fallen," Ty replied. He reached out and grabbed Terra's rifle. Terra was so stunned that she let it happen. He opened the chamber with fingers that trembled and removed the cartridge. "Customized non-lethal rounds, Miss Kris."

Terra took it and examined it closely. "Non-lethal?"

Ty nodded. "Tamara switched them out when you were unconscious. Your weapon acted as a true firearm, but the rest was the great work of my team." He raised an eyebrow. "I couldn't have you hurting my people now, could I? Not when this was all a test."

The rage burning inside Terra grew. A test? Who did they think they were?

"What did your test prove?" Terra asked. "What possible reason could you have had for testing my intellect, skill, and combat ability?"

"To prove that you were true to form," Ty replied. "To ask the question that needed answering. Is Terra Kris up to code."

Terra's nostrils flared. Ty stood staring at the screen as Tamara scrubbed the footage and showed Terra in combat with the anonymous assailants. "Great technique. A quick mind. A power inside you that has never been seen or utilized on Atlantica… Maybe, just maybe, you *do* have what it takes to turn the tide."

"Enough riddles." Terra turned to face Ty. "I came to find you. I've achieved my mission. Now, tell me why it's so goddamn important to Nora that I find you."

Ty smirked, his cheeks wrinkling. "Nora…That woman has been after me for years." He turned toward the door and started back into the other room. "Follow me."

Terra clenched her fists, her patience failing. Would it be so bad to torture an aged man to get the information she sought?

Ty returned to his seat and pressed the oxygen mask to his face. Tamara knelt beside him, offering a hot drink in a wide cup. She offered Terra the same. Terra declined.

"The island of Atlantica is dying," Ty started after finally refilling his lungs. "Not its nature or its people, but in the integrity of justice that the island once held. Its edges are cracking. Its people are dying. Drugs and murder and all criminal activity are at an all-time high, despite the hard work of our people in blue."

"Tell me something I don't know," Terra replied.

Ty continued as if Terra hadn't spoken. "The criminal justice system is at the heart of it all. Once there was a time when a person could be held accountable for their actions, a time where murder was outlawed and crime was something unworthy of protection. Where an elite group of law enforcement officers took the reins and whipped this island into shape." A nostalgic smile crept over his lips, eyes glazing over slightly.

"The Executioners?" Terra asked softly, curiosity drawing her in.

Ty met her gaze. "You know of them."

"No," Terra answered. "Not really. I hear whispers…"

"Whispers are all that remains," Ty replied. "The Executioners consisted of six of the city's most hardened officers; combat agents hired to whip this shithole into shape. In Atlantica's early days, when the island was fighting to find its identity, The Executioners fought for justice—by any means necessary."

"Justice before mercy," Terra muttered.

Ty nodded, clearly impressed. "They fought for the island.

They fought for good, tearing down the corrupt and the power-hungry and delivering their brand of justice that had the rest of the world watching with fearful eyes.

"Atlantica was going to be a beacon of good for the world, a place where peace reigned sovereign, where technology would advance farther than the world had seen. Atlanticore had been discovered and harvested. Advancements were coming at a mile a minute. The money invested into the island was unlike anything else on the planet."

"I sense a but," Terra commented.

"But they failed," Ty stated softly before adjusting. "Not failed, exactly…but things didn't go the way we wanted."

"Well, no," Terra replied. "Because now we have a city that provides a thousand safe places for criminals to hide. The justice system forces law enforcement officers to stand on the outside looking in, even if the crimes committed are within sight through the windows. The bad guys won."

"The politicians won," Ty corrected.

Terra scoffed. "Isn't that what I just said?"

Ty chuckled. He brought the mask up to his mouth and drew a deep breath. Tamara assisted, holding his drink while he recouped.

"It was a sad day for the island," Ty continued at last. "A sad day for The Executioners. The moment they laid down the law, they knew it was over for now. They fought and lived for justice, but justice wasn't what the island wanted.

"The moguls and those with the greatest influence bought the politician's votes, and in the end, the bill passed and the law came into play." His brow creased, anger flaring in his eyes. "They were so close…*so* close to making the right decision. The island has only suffered ever since."

"Money talks," Terra offered.

"Money and power," Ty replied. "The Executioners disbanded

not long after that, although that's perhaps a story for another time. The bigwigs in their ivory towers claimed Atlantica, and the horizon has darkened ever since." He shook his head sadly. "It's a damn shame."

"What I fail to understand is this. If The Executioners were as influential and powerful as you say, where are they in the history books? I've been on the AJS for years. The first I heard of this was in a passing comment from a stranger a few weeks ago. Where did The Executioners go? Where is their legacy?"

"Here," Tamara stated sharply, drawing Terra's eyes to her. "Their legacy is before you."

Before Terra could ask more, Ty added, "Don't you think there's a reason you haven't heard all of this before? The AJS has covered up the work we've done, hiding us from any history books. Do you think it would look good to have a neutered AJS regaled with the tales of the good old days when they could hold people to account and get their job done?

"No. It wouldn't reflect well on the force. From the moment the law came into place, the AJS wrote us out of the scripts. Generations came and went, and our work became lost to history. Who is history written by?"

"The victors." Terra side-eyed Tamara.

"Exactly," Ty confirmed. "The victors write history. The AJS of today has nothing on the foundations of the very thing we built it on."

Terra lost herself in her thoughts, processing all of this information. Could it be that there was once a force out there fighting for the city in the same way she'd dreamed of all her life? Could it be possible that justice once prevailed in the way it did for the rest of the planet? Would there ever be a way to return to that kind of rule?

Then the last piece of the puzzle sank in. Terra frowned as her gaze locked onto Ty. He sipped his brew, then turned to Terra.

"You said 'us,'" Terra stated. "You said 'our' work became lost to the history books."

Ty held her gaze.

"Were you one of The Executioners?" Terra asked.

Ty smiled, a memory dancing somewhere in the depths of his mind. "I was the first Executioner."

CHAPTER TWENTY-TWO

An hour later, Terra followed Tamara back through the underground marketplace.

The crowd had dispersed a little, but there were still more people present than she'd like to see. The ceilings were high, and the stalls were many, the marketplace running like another huge labyrinth in this unknown location beneath the city.

"What is this place?" Terra asked Tamara, keeping her wits about her and using APRIL to scan for any threats.

"Marché du Diamant Noir," Tamara replied with an impressive French accent.

Terra paused. "The Black Diamond Market?"

Tamara grabbed her wrist and pulled her onward. It seemed the general rule here, based on the activity of others, was that you either kept moving, or you sank. The only times people stopped were at the market stalls themselves.

"Yes," Tamara replied. "The market of myth."

Terra looked at the world around her in a whole new light. The Black Diamond Market was infamous for dealing in much of the underground trade that Atlantica had to offer. For years, AJS officers had searched for the market but had been unable to enter since the entire length of this strange real estate qualified as private property. Not only that, but of the few officers who had managed to gain entry, zero had returned. This place had a penchant for silencing those who should not be walking in their midst.

That would explain all the stink eyes, Terra thought. *And perhaps why we're moving so fast.* APRIL had tracked three small groups of civilians who were tailing them and keeping a close eye.

Tamara took Terra through a side alley, then into another building. This time, Terra was pleased to see some of the normalities of overground life, with the apartment unfolding before her. It wasn't too dissimilar to the place she'd acquired when she first ventured out into the city by herself.

There were no TVs or radios, and Terra could understand why. It seemed that this entire place was a haven from external forces, which made it no wonder that Terra and the rest of the AJS had difficulty trying to discover what exactly went on here.

"You can stay here for the night," Tamara offered, motioning to a bedroom. "Mr. Katakura needs his rest and will attend to your questions on the morrow. You have done well today, and I imagine that rest will be on your agenda, too."

"I mean, I slept pretty well on that stone table you guys gave me." Then Terra felt a wave of drowsiness. "Perhaps a few hours of sleep will help me some, though."

Tamara showed Terra around the place, ensuring she had everything she needed, then left her alone. Terra watched her out the door, then closed it behind her. There was only one lock, and it operated with a key. Terra couldn't help but imagine any one of the civilians out in the market deciding to shoulder through the door and break in.

She wandered around the room, the sudden silence almost overwhelming. Her brain whirred at a mile a minute, processing all that had happened and all the questions that remained unanswered. What did Nora expect Terra to do with Ty, and why was

Ty testing Terra with such an extreme simulation? The actors might have been faking, but the bruises on Terra's body were certainly real.

She made herself a coffee from the machine on the side then sat on the couch, deep in thought. The coffee was bitter and warm and helped her relax a little. She questioned APRIL and tried to see if she should utilize the technology in her head, but the responses were limited. This deep under the ground APRIL could yield little in the way of live info.

Eventually, she settled for sleep. She made her way to the small bedroom and looked around for something more comfortable than her uniform. When nothing showed, she decided that maybe it was better to be armed and ready than to have someone break in and get caught with no defense.

She placed her utility belt on the bed beside her. She tucked the rifle beneath the sheets. For a short while, she stared at the ceiling, colors swirling in the darkness.

Eventually, she closed her eyes, and sleep came.

Although it didn't come for long.

The first she heard of the intruders was the scuffling in the other room, the soft padding of trained feet.

Terra, wake up. Immediate threat nearby.

Terra opened her eyes and rubbed away the sleep. She sat up in the darkness and listened to the sounds magnified by APRIL's technology.

Who are they? Terra asked.

Unable to determine, APRIL replied.

Terra reached for her rifle as the door kicked in, and several bodies rushed toward her.

One of the bodies leaped through the room, arcing through the air in an attempt to bellyflop on her, it seemed. Terra barrel-rolled sideways, collecting her utility belt and the rifle. She dropped off the bed, then climbed to her feet as a beam of light focused on her eyes and momentarily blinded her.

Another figure ran around the bed, charging toward her. It swept Terra off her feet, and she smacked into the wall. She grunted as her attacker squeezed the air from her lungs.

"Keep her pinned," a gruff voice called. "Don't let her get comfy."

"APRIL, night vision," Terra demanded.

The person squeezed her even tighter, pinning her arms to her sides. Four more figures lit in the darkness behind the beam of the flashlight.

"Who's she talking to?" another voice called, causing one of the figures to turn and examine the room.

"Me," a voice retorted that caught Terra by surprise. She glanced down at her chest as a bright blue diamond appeared on the console's screen. "I'd recommend releasing your target," APRIL's voice called loudly.

The screen lit up in a brilliant light, illuminating the face of the person who held Terra. Dark stubble, deep wrinkles, and yellowed teeth were inches from her face. The man's eyes filled with concern as he looked back at his comrades for some kind of help.

"They can't help you." Terra pulled her head back and drove it forward into his.

The man groaned as blood exploded from his nose. His grip loosened a touch, allowing Terra to wriggle and bring her knee to his stomach.

"Don't let her go," one of the figures called.

Terra paid no heed to their comment as she worked on the man before her. He tried to regain his grip, but she had momentum. Terra freed an arm, then drove it toward his shoulder.

The man wasn't down. Forsaking his attempt to restrain her, he pulled his arm back, then jabbed at her face. She ducked that, but it was a feint to cover his foot hooking behind her knee and pulling.

Terra's knee buckled. Over on the far side of the room, another scuffle broke out. The light from her chest hit the man in front of her. It cast dancing shadows that made the room feel as though it was melting and warping around them.

Another grunt. "What the…" someone shouted as the sounds of flesh beating flesh met their ears.

Terra focused on the job at hand, sparring with the man before her. Now that he was a step back, he was matching her blows, blocking attacks, then sending them right back at her. Sweat formed on Terra's forehead as another figure came to join them, running over the bed to get her.

More sounds of fighting from across the room. Terra wondered what the hell was going on over there but didn't have time to look.

She grabbed the first man's wrist and twisted it sharply to the right. The man yelled in pain, then swung his elbow toward Terra. Terra blocked with her forearm as another fist struck the top of her head.

She grunted, a sharp pain exploding behind her eyes. Something metallic sounded across the room. Terra tried to see, but with the light bursting from her chest and the pain behind her eyes, there was no way to get a clear picture.

She twisted, throwing a swift uppercut to the crotch of the attacker on the bed. The woman cursed, then brought her knee to Terra's face.

Terra threw her head back, knocking into the wall. She wasn't sure if she would have been in a better position just taking the knee to the face.

The man punched her in the ribs. Her uniform flared. She gritted her teeth, then took the man's face in both her hands, once more throwing her head toward his.

Before she could make contact, a fist grabbed her hair. Terra's anger grew. She turned her attention to the woman on the bed and grabbed around her hips. Kicking off the wall, she threw the woman backward.

She mounted her, then hit her with a flurry of blows. APRIL's light from her chest blinded the woman, casting her in violent tones of white. The man behind clawed at Terra's leg, then let out a haunting gasp as that metallic sound came once more.

Terra didn't notice that the rest of the action in the room had died. She focused only on letting out her anger on the woman beneath her. After a few more punches, the woman's eyes rolled back, and she stopped fighting.

Terra let her arms drop by her sides. She was exhausted. The aches from her escape in the labyrinth and the figures she had fought still weighed on her. Now she had to wake up and deal with these?

She drew a few long breaths. Footsteps padded behind her. Terra turned sharply, jumping to her feet, swinging her rifle around to guard her.

The face that met her made her breath catch.

Blood painted the wall behind him. The man who had Terra cornered lay on the floor, a deep groove in his back. Terra's gaze fixed on Ty Katakura's, the ninety-something man who shouldn't have been standing as proudly as he did.

He held the wakizashi in a white-knuckled grip, the long silver blade speckled with red and rising toward his face. He was panting, but only a little. There was no sign of his oxygen mask nor his cane. For all Terra could tell, the man had time traveled, and here before her stood a proud warrior who was at least thirty years younger than she'd seen him before.

"Are you okay?" he asked, eyes laced with concern.

Terra nodded, unable to form the words she needed to.

"Killers," Ty confirmed for her. "Part of a clan down here who have erased at least eight AJS officers from existence." His eyes darkened. "I won't let them take another. Especially one such as you."

"I had it handled," Terra replied at last, not sure her own words convinced her. The fight had been tough.

"I have no doubt," Ty replied. "Although, as I have learned, and so too shall you, boldness and bravery don't diminish with aid. They only grow if one can learn to harness the power of trust in her kinsmen."

Nostalgia flooded behind his eyes. He lowered his blade and wiped the blood off with the hem of his robe. When he was satisfied it was once again spotless, he slid the wakizashi into its sheath.

Terra's eyes narrowed as his gaze returned to hers. "Just who the hell are you, really?"

Ty smirked. Kindness softened his features. "You know who I am. The real question you want to ask is how can I help you achieve your aim?"

Terra nodded. "That, then."

Ty sat on the bed. "Sit. It's time."

CHAPTER TWENTY-THREE

"You know the truth of The Executioners," Ty started, his soft voice soothing in the gloom of the room. APRIL's light on Terra's chest was now just a mild glow, casting shadows on the bodies of the fallen and keeping them out of her field of view. "You know now what the island once was."

"That was then," Terra noted. "That was years ago."

Ty nodded. "So it once was, so it shall be again." A distant glaze settled over his eyes. "The island changed back then. When the rules changed, so did our work.

"I was one of the proponents of keeping things as they were, but the island chose another fate. I slipped out of the public eye, along with my comrades, and we truly hoped that things wouldn't turn as badly as they did."

He sighed. "Alas, here we are, half a century later. An island operating on its self-destructive tendencies and ruining what had once promised to be a utopia. Some believed we'd truly found the island of Atlantis, and somewhere on this island we'd find the forgotten technologies and create a revolution unmatched in the history of humankind.

"Humanity is a cursed beast." Ty rubbed his forehead, his age appearing to catch up with him as his back hunched.

"We're now on the edge of a revolution, but it's not the one they hoped. It's a revolution where the bad guys will win. The influence of the corrupt over the AJS is growing. You highlighted one of many instances recently with your capture of Captain Garcia."

"You know about that?" Terra asked.

Ty grinned. "I've made it my job to know. I might not play an active role aboveground now, but I keep abreast of all that's going on. Magazines, radio broadcasts, whatever I can snatch to keep on top of current goings-on, I do. Things are reaching a horrendous shake-up."

Terra listened closely.

Ty continued, "Technology is evolving. The APRIL technology that resides inside your mind has limitless potential for good, but it also has infinite possibility to be warped, distorted, and put to nefarious uses."

Terra held back on asking how Ty knew about the system logged in her head. "I know this. I've seen what can happen in the wrong hands. They were trying to control *me*."

Ty nodded sadly. "What has happened since you've freed yourself?"

Terra thought about this. She wasn't sure what Ty was getting at. Since Valentina had helped her rid herself of the connections with Cross, Terra had been free to operate how she liked with the technology. "I don't know..."

"Think harder," Ty offered, eyes intently boring into Terra's.

Terra thought harder. She considered the AI, thought about her meetings with Black...

The stack of boxes in the corner of the room filled her mind. Black had told her that the latest instructions had APRIL glasses working on every police officer in Atlantica. Imani had a pair.

Slim had a pair. Hell, Black had even separated Hewlett and Dunston to operate with the APRIL glasses.

"They're citywide," Terra replied. "But…we captured Garcia. We dealt with Cross. Surely the heat is too high now, and the glasses can only operate as intended?" She thought back to her conversation with Slim. "Captures are on the rise. The AJS force is more effective than it's ever been."

Ty gave a slow, sad nod. "In a sense, yes. In a sense, no."

Terra grumbled. "Can you just be straight with me, please? I'm tired of your games and riddles. I've passed all your tests."

"You have one more to pass," Ty replied. "I can't force you to see the truth. You have to get there for yourself. All of this," he motioned around the room, "everything that exists on this island…it's at a tipping point. We need you to understand the magnitude of what we're dealing with here."

"So, tell me!" Terra cried. "Tell me what it is I need to know. If it's not Nora, or Imani throwing around riddles and not being clear with me, it's some old has-been who once used to clean out the city but decided to forsake it when times got tough!"

Ty held her gaze. Terra's chest rose and fell, her internal body heat higher than it had been for some time. APRIL worked its magic, cooling her systems, but still, Terra was tired of skirting around the edges and heading on wild goose chases from those who seemed to know the answers.

Ty cast his eyes at the dead body in front of him. "You of all people should know the limits of bureaucracy. My people did what we needed to in the time we had. It's now up to the new generation to carry our torch."

"So, tell me where to go," Terra commanded.

Ty replied, "I have. Listen. Think…"

Terra did so. In the quiet room, she thought about what Ty had said, about the APRIL glasses and their use on the force. She thought about Slim's increase in captures and the effectiveness of the AJS in the city. It all seemed like a good thing…didn't it?

Her brow creased. Her mind rolled the highlight tape of her experience with the glasses. When she had first worn them on a mission, hadn't the glasses stopped her in the middle of arresting a bad guy? Hadn't they played with her internal circuits to black her out and stop her going too far?

The glasses hadn't been about justice. They'd been about control—controlling the AJS officers and ensuring that those in their ivory tower could keep a handle on their minions.

Terra screwed her eyes shut, thinking hard.

Yes… The APRIL system she had now wasn't like the one she first trialed. She'd had to jump through hoops lit with fire to make sure that the technology worked for her. Other people were controlling her strings. She'd had to fight for freedom.

Who was pulling the strings now?

And why?

If the entire city deployed with APRIL glasses, whoever controlled them would have total autonomy over how the AJS operated. Sure, the captures and the arrest rates in the city could skyrocket, but…

Shit.

"It's all a ploy," Terra muttered at last. "The APRIL glasses, the increase in the AJS' effectiveness. The captures aren't high-level…they're distractions. Whoever's pulling the strings behind it all is making the AJS *seem* more effective when what they're doing is distracting them away from the arrests that matter. If that person has control over the entire AJS force, it means they can pull them away whenever they want to. If a big deal is going down on the south side of the city, they can turn the heat up in the north and keep the eyes of justice away."

Ty gave a small nod. "You're getting it."

Terra ran a hand through her hair. "Holy shit, this is huge."

Terra rose from the bed and paced around the room, swerving around the fallen bodies. "So the AJS is under attack. The whole system is finally bracing the AJS in its palms and telling it where to go, and the whole time nobody knows what's going on? It's a win-win. The AJS look like they're doing amazing, gaining public trust and reputation, while in reality, they're not truly effective at all."

Terra looked down at the nearest body, a man in his thirties with a scar running across his cheek. His handgun lay in his open palm, presumably unused due to Terra's proximity with his comrades. Terra looked closely at the black material on his chest and the diamond embossed in black stitching. It matched the one on Terra's chest plate.

"Who were these people, really?" she asked.

Ty followed her gaze. "We don't truly know yet. All we know is that they're embedded in the founding of the APRIL systems.

"But…" Terra looked out toward where the market was. "Isn't this place the Marché du Diamant Noir?"

Ty nodded.

Terra's head spun. "The owner of the market is embedded in this plot?"

Ty raised his head. "That's one thing I don't know. It's one of the many reasons I took to hiding down here in the first place. The closer I could get to this mystery, the more information I might be able to pass on to whoever was smart and agile enough to carry the torch for us."

Terra pressed her hands to her head. "This is a lot to take in."

"I know." Ty rose to his feet, then limped toward Terra. She couldn't understand how he'd been so agile when fighting but how he was now regressing once more. He laid a hand on her shoulder. "Terra…it's up to you to find the answers for us. I can't perform like I once did. Age has taken a lot of the agility I once had."

"If this is you when your talents are dull, I'd be fearful of seeing what you were like at full strength," Terra commented.

Ty narrowed his eyes. "I was much the same as you."

Terra didn't know how to reply to that.

Ty glanced at his waist, then fumbled with his wakizashi sheath. "Here." He slowly lowered to one knee, then presented the wakizashi to Terra. "May this be a symbol of hope for you. A reminder that within you, there is greatness and that you are the next generation of what The Executioners once stood for. The fate of the AJS, of justice, rests on your shoulders."

Terra scoffed. "You're not asking for much, are you?" She looked into his eyes and beheld his earnestness. "Fine." She took the wakizashi from him. It was lighter than she imagined. She secured it around her waist as Ty stood again. "A couple more questions from me."

"Sure." Ty smiled softly.

"Why are you in hiding?" Terra asked.

Ty drew a long breath. "It's a long story. Suffice to say it's better this way. When those in power know that the very force to threaten their existence is still alive…they go to great lengths to silence them."

Terra nodded.

"Last question," Ty informed her.

Terra stood straight. "Where can I find the owner of this market? I have some questions for him."

"Her," Ty shot back.

Terra raised an eyebrow.

"Lucille Orlando," Ty stated. "Come. I'll show you the way."

Ty led the way out of the room, ignoring the dead behind them. More bodies lined the apartment as they made their way toward the door.

"You might want to cover up." Ty handed Terra a long robe that would conceal her uniform.

"You couldn't have told me that when you first met me?"

Ty turned back to the door. "I had to test your mettle."

"Are you satisfied yet?"

Ty didn't reply. Instead, he swept out into the bustling underground market.

Terra followed, wondering where he was leading her. If Lucille Orlando somehow tied into all of this, could they simply walk up and knock on her office door? Surely she'd be guarded by a thick layer of security, guards falling out of her place of residence?

Terra found out the truth fifteen minutes later. It was oddly unsettling.

CHAPTER TWENTY-FOUR

They walked to the edges of the marketplace, this time avoiding drawing the eye of the other civilians. Terra kept APRIL active, ensuring that this time no one followed them and they could arrive safely at their destination.

Not that she knew where their destination was. After an unknown time beneath the ground, devoid of sunlight or fresh air, she was beginning to crave the outside. The market swelled and narrowed as they walked along the walkways until only a smattering of people remained.

Here, the ceilings were nearing thirty feet high, with strange carvings etched into the stone near the top of the walls. Terra zoomed in with APRIL's technology and saw engravings that showed stick men and women building great structures with glowing blue stones in the center.

Ty followed her gaze. "Don't get hung up on the stories. A lot of people on this island have searched for the lost city of Atlantis. No one has ever been successful. You'd think with the technology we have, the increasing density of the population, and the hungry fever of people trying to find their next big discovery, that we'd have found it by now. Urban legend. That's all it is."

Terra thought back to her phone call with her friend. Maybe she'd have further information on this kind of stuff. After all, she was known for her adventurous spirit and love of Atlantica's wilds. Terra wondered if she'd make the surface in time for their drinks.

This is more important...

They arrived at a large archway decorated in artificial vines. The air grew quiet when they passed through. Ty led the way with Terra only a few steps behind. Long steps rose on either side of the walkway, decorated with dozens of guardians.

They stood with their rifles clutched in one hand, the barrels pointing at the ceiling as they rested against their shoulders. They stared ahead, not one of the figures turning to face the pair walking in their midst.

"They're not statues," Terra remarked.

"They are not," Ty replied softly. "They are the legion of the Black Diamond. Protectors of the market and Lucille."

"What are the chances that we're going to have to fight our way out?" Terra was thinking of the getaway plan if they suddenly had to go up against an army of guards.

"It better not come to that."

The walk was long and ended with a second open archway. They passed through into a set of chambers that were wide and long. Thick pillars supported the ceiling, each one lined with long strips of gold. Fires took their place along the walls, filling the room with a sleepy warmth that surprised Terra.

More guards lined the way toward a large, empty throne. Terra couldn't help but think of kings and queens from medieval times, looking down at their villages from on high. Ty stopped at the bottom of a set of steps and waited patiently.

Terra stood by his side.

The room was silent but for the crackling of the fire.

They waited for what felt like hours before finally, a set of footsteps echoed from somewhere out of sight. Terra turned toward the sound and saw a beautiful, elegant woman walking toward the throne.

She wore a silky robe of midnight black, the weaving speckled with sparkling jewels that looked like stars amid the black. A net veil obscured the top half of her face, but her ruby red lips shone with a wicked smirk. Long, alabaster legs protruded from the hem of the skirt as she took her place at the throne.

Before sitting, she clapped her hands twice. The guards all stomped in unison, then marched from the chamber. Terra watched them file neatly out the door.

Lucille sat. Her elegance washed over Terra in waves, leaving her almost breathless. It was hard to think that a jewel like her would spend her life beneath the city, ruling over a bandit's market.

"It is not often that such a noted figure requests my presence," she announced, words echoing enthusiastically around the chamber. Her voice was silky smooth, almost hypnotic. Her dark eyes glittered behind her veil. "To what do I owe this pleasure, Ty Katakura?"

Ty gave a subtle nod. "Thank you for your audience."

They held each other's gaze a moment before both broke out in a smile. Lucille rose from her chair, then walked down the stairs toward the pair. Terra kept poised, ready to defend if needed, but it wasn't necessary. Lucille folded her arms around Ty, and he embraced her back.

Terra couldn't understand what was going on. What the hell was the dynamic between these two?

"My old friend," Lucille remarked, holding Ty at arm's length. "It's been some time. Where have you been hiding."

"In plain sight," Ty replied. "The best place to hide."

"In my market?" Lucille asked.

Ty nodded.

Lucille laughed, the sound like the tinkling of seashells. "You're an impressive man, Katakura. You always have been." She turned to Terra as if seeing her for the first time. "And who's your friend?"

Ty opened his mouth to speak for her, but Terra interjected. "Terra Kris. Atlantica Officer for Justice."

Lucille's cool demeanor faltered, only for a moment. She regained composure, then extended a hand to Terra. "It's a brave move to have an AJS officer in these parts of the island. I can't hold my people responsible for the hostility they exhibit to the AJS." She straightened her spine. "If you're looking for justice for the fallen, I'm afraid you'll have to look elsewhere."

"That's not why we're here," Ty replied.

"Oh?" Lucille cast an amused glance at Ty. "Then why *are* you here?"

Ty explained the situation they found themselves in, about the black diamonds etched into the outfits of the people who had visited Terra late in the night, about the diamond symbol found on the chest plate beneath Terra's cloth robe. Terra studied him closely, curious as to how he could be so frank with a woman who seemed to wield so much power. He wasn't accusatory in any way but explained it all as if reading from a recipe, going through his thought process step-by-step.

When he finished, Lucille let the silence fill the room. Her expression was thoughtful, her bright lips crooked as she chewed her lip and pondered what was said.

Lucille turned to Terra. "Show it to me."

Terra opened her robe, revealing the dark black chest plate.

"Activate it," she instructed.

Terra obeyed, holding Lucille's gaze as she muttered, "APRIL, activate chest plate."

The chest plate lit in blue, the diamond logo spinning and forming on her chest before fading into blackness. Soundbars replaced it as APRIL commented, "Chest plate activated."

Lucille brought her hands to her face. She pinched the veil and lifted it away from her eyes. They were dark, the pupils bleeding into the whites. Only one seemed to focus, while the other remained glazed over. "Impressive."

"The match is uncanny," Ty stated. "You can understand our line of questioning."

"I can," Lucille replied. "Although I'm sure it won't please you to know that this is not my doing and something that I am unaware of. If someone is out there taking my emblem and using it for nefarious purposes, that is something that must…"

Terra looked between Ty and Lucille as the beautiful woman fell deep into thought. "It can't be…"

"I imagine it can," Ty answered.

Lucille's expression changed from one of serenity and calm to one of extreme irritation. "There may be someone…"

"Who?" Terra asked eagerly, keen to end this strange meeting and get the show on the road. "Who is it?"

Lucille narrowed her eyes. "When the founders birthed this marketplace, it was born from the vision of providing a place safe from law where outlaws, bandits, and the assholes of Atlantica could thrive in peace. It was an amalgamation of ideas, bonded together by a ruthless few who liked the power that providing such a venue would bring.

"Over time, things shifted. My father was one of the founders of this place. They assembled a council to enforce law on the unlawful and ensure this place remained what it was always born to be. We attract citizens from all over Atlantica. We monitor trade, ensure that calm—or as much calm as we can rule—is kept. Then the council broke…"

"How does a council break?" Terra asked. "Don't you repopulate the seats of those who break away?"

Lucille shook her head. "There was a split of ideals. Some liked the rule of the council. Some preferred the governing of the iron fist. As the original councilors passed from old age—well, some of them, others were found brutally murdered in their sleep

—their number shrank, and over time the council grew smaller and tighter than ever before.

"When I was born, only three council members remained," Lucille continued. "Over time, Noritz Landsdale passed, leaving only my father and one other councilwoman, Rita Nash."

Lucille's eyes glazed over with the memory. "The pair did everything together. My father and Rita shared the market, shared their time, and both had single daughters.

"Rita's daughter, Laura, and I did everything together because so did our parents. They were obsessed with this market, and we became obsessed too, learning the ways of operation. Upon reaching age, we took the vow to take over in their stead once they could no longer perform as needed."

Lucille walked over to the far side of the room. Terra and Ty followed. On the wall were several framed pictures near the fire, the glowing embers making the images dance. They showed black and white photos, all the way through to recent photos of men and women, children, and the aged.

Terra recognized a younger Lucille with her arms around a young girl with big brown pigtails and a toothy smile. "We were meant to do this together. Me and Laura...they left it all to us."

"What happened?" Terra asked.

Lucille continued to stare at the photo, one finger softly tracing its surface. "She said she couldn't do it anymore."

Ty frowned.

"Why?" Terra nudged.

"Because of what this place represents," Lucille replied, her voice whisper-soft and barely audible. "Because of all the darkness that we govern. Because it was in this very marketplace, she stumbled across the desecrated corpse of her father."

A single, solitary tear rolled down Lucille's cheek. "She vanished after that. I couldn't stop her. I didn't want to. I knew why she'd gone. Instead, my father helped me shape the new market around our system, a system that employs one single ruler to govern all."

Terra scoffed.

"Is there a problem?" Lucille asked.

"Nothing. I mean, you sound like Sauron," she commented.

Lucille turned to Ty for clarification. He stayed stoically silent.

"The point being," Lucille continued, "that this is my operation now, and I haven't seen Laura since she left this place."

"How long ago was that?" Terra asked.

"Three years," Lucille replied. "Three years and this place has never operated so smoothly. Our casualty counts are at their lowest, and trade is roaring." She frowned. "Amazing what one woman can do when left to her own devices."

Ty nodded. "A worthy operator, to say the least. You truly have grown into a queen among these people." He took her hand and kissed the back. "Thank you for the information. We can take it from here."

Lucille raised an eyebrow. "You're going to track her?"

"I'm not," Ty replied. "Terra will."

Terra narrowed her eyes. "I'll do what I must."

"Be careful," Lucille warned. "When Laura left, she was a bitter woman, scorned and hurt. There's no telling what she'll be up to out there in the open world."

"I'm sure we'll manage," Terra replied. "I've come this far without a problem."

She chuckled as Ty led her out of the room and past the silent guards.

CHAPTER TWENTY-FIVE

Ty stopped Terra at the face of a thick, steel door not dissimilar from the one she had unlocked to find Ty not too long ago.

"The road ahead will only get more dangerous," Ty offered with a concerned look. "You must keep your wits about you. Take what you have learned and use that as your guiding focus. Atlantica is counting on you."

Terra gave a solemn nod. "I'll do what I must."

Her head swam with all that she'd learned in the underground market, the weight of it all settling on shoulders that were tired and aching.

Ty placed a hand on her shoulder. "Carry our legacy. Carry the flames. The soul of The Executioners lies with you. I have unfaltering faith that you will restore the values we once held." He glanced at the wakizashi fixed to her side. "Treat her well."

"Thank you," was all Terra could think of to say before Ty opened the door and gave Terra a view of the crude tunnel beyond.

"Follow the tunnel straight," Ty instructed. "There are many bends. Ignore them all. The tunnel will lead you right."

Terra stepped through, only casting a fleeting glance behind at the wizened man as he closed the door and cast her in darkness.

The silence was deafening. "APRIL, night vision, please."

APRIL obeyed, casting the tunnel in strange shades of green. Terra began her long walk.

The tunnel stretched on for a couple of miles. Occasionally a path would open on either side, but Terra did as instructed and continued ahead. Now and then, she heard footsteps and the frustrated grunts of others who sought to find the market. Only once did she walk directly past someone who begged Terra for directions. Terra sent her off to the left, then continued ahead.

Eventually, she came to a set of stone-carved steps. Terra scaled them until she encountered one final door.

"I hope this is it," Terra muttered, pushing against the thick door.

The door creaked on its hinges. Daylight flooded Terra's vision. She brought an arm up to shield herself from the onslaught, gasping as fresh, cool air soothed her sweating skin.

The smell of wet grass and water drainage reached her nostrils. She stepped out into the air and let the door close behind her. For a moment, she simply blinked in the dazzling sun, uncertain how it was this bright when all she'd ever known was a dense layer of fog covering the island.

There had been sunny days without haze, but they had been few and far between. The newspapers and media carried stories of those days for years, sharing pictures on each anniversary as though it would never happen again.

She lowered her arm, realizing that the fog was still there. The brightness was simply the contrast from the dark tunnel she had exited. She let her eyes adjust, trying to gain her bearings.

She was standing on a small cement ledge. On either side of her, a steep bank of concrete slid down toward a drainage ditch. At the top of the slope was a thick bank of grass.

Behind her, she marveled at the doorway's disappearance.

Hidden beneath the shadows of a concrete shelf above the door, someone had expertly painted the surface to look like the entry into a large sewer. Metallic paint glimmered in the shape of iron bars. The rest of the surface was black.

*Clever...*Terra thought. She wondered how many more places like this hid around the island.

She moved over to the concrete bank and worked her way up on all fours. The concrete was slippery, but she managed to hold on. When she reached the grass verge, she gripped handfuls to support her the last few feet.

She clambered to her knees, thankful to feel the earth beneath her again. The luscious green grass surrounded her, neatly groomed by someone's mower. A short distance ahead, a road shimmered under the sun's heat.

Something glittered, catching Terra's eye.

She smiled, then climbed to her feet. The bike was immaculate, its paintwork silky smooth and gleaming. Once more, she wondered who the bigger players were in this scheme, if Ty had readied her AJS bike for her, or if perhaps Nora had advance notice of her exit from the market.

She supposed it didn't matter. What did matter was that Terra was in desperate need of some TLC. She kicked the bike into life, twisted the throttle, then sighed at the lack of roar as the maglev technology zipped into action and sped her on toward the city.

She was silent all the way to Nora's facility, only engaging in a brief interaction with the guards at the gate.

She parked her bike, then headed inside. For the first time in a long time, she hoped she wouldn't encounter anyone that she knew along the way, and for once, she was granted her wish.

Terra settled in her room, removing her uniform and brewing herself a strong cup of coffee. She stripped to her underwear, a sour smell reaching her as she released her sweating, tired body to the air. Her nose wrinkled. She chuckled, then headed to the bathroom.

The shower was hot, filling the room with steam. Terra scrubbed her tired muscles, then lathered her hair with shampoo. The water was comforting, the smell of lavender and eucalyptus rising with the moisture around her. When she finished, she dried herself off with a towel and headed back into the living room.

Cool air plucked her skin with gooseflesh. The open balcony doorway provided an unhindered view of the Atlantican forest. Terra sat on the couch and drank her lukewarm coffee, closing her eyes and appreciating the small creature comforts of this world. How long had it been since she'd been able to have some time for herself?

The ghost of a bark reached her ears. She grinned, imagining Skooch jumping on her, tail wagging, tongue lapping her cheek. She thought of her smiling parents, back in their home, not hidden in a bunker beneath the precinct, in a time when the world was easy.

It would be easy again. She was sure of it. She could make that happen.

She glanced at the wakizashi that lay on the floor with her clothes. She picked it up, holding it carefully and with the reverence she knew it deserved. She drew the sword from its sheath, the metal ringing and echoing like silver bells. The blade was immaculate, not a notch in its razor-sharp edge. Intricate carvings graced the handle. The entire sword was lighter than she could imagine.

She held it before her, the blade dividing her face into two, then gave a soft nod. She sheathed the blade and carefully set it aside.

Despite the coffee, Terra grew drowsy. She looked at the couch but instead moved to the bedroom. It was cool inside and dark. She climbed beneath the covers, then checked her cell phone.

There was only one message. She smiled, then sent a reply. She would get to work. First, she'd blow off a little steam. After all, if everything didn't go to plan and Terra found herself on the wrong side of a blade, she'd at least go out of this world knowing that she'd learned how to have a little fun.

CHAPTER TWENTY-SIX

It was around 9:00 p.m. when Terra dismounted the motorbike and stared across the street at the vibrant bar.

Music *thumped* loudly in the night. There was a string of patrons queuing to get inside. Neon lights showed animated cocktail glasses pouring their contents into one another.

Terra grimaced.

She was thankful to have left the facility. She hadn't encountered Imani or Nora on her way downstairs, which was a bonus. For the first time in a long time, she felt a modicum of freedom and autonomy, as though she was allowed to have a life outside the AJS.

Make the most of it while it lasts, she thought to herself.

She listened to the music, trying to determine what the song was and if it was one that she recognized. After a short while, it became clear that Atlantica's music trends were another thing that totally escaped her. She dug her hands in the pockets of her leather jacket and made her way across the street.

She glanced up and down, looking for her. After a minute or two, Terra's frown broke into a smile as Santana Sokolov strode toward her.

She couldn't remember how long it had been since she last saw the other woman. Time had warped thanks to the events of her time spent with APRIL. Terra had first met Santana when they were both children at school. Santana had recently migrated to Atlantica along with her Russian father and Mexican mother. Terra still remembered those first few weeks of Santana's time in school, a ten-year-old who could hold her ground and wouldn't allow the bullies to get near her.

That all became harder when Santana's mother died in an unfortunate cave-in accident. It wasn't long after that her father took her back to Russia where they could grieve for her loss.

Terra was surprised when she got the call some years later to tell of Santana's return to Atlantica. By that time, she was a young woman and soon made fast connections in the city, taking over her mother's role as a dependable island explorer. Terra always wondered if there was more to it than that. If perhaps Santana had other motives—chiefly, discovering what happened to her mother's body.

They hugged, stepping to the side of the queue to remain out of the way of the other patrons. Terra chuckled. "You know this is a fancy place, right? You could have at least have made an effort."

Santana looked down at herself. She was wearing short cargo shorts and hiking boots, complete with a white tank top and a beige jacket. She made no bones about the pistol holstered on her hip nor the long looping curl of the bullwhip.

Santana returned the smile. "Hey, not all of us have the luxury of going home to get ready before we hit the town. Some of us have to work, you know."

Terra rolled her eyes, then pulled Santana close to her again. She glanced back at the queue. "You still up for this place?"

Santana's nose wrinkled. "I can tell that means that *you're* not." She studied the queue, her long brown ponytail keeping her hair free from her eyes. "To be honest, I'd rather go somewhere quieter. You know of anywhere that doesn't give the impression that we're going to have eighteen-year-olds hitting on us all night?"

Terra laughed. "Hold on." *APRIL, can you find us a quiet bar?*

Terra's eyes glazed over. After a moment, APRIL replied.

"There's a place two blocks over." Terra ignored Santana's curious look. "Follow me. You can tell me all about your latest adventures while we walk."

"First, you have to tell me how you did that," Santana replied.

Terra grinned. "All in good time."

As they walked along the sidewalk, Santana told Terra about her life out in the jungle. Between several buyers all looking to try and find lost artifacts in the Atlantican wilds, and the ongoing pursuit of some billionaire mogul that Santana had crossed paths with, life was busy. Most of her nights were spent out beneath the canopy of leaves, fighting off the wildlife or helping guide potential treasure hunters through the thickets.

Terra pried into the specifics of her tasks, but Santana wouldn't go too in-depth. As an avid explorer of the island with a good reputation for getting things done, she asked Terra to understand the boundaries of confidentiality.

"You're talking to an Officer for Justice," Terra replied. "Of course, I know the value of confidentiality."

They arrived outside the little hipster bar, then entered. The sparsely populated place boasted tables made of upcycled wood. The stools were upturned casks, and the barman standing behind the counter sported a styled handlebar mustache.

"At least it's quieter in here." Terra chose a seat.

"Does that mean we're getting old?" Santana asked. "That we choose the quiet and the empty over the vibrant and bustling?"

"You've never gone for the clubbing scene," Terra shot back. "You've always loved your solitude. It's a wonder I managed to catch you on a down day for a drink."

"They happen once in a blue moon. You got lucky." She leaned one hand on the table. "What you drinking?"

"Coffee," Terra replied.

Santana nodded then went to the bar. The few men in the place followed her with their eyes, hungrily feasting on her flesh. Terra couldn't blame them. Santana was in fantastic shape. Her muscles were toned and defined, and Terra noted she'd have to ask Santana's secret for keeping her legs so smooth.

The barman nodded and fetched the drinks. A man sitting at the bar tried to talk to Santana but she kindly brushed him off. The place smelled of the sweet mix of liquors and juices.

Santana thanked the barman and returned to the table. She set down a cloudy white drink in front of her seat and handed Terra a bright blue beverage that reminded her of Atlanticore.

"Strange-looking coffee," Terra remarked.

Santana smiled. "You didn't invite me out here to get caffeinated and awake. You brought me out here to loosen up and have a good chinwag." She raised her glass.

Terra *clinked* hers against it. They both drank.

"So, you going to tell me what's new with you?" Santana asked. "Got a new fella in your life?"

Terra scoffed. "You could say that."

Santana's eyebrows raised. "Well, I wasn't expecting that. Terra Kris, the perpetually single, taking another into her life. What's his name?"

"APRIL," Terra replied.

Yes? APRIL stated.

Not you, she shot back.

"April?" Santana mused, realization dawning on her. "Oh… Have you? I mean… Are you?"

"No, no," Terra interjected. "Nothing like that. I've… Well… This is going to sound a little crazy."

Santana sipped her drink and crossed her legs. "I love crazy."

Terra divulged the fact that she had an artificial intelligence system embedded inside her head. She told Santana of the unfortunate circumstances that had led to the life-saving surgery and the abilities that APRIL was capable of. She avoided the drama and all of the information revolving around Cross and Parker and all that had happened over the last few days, knowing that the less Santana knew, the better.

Santana smiled and shook her head disbelievingly. "Shut up."

"It's true," Terra replied. Her drink was nearly empty. "Ask me a question about you. Anything."

"What's my mother's name?" Santana teased.

Terra rolled her eyes. "A question you know I wouldn't know the answer to. Something you've got on record that would be impossible for me to know."

"Fine." Santana thought long and hard. "What's my social security number?"

APRIL, what's Santana Sokolov's social security number? Terra's eyes narrowed at Santana. Then she recited, "078-50-1120."

Santana's eyes widened. "Okay… That's impressive but could be coincidental."

"Coincidental, how?" Terra replied.

"You could have looked at my records on the AJS database before we met up," Santana replied. "Who were my last three clients to pay fees into my account?" She sat back and folded her arms, a smug grin on her face.

Terra asked APRIL the question. Financial listings appeared around Santana's head, lists of transactions scrolling and highlighting themselves. Terra couldn't believe APRIL could dive this deep.

"Taylor Yungheim, Bonita Ung, and Charles Trevors," Terra replied.

The mirth left Santana's face, replaced with deep fascination. She leaned closer to Terra, looking intently into her eyes. Terra saw her reflection in Santana's. Some small light blinked in the corner of her eye. "You weren't kidding."

"No," Terra confirmed. "Why would I kid about any of that?"

"I don't know," Santana replied, sitting back. "Sometimes people play pranks."

"About AIs sitting inside their minds?" Terra replied. "I don't think so."

"Fascinating." Santana's eyes glazed over for a moment, her mind turning inward as though reaching a mini-revelation. "It can do everything you say it can?"

"Everything and more," Terra replied. "Even now, I'm still finding out things that it can do that I was unaware of." She nodded at Santana's drink. "Another?"

Santana thanked Terra. The AJS officer returned a moment later with two of the same orders. "I'm surprised you didn't go for a coffee again," Santana commented.

"Go big or go home."

Santana rolled her eyes and swallowed her mouthful. "Do you remember the guys that used to live by that as their mantra? I wonder what they're doing these days."

"Mostly rotting in prison cells or drug dens hooked on ink. We caught Phillip Vaughn, by the way."

Santana nearly spat out her drink. "Little Pippin?"

"The very same. Caught him a few months back dealing ink to a bunch of school kids. When we dug in further, there was... Well, let's just say that there were more kids where they came from."

"Damn. This city hits its people hard, doesn't it?"

Terra nodded. "What about you, anyway? Any more trips back to the motherland recently?"

Santana shook her head. "Afraid not. It's been a few years since I've been back to see Papa. I have far too much to keep me busy here." She looked as if she wanted to say more but held it back. "Atlantica has a way of swallowing you and holding you here."

Terra smirked. "Tell me about it."

"I do miss the mountains, though," Santana continued. "Nothing like staring up at the canvas of stars from the top of Mount Elbrus. I can't describe it… It's like the gods birthed all their colors and swirls and slapped it on the black. You don't see that here. Only fog, fog, and more fog."

Terra looked down at the table. "I'd love to visit one day."

"You should," Santana replied. "If our days off ever cross, I'll take you there. I'll show you the best trails to the top. We'll wrestle mountain lions and hug goats and…"

"And fall from the top?" Terra laughed. "Just the straight and up, please."

"You got it." Santana drained her drink in one. "You down for another?"

Terra finished hers, enjoying the dizzying effects of the alcohol on her system. Her head spun until she detected a cool wash running through her. *APRIL, don't balance my biochemistry.*

Pausing biochemistry protocol.

Good, Terra thought. *I want to feel what it's like to be fully human for one night, please.*

She rose from the table and took Santana's glass. "I'll get this round."

"Fine." Santana smiled. "I've got next."

Terra moved over to the bar and gave the orders. She stared at the back of Santana's head, admiring one of her oldest friends. She scanned the patrons, catching those hungry stares of the male patrons and a few of the females, and scoffed.

She turned to the front of the bar, ensuring that nobody was watching either of them. The alcohol did a great job of letting her relax, but she knew she needed to stay watchful.

She thanked the barman for their drinks, paid the fee, then headed back to the table.

For one night only, she would be a regular Atlantican.

CHAPTER TWENTY-SEVEN

Terra woke up to a pounding head.

She grimaced, not enjoying the pulsing waves of pain that washed over her. A breeze fluttered past, and birds sang outside.

She peeled open her eyes. It was bright. She shielded the worst of the light and groaned. "APRIL, you can balance my biochemistry now."

Balancing biochemistry.

The cool sensation washed through her body, spreading from brain to toe. Slowly, the pounding in her head eased until all that was left was a dull ache. She felt the strength returning to her muscles. She rose off the cool floor tiles, taking a moment to gain her bearings.

She was in an apartment. Everything was a clean white, with painted white walls, white ceramic tiles, and a white ceiling. Furniture was sparse, with only a single couch nearby that looked as if it had seen better days. There was no TV, no radio, nothing that would suggest that anyone lived in this place these days.

She rose to her feet, eyes lingering on the couch, wondering why she wouldn't have just slept there instead of on the hard floor. Snippets of last night's events came back to her. Flashes of Santana and Terra laughing as they walked along the sidewalk and hopped from bar to bar.

Terra smiled. It was great while it lasted.

She looked around the apartment, stopping when she noticed a couple of strange-looking mechanisms on the floor by the front door. She glanced over her shoulder and found the same mechanisms by the open balcony door.

As she passed the kitchenette counter, a note blew gently in the breeze.

She picked it up and read it.

Terra,

Thanks for a great night last night. Always fun to catch up. We say it a lot, but we really should do this more often.

I have to head out and meet a client. Help yourself to whatever's in the fridge. Coffee is in the pot. I've activated the bare minimum of trip-wires and booby traps to ensure you can get out of the apartment.

Don't close the balcony door.

See you soon.

SS x

Terra re-read the letter twice, a smirk on her face the entire time. She knew Santana tended to booby trap her apartment to stop others from breaking in. However, she was uncertain whether she felt positive or negative about being booby-trapped *in* the apartment.

"APRIL, activate scan. Look for traps and places to avoid," Terra commanded.

APRIL took over her vision, highlighting several pressure tiles, laser systems, and tripwires dotted around the apartment. Some were inactive. Others were prepped and ready to go. Terra laughed. "Nice one, Santana."

She crossed to the balcony, avoiding the trips along the way. She was high above Atlantica, looking out across the tops of skyscrapers that punctured the clouds and rose into oblivion. She glanced up, finding that she was on the topmost apartment floor, but spotted a small length of rope dangling from the edge of the roof.

She returned inside and fixed herself a coffee. Despite Santana's recommendation to raid the fridge, the damn thing was empty. Terra's stomach rumbled.

"I know, pal," she stated, patting her stomach with her hand. "Let's go grab you some grub."

She took the mug of joe with her, avoiding the last few booby traps as she exited the apartment. When she closed the door behind her, several systems *beeped* into activation.

She really has got this nailed...

Terra left the apartment in search of food.

She filled her stomach in the closest diner, tucking into a steaming plate of beans, sausages, French toast, and black pudding. She ordered a second coffee. When she finished, she went in search of her bike.

The twelve-block walk was smooth, with Terra blending in among the Atlantican civilians in a way that she hadn't for some time. Out of her AJS blues, she was unused to civilians not paying her attention. The fog trapped the sun's heat, and as Terra spotted her bike and crossed the road, she wiped away the beads of sweat dripping down her forehead.

The bike was untouched. She mounted the vehicle, then sped off toward Nora's facility. The wind cooled her, the wheels eating the road until the city was far behind them and Nora's place came into view.

She passed through the guard gate, then parked. She climbed the stairs and made her way to her apartment. Determination settled over her as she suited up in her AJS uniform. She shouldered her rifle, then strapped the utility belt around her waist.

She fixed the wakizashi, taking a moment to thank Ty again for his contribution silently.

"Justice before mercy," Terra muttered.

A knock came from the door behind her. "Come in."

Imani entered, looking tired. Her hair was messy, and there were bags beneath her arms. "Nice to see you're finally back."

"You look awful," Terra noted.

"Thanks." Imani smirked. "It's been a long night."

"Mine, too," Terra replied. "Do you know how cheap drinks can be when you avoid popular places?"

Imani raised an eyebrow. "Drinking?"

Terra smiled.

Imani laughed. "Well, not all of us have a system inside our brains that can erase a hangover. Or tiredness. Or pain." She shook her head. "Actually, screw you, Kris."

Terra laughed, seeing the harmless fun in Imani's eyes.

Imani closed the door and sat near Terra. "Did you find what you were looking for out there?"

Terra nodded. "I found all that and more. I'll be gone for the next few hours, too. Could be a couple of days." She looked at the pair of APRIL glasses settled on Imani's forehead. "Don't wait up."

Imani stretched. "I won't. Trust me. I need sleep. Ever since I got these glasses, the precincts are going crazy. Arrest after arrest after arrest. I've never seen anything like it."

Terra gave a knowing nod. "No. How about that."

Imani rose and yawned. "Keep us posted, Kris. I know Nora has put a lot of faith in you to get things done. Go make it happen. For both of us."

"Don't worry. I will."

When Imani left, Terra adjusted her fatigues, ensuring that everything was where it needed to be. Satisfied, she went down into the bowels of the building, hunting for ammunition and top-ups to the gadgets and gizmos she'd used.

A kind man with spiky hair and a ginger beard led her to the stockroom—another large garage-type structure in the building. A man dressed all in black, wearing sunglasses indoors, showed Terra around and helped her get kitted for her mission.

Once Terra was fully stocked again, she thanked the man, then headed outside.

Terra found her bike and straddled it. She looked out at the open air for a moment before she throttled up and eased out of the facility. Once outside, she cruised along the long, straight roads back to the city proper.

"APRIL," Terra commented.

Yes, Terra.

"I'd like you to start a scan, please. Find Laura Nash." Terra leaned lower over her handlebars, twisting the throttle that was absent of her signature roar.

CHAPTER TWENTY-EIGHT

After nearly toppling off her bike, Terra compartmentalized the information that APRIL provided into the lower corner of her vision.

Images and documents had barraged her sight, causing Terra to stupidly blink as she looked through the whirlwind of documentation on Laura Nash. After a quick call for APRIL to shift so she could see, she regained control and closed in on the city.

The information was interesting, but as more revelations flooded toward her, she became less surprised. All of the pieces of the puzzle were starting to slot into place.

According to the registered information on the city's public database, a Laura Nash that matched Lucille's description was part of the APRIL glasses manufacturing operation. A Tynamo Inc. company set in the center of the city produced the glasses and listed her as one of the lead developers on the project.

Terra thought through each step, making sure she had everything in place. Although she still didn't know what Nora's role was in all of this, all that she had said to Terra was beginning to unravel and make sense. To find Ludlow, Nora had told Terra to find the former Executioner, Ty Katakura.

Ty had revealed the information regarding the APRIL glasses utilized in the city to distract and deter the AJS. The diamond-shaped installation on the APRIL system on Terra's chest plate matched the uniform of the market guards, and now the common tie to link those two together was the one and only Laura Nash.

"If only we could narrow in on Kravitz…" Terra mused.

They made their way to the manufacturing plant, a strange geometric building comprised mostly of one-way glass. The outside was black and crisscrossed with metal beams. Gardens littered the front space, with water features and colorful flowers springing from the bushes. There was serenity at the doorstep.

Terra made a loop of the building, investigating from all angles. At the back was a loading dock where trucks transported the goods away and brought in the raw materials. Several semi-trucks were parked, one or two loading, the others unused. Terra skirted back around the front. "Is she inside?"

APRIL scanned the building, highlighting a significant number of workers on the various floors. "Unable to determine."

Terra glanced at her chest. "Indoor voice."

Affirmative.

Terra strode along the stone walkway toward the reception. Automatic doors parted for her. She stepped into the cool lobby and approached the main desk.

"Hi there," a chirpy voice declared. "May I help you?"

The woman was petite, with dimples in her cheeks. Her light shade of lipstick almost vanished on her rose face.

"Hi," Terra replied. "I was wondering if you could point me in the direction of Laura Nash?"

The woman kept her smile and examined her computer screen. She typed a few letters, then scrolled down a list. "Do you have an appointment?"

"No," Terra replied truthfully.

"Unfortunately, Mrs. Nash's calendar is full for today." The woman's brow creased. "May I recommend you make a booking in her next possible slot?"

"When would that be?"

"Let's see." She clicked her tongue, scrolling through appointments on the calendar. "How's next month for you?"

Terra narrowed her eyes. "That won't work for me. It's of some importance."

The woman kept her plastic smile fixed. "Unfortunately, that's the best I can do."

Terra thought hard, deciding to try something else. *APRIL, any chance you could open up her calendar for now?*

Searching...

A list of coding information appeared in Terra's vision. She chewed her lip, stalling the woman while APRIL performed its magic. After a moment, APRIL stated, **Complete.**

Terra had to hold in her laugh. It couldn't be possible... "Could you take another look at today? For me? Please."

The woman showed her first sign of patience wavering, then returned her gaze to the computer. After a moment, she sat back a little. "Oh. Well...it seems that something has opened." Embarrassed, she typed into the computer. "What did you say your name was?"

"Terra Kris."

"Terra, do you know your way to Mrs. Nash's office?"

"I do not."

The woman motioned to a man standing near a door leading into the facility. "Brett will take you through. He'll give you the mini-tour as you proceed up to Mrs. Nash's office. Thank you for your patience."

"Oh no." Terra offered her a sardonic grin. "Thank *you*."

Brett took them inside.

He walked toward an elevator made of clear glass, aside from the floor. They stepped inside and were soon ascending into the facility. Terra noted the size of the operation as the facility's floors opened around them to reveal long lines of conveyor belts with items rolling along their surface.

Machines swept around their stations, drilling and hammering and putting parts together. Dotted around the conveyor belts were men and women in royal blue uniforms holding tablets and examining stages of the process.

"We have the most sophisticated manufacturing process in the world." Brett nodded toward the machines. "These machines are infused with artificial intelligence programs deployed from the world-renowned Tynamo Inc. to ensure that we craft each product to the highest possible standards.

"Our staff runs daily checks to ensure that each part of the process is perfect. With this human-technology system working in tandem, we've been able to deliver the first one hundred percent effectiveness of product program."

Terra spotted a corner of the plant where white boxes were stacked high. She zoomed in with APRIL and spied the "APRIL" lettering on the side of the packages. "What are you currently making?"

Brett offered a warm smile. "That is confidential."

The reception area disappeared beneath them as they rose ever higher. Terra estimated they ascended at least two hundred feet before the facility fell away and the upper offices came into view.

The offices took the entire length and width of the upper floor. The glass windows circled the entire building, offering a stunning view of the city proper.

Brett led Terra through the hallways, although the walls were also glass so it was easy to see what was going on and where. Dozens of professionals in suits and ties sat at computers, viciously tapping away at the keys. Some were on the phone. A few were involved in meetings.

They reached an end office where a grim woman sat behind a black glass desk. Terra was surprised to find that she wasn't engaged in a meeting. If APRIL had deleted the meeting block, where was the person she should be with?

Brett knocked on the door. He waited for an answer before ushering them inside.

Terra entered the room. As Laura Nash looked over her computer, something akin to recognition flashed in her eyes. She lowered her gaze to the screen, the light illuminating her face turning off a moment later. She rolled her chair to the side to look at Terra across the table.

"I wasn't expecting company at this time," Laura announced, her voice clipped.

But you were...

Terra sat and leaned forward in her chair. "Apologies for the last-minute booking. I had some questions I'd like to ask you if it's not too much trouble." She flashed her kindest smile and waited, studying each move Laura made.

Laura sat back in her chair and crossed her legs. Behind her, an airplane flew low over the city, coming in to land at Atlantica Central Airport. "My name is Terra Kris..."

That same flash of recognition crossed Laura's face. She kept her composure, although APRIL detected a slight increase in her temperature and heart rate.

Terra continued, "...and I'm from the Atlantica Justice System. I've been dealing with a case that I'd like to make progress with, and it seems that you might be in a position to help me."

Laura didn't blink. Her dark eyes reminded Terra of a hawk's, sizing her prey for the kill. "What do you imagine I could do to help you?"

Terra drew a steadying breath, then went for broke. "I know your past. I know your former connections with Lucille Orlando at the Marché du Diamant Noir. I know that your diamond emblem is on all the guards and sentinels at the marketplace, the very same diamond imbued on my protective chest plate." She held Laura's stare. "APRIL, speak through the chest plate."

A diamond icon appeared. "Speaking, Terra."

Laura's head lifted a touch as if that confirmed something in her mind. "That's some fancy technology."

"Technology that seems to tie into the APRIL systems." Terra narrowed her eyes and leaned closer. "Do you know who I am?"

Laura nodded. "You are Terra Kris. You've told me this."

Terra smirked. "You know more than that, don't you? Your investment in this company…the role you play in manufacturing the APRIL systems…you know far more about the operation running behind the curtain. You don't have to answer the question. I know you do, so save yourself the embarrassment of protesting otherwise."

Laura frowned. "I'm not sure what you're alluding to, Miss Kris."

Terra held her smirk. The only way to truly know if this woman had something to hide was to press her on the issue, to watch her slip. Terra could tell that she was holding back. The question was what, and how much?

"I'm alluding to the fact that you know someone is trying to manipulate the AJS."

Laura kept her cool and laid a hand on her chest. "This is news to me. Why would someone be doing that?" She sat forward. "Are you insinuating that I'm somehow involved in a conspiratorial plot?"

Terra leveled her gaze. "I am."

"My dear," Laura replied, rising from her chair and moving to the window. "This entire facility is producing state-of-the-art technology designed to *help* the AJS. Everything you've seen on your way here is building on the premise of helping the Atlantica Justice System. What possible reason would we have to do otherwise?"

APRIL, log into her computer and scan Laura's messages for anything awry that may link to wrongdoings or misdeeds.

Initiating scan.

Laura continued to face away, fingers laced behind her back. "You do understand that it's only through my kindness that I allowed you to enter this room. When Carla at reception told me that an officer had arrived, I wondered if there was genuine help I could offer. But this…" She spun, eyes narrowed. "This is taking liberties not afforded to you on private property."

Terra rose to her feet. "You have answers."

"I have another appointment," Laura coolly replied. "Please leave the premises."

She moved to the desk, hovering with a finger over a button. Terra didn't need to know what the button did to understand that it would call security to escort her from the building.

Terra gave a small nod, lips thinned. "Very well. Just know that this isn't over. I have my eye on you, and whatever the hell is going on, I'm going to get to the bottom of it. You know why?"

Laura remained stoic and stared.

"Because you made me," Terra replied. "You and all this bullshit APRIL operation. You made me what I am, and I'm not going to stop until I've pulled every last pillar to the ground."

She spun, leaving Laura in silence.

"Tell me you got something useful." Terra walked across the street to her bike.

I have found several interesting pieces of information, APRIL replied. **Would you like me to list them all to you?**

"Not yet." Terra cast a look back at the top of the building. Although she couldn't see her, she imagined Laura watching as Terra walked away.

Terra rounded the corner and headed a few blocks over. There, she stopped at a local diner. Once tucked into her booth, she ordered a Caesar salad with a side of cheesy fries.

After the waiter had gone, Terra thought, *Okay, tell me all.*

There were several anomalies and inconsistencies in Mrs. Laura Nash's inbox.

Terra grinned, eliciting a concerned look from an older woman at a nearby table. *You managed to crack into her emails? As always, delivering above expectations.*

Thank you. She sent several personal emails via the mail server exchange, but that isn't the part that might be deemed interesting.

Well, what is? Terra munched on her French fries.

She sent several other messages through an encrypted server that isn't registered anywhere on Atlantica. The code's origin is somewhat difficult to decipher, although the notes are easy enough to interpret.

I don't understand, Terra replied.

APRIL clarified, **There is a string of messages from an unknown messenger. They were all sent across in a code that is surprisingly simple for my system to translate. However, it is difficult to determine their origins because the message came from outside Atlantica.**

Okay. Terra sipped her coffee. *So you're saying that someone* off *the island is talking to Laura and sending secret messages. What's the content?*

Snippets of emails showed in Terra's vision. There were snatches of a conversation discussing the APRIL technologies, some with direct instructions on altering the master coding. Occasionally a message would detail specific coordinates on the island, followed by a command reading, "Deploy."

Terra chewed on this information. Was Laura being directed and guided to divert the APRIL glasses and lead the charge for the AJS officers under their control? Why would it be Laura's job to enact the commands on behalf of the other messenger?

Unless it was because they were trying to keep themselves as far away from the danger as possible. If someone gave Laura commands, that meant this person might be farther up the chain. Who else would want to keep themselves at arm's reach from being captured by the person who was originating the whole operation?

APRIL, what's the location that the server is giving? Terra asked.

A map appeared, showing the island of Atlantica. A small "X" appeared in the waters a few miles off the coast. Terra zoomed in, finding a few stray rocks floating around in the middle of the sea.

"Strange," Terra muttered.

The waitress walking past paused. "I'm sorry. Did you need something?"

"No, thank you," Terra replied. "I'm good."

When the waitress had gone, she thought, *Why would the signal be coming from the middle of the ocean?*

Only one way to find out, APRIL replied.

Terra smirked.

You're becoming more human day by day, she offered.

I'm not sure that's a compliment.

The weather began to turn as Terra stepped out of the diner.

Her stomach was full, and her focus was high. She glanced back in the direction of the manufacturing plant, unable to see the building but wondering about the woman inside. Above her, the clouds darkened as small raindrops fell into the city.

Terra climbed onto her bike and headed toward the location detailed on the map. In the distance, she heard the blare of AJS sirens heading toward their next destination.

Terra streamed past the queues of traffic, expertly navigating through the city. The sky darkened further, rain slicking the asphalt and showering civilians. Men and women rushed to get undercover as the downpour grew.

Terra rode closer to the coast. The stores and diners of the city turned to hotels and themed restaurants for tourists. The blaring AJS sirens grew louder, and Terra wondered what was going on in the city. Occasionally, she spied the glare of red and blue lights as she drove on a parallel street and crossed an intersection.

"Something's going on," Terra remarked as they approached their destination.

They had reached the coast. The road stopped at the golden sands of the beach. To their left, a large expanse of dark rock stretched for a good mile or so. Large formations spiked along the land. She drove adjacent to the rocky landscape as waves crashed and crested in sprays of white foam until she found the commotion's source.

AJS had set up a blockade to prevent entry on a small slip road to the ocean. Terra couldn't see what was down there, but she recognized a few of her comrades.

She parked her bike and strode toward the two men she recognized. Both Hewlett and Dunston wore their APRIL glasses as they scanned around and set up a perimeter with AJS tape.

"I heard that Black separated you guys because of your glasses," Terra commented. "What's so big that you're back together for a single purpose?"

Hewlett continued to lay out the tape, ignoring Terra.

Dunston straightened. "We got a report about a possible terrorist intervention in this location. A boatload of terrorists heading toward the coast with a series of bombs ready to detonate at any moment. Our instructions are to ensure that no civilians come to harm as the bomb squad intervenes."

Hewlett cast Terra a sour glance. "I would've thought your brain-bot would have told you."

Terra looked inward as APRIL brought up the information. It seemed they were right. An anonymous source had tipped off the AJS about a boat coming in from the Atlantic, the entire vessel strapped with explosives.

Terra glanced past the tape, looking out at the dark ocean. Could it be that the exact time she wanted to check where the signal had come from, the AJS was put in place to block her?

"Okay, well, I need to get past," she commented, shouldering past Dunston.

Hewlett rose, moving toward her. Another few officers who were nearby moved to stand in her way. "Sorry, Kris," Hewlett commented. "In this instance, you're no more special than the rest of us." He grinned. "For once, maybe you should think about falling in line."

Terra's lips thinned. She nodded, then stormed back to her bike.

She mounted her vehicle then drove a little way back. The rain hid the others from view as she looked to her left at the rocky formations leading to the sea.

"Perhaps..." Terra mused.

She parked the bike once more, then approached the rocks. A small path led ahead, which she took. She used her hands to support her while she trod the uneven ground, hiding from the AJS blockade. When she neared the ocean, able to taste the salt spray from the waves, she utilized APRIL's technology to look at the water.

Nothing leaped out at her. There was no boat laden with bombs, no place where a signal could appear from. All she could see was a series of treacherous rocks spiking from the water, a sailor's nightmare.

She sighed, then glanced to her left as something caught her eye.

Strange...

She inched closer. Occasionally her foot slipped, twisting almost to the point of pain. She guided herself through the rocks, nearing the waves.

A spray of foam soaked her. All she could hear was the roar of the ocean, each droplet catching the flashing red and blue of the lights behind.

Terra continued, curiosity rising from deep inside. She activated APRIL and snuck toward the object of her attention, pausing just out of sight.

Where the rocks broke into a small beach, a woman stood on the edge of the shore. She wore a waterproof jacket and puffed on a cigarette. In the water nearby, a boat rocked and rolled with the waves.

Terra checked the coast was clear, then approached the woman. "Excuse me!" she called, loud enough to be heard above the wind and rain but quiet enough to avoid detection from the officers.

The woman turned with a frown. "You shouldn't be down here."

"Says who?" Terra grinned, showing a playful side.

The woman leveled her gaze at Terra. "Your cop buddies." She nodded at the thin trail which led to the blockade. "Nobody in, nobody out." She shook her head. "Way to spend an afternoon, don't you think? Trapped on the shore, the rain pissing down."

Terra took a step closer, looking at the boat. "Looks like you have a place to wait out of the storm."

The woman sighed. "Supposed to be waiting for the next batch of travelers. Looks like nobody'll be getting through now." She shook a fist at the blockade. "That's several grand I'll never see again."

Terra blinked in the rain, some of the salt spray stinging her eyes. "Where are you taking them? It has to be way too far to take them across the Atlantic."

The woman puffed on her cigarette. Terra wondered how it stayed lit. "Liberty Crag. The only way to and from the island when things get rough." She narrowed her eyes, studying Terra up and down. "You want across, that'll cost you ten grand."

Terra's eyes bulged. "That's quite the cost."

"I'm quite the sailor."

Terra initiated a scan. APRIL revealed the woman's name to be Kristin Jackson. Her record was clean enough, with only a couple of minor juvenile convictions to her name. Seemed Kristin knew how to keep out of trouble.

"What's at Liberty Crag?" Terra kept a watchful eye on the blockade as she sensed movement among the officers.

Kristin gave Terra a strange look. "You have no idea?"

Terra shook her head. *APRIL, any ideas?*

None.

Kristin extinguished her cigarette and tossed it into the ocean. "Tell you what, for an even fifteen grand, I'll take you there right now."

Terra raised her eyebrows.

Kristin smirked. "Business is tough tonight. So, sue me."

Terra noticed a few of the officers walking down the strip toward them. Kristin walked toward the boat, taking a length of rope in her hand and giving it a swift tug. A floating dock slid down with small strips of wood to help boarders keep their footing.

"What the hell," Terra muttered and followed her on board. She caught up with Kristin and tapped her on the shoulder. "How's twenty grand sound for keeping my presence on this ship quiet?"

Kristin glanced back at the shore, spotting the approaching officers. "Sounds fine by me."

CHAPTER THIRTY

Terra stowed away below deck, keeping a keen ear out and relying on APRIL for greater sound enhancement. For the most part, she could only make out the whistling wind and crashing waves, but amid the raucous noise, she detected the sounds of people talking.

A few minutes later the boat lurched. They were out in the ocean now, the waves pitching them up and down in a relatively steady pattern. Terra waited a moment, then popped her head out of the hatch that led above deck.

Kristin was at the helm. One hand gripped the wheel while the other adjusted the throttle to power forward on the incoming swells and slow on the descent. Her focus was intense, eyes straining to see the ocean through the glass panels that shielded her from the weather. Terra joined her.

"They were looking for you," Kristin stated.

"They were."

"Are you an outlaw?" She glanced at Terra's reflection. "You're not wearing the uniform of an outlaw."

"I'm an AJS officer. Same as them."

"Sure didn't seem that way." Kristin's muscles tensed as she braced against a strong wave. Terra spotted the large rocks on either side of the boat and wondered if she'd made the right move. After all she'd been through, the last thing she wanted was to die in the ocean, tossed overboard or smashed against the crags. "What have they got on you?"

"Nothing. I told you, I'm one of them."

"You sure don't dress like them," Kristin shot back.

Terra remained quiet for a moment, choosing not to follow that line of questioning. "Are you going to tell me what's at the Crag?"

Kristin's tongue poked out the side of her mouth. The way she handled the waves was impressive. She held the boat steady, facing into each wave to ensure they didn't capsize in the frigid ocean.

"The Crag is for the crème de la crème," Kristin replied. "Now, I don't know all that much since most of those guys pay me to be quiet and ferry them across the ocean, but even I can tell they're Atlantica's elite. The Crag is a guarded facility, fenced all around, experimenting with some of the latest technology that Atlantica offers. It's for people who don't want to be disturbed, if you catch my drift."

Terra's heart raced. *People who don't want to be disturbed.*

"Why haven't I heard of it?" Terra asked. "If this place holds Atlantica's elite, why wouldn't an AJS officer have heard of it before?"

Kristin shrugged. "Maybe they're trying to keep it hidden. Not my business to know. As I say, I'm the ferry. Got a question? Take it up with the big guys."

A sudden wave crashed against them. The boat lurched. Terra bumped her head against the entrance.

"You might want to go below deck," Kristin warned. "Things can get a little choppy out here."

"Are you saying that this isn't choppy?" Terra asked.

Kristin grinned, holding her steely gaze to the water.

The journey was nauseating. Even with APRIL controlling Terra's biochemistry, her stomach tossed and roiled with the waves. The ocean's roar was deafening. Terra bided her time and waited, wondering what awaited her on the other side.

Liberty Crag... What was this place she'd never heard of before? She thought back to Kristin's words, "Maybe they're trying to keep it hidden."

"APRIL, are you sure there are no records of Liberty Crag?" Terra asked.

Affirmative, APRIL replied. **Nothing in the database for Liberty Crag.**

Terra pondered the type of people they might meet on the island. They would be well-connected, those with billions of dollars to spare. As a lone AJS officer, how was she going to explore the island and find answers?

She wondered if perhaps she'd gone a step too far.

She pulled her rifle over her shoulder and maintained her grip on the firearm. It was reassuring being close to her body, but what would one gun do against an unknown assailant? What about an army of assailants?

She shook her head and pushed away the images. There was no sense fretting until she got there.

At some point in the journey, Terra closed her eyes. She slipped into an uneasy slumber, waking every time her head knocked against the hull. An unknown time later, Terra opened her eyes to find the hatch had opened and soft yellow light poured inside.

"Wakey, wakey, sleepyhead," Kristin called. "We're here."

Terra rubbed the sleep from her eyes and moved toward the steps. She emerged on the deck and looked around.

The boat still rocked gently, even docked against the pier. Through the rain, she made out a small beach surrounded by rock and a set of steps leading up toward a destination she couldn't see.

"Over to you," Kristin stated. "That'll be twenty grand."

Terra took her cell phone and tapped it to Kristin's. The Satiata Cash App *chimed* to confirm the transaction.

"Thank you," Kristin added.

Terra looked at the beach, the sand dampened into a brown, muddy color. "Where to?"

Kristin chuckled. "That's on you, now. You can either take the stairs to the front gate or brave that cave through there." Her laughter grew. "Not that anyone has found their way back out again who has tried it." She turned her attention along the shoreline. "Or you could try the random little phone booth thingy over there, I suppose."

Terra raised an eyebrow. "Phone booth?"

Kristin waved a hand. "Probably nothing. Just ignore me." She puffed her chest. "Well, if you don't mind, I have no more passengers to collect, so you better fuck off and let me get back to my business."

"What's that?" Terra asked.

"None of your business." Kristin winked.

Terra stepped onto the pier, careful to keep her balance on the slick wood. When she made it to the beach, she looked around at her options.

Lights shone above her, murky through the thick curtain of rain. Next to the start of the stairs, a small cave loomed like an inky mouth, devoid of light. Terra turned along the shore, looking for what Kristin had mentioned. Why would there be a phone booth along the coast?

She asked APRIL to scan, but nothing came into sight. She approached the cave, knowing that to try the stairs would likely be folly, and sheltered from the rain.

The cave smelled of salt and sand. There was a warmth that

sprang through an unknown breeze. "APRIL, night vision, please."

APRIL illuminated the way before her. The cave lit up to reveal every nook and cranny. Terra looked up, wondering if APRIL could show the island above through thermal imaging, but the rock was too thick.

"Worth exploring?" Terra glanced to the right, looking at where the cave bent along the shoreline, occasional drifts of light breaking the black.

The ground was slippery. Now and then, Terra found an opening that fell into a dark cavern below. She skirted the cave and the shore until she came to a small crack around head height that looked onto a rising bank on the shore.

Sure enough, Kristin was right.

There was a booth there, standing at the size of a phone booth. Had it been painted red, Terra might have believed she'd accidentally tunneled to England. "What is that?"

She looked around for a way to escape her hidey-hole. A little farther along, another cave entrance gave her access to the shore. She stalked up the bank, bracing herself against the wind and rain.

The structure had a metallic frame. A keypad with a numerical lock stood next to a fingerprint scanner. Terra skirted the booth, wondering what the hell this strange contraption could be for.

"APRIL, do your magic," Terra commanded.

APRIL examined the object. **Unable to determine interior contents. Booth is lined with impenetrable lead, apart from one vulnerability point.**

"What's that?" Terra asked.

APRIL highlighted a small antenna protruding through the top.

"Hmmm." Terra examined the keypad. "Can you do anything about the locks?"

APRIL took a moment to scan. After a moment, the reply came. **Negative.**

Terra frowned. She had started to believe that there was nothing APRIL couldn't do.

I can, however, help you determine the location of the most recent visitor to this spot.

Terra raised an eyebrow. "You can?"

APRIL drew her attention to the ground, where someone had left deep, thick footprints in a patch of dirt. They were muddy, almost lost by the water that filled them, but APRIL highlighted them and showed Terra the set leading off and up the hill.

"Guess we better investigate," Terra muttered.

She trekked up the hill, fighting against the wind and rain and trying not to slip down the slippery rock. A couple of times, she jabbed her fingers into crevices to prevent herself from falling.

When she finally neared the top, she came across a long wall that ran along the island's perimeter. At the top of the wall in intervals was a round metal orb. APRIL scanned them, revealing that they were some form of explosive defense.

Terra moved closer to the wall, moving slowly under their idle glare. She looked along the barrier's length but couldn't understand what had happened to the owner of the footprints. They approached the thick wall, then seemed to pass right through, as if a doorway should be present where there was none.

Terra moved closer, keeping an eye on the orbs. She traced a hand along the wall's surface. "APRIL, do you see anything here?"

APRIL was silent.

"APRIL?" Terra nudged.

Her vision glitched. The wall shuddered in strange stripes and colors. A small pain shot through her head. "APRIL, what are you doing?"

Another glitch rocked her vision. Terra pressed her hands to her ears. She crouched, eyes squinting shut against the strange sensation. After a moment, the glitching stopped.

Terra waited, cautious about opening her eyes. When she did, the etched outline of a door had appeared in the wall. A digital panel sat to the side. Deciding to take her chances, she pressed her thumb to the fingerprint reader. The mechanisms in her metallic thumb shifted, and the light granted her entry.

"APRIL, what have you done?" Terra asked.

The door slid open. Terra entered. The door closed behind her, the outline of the doorway disappearing almost instantly.

APRIL remained silent.

CHAPTER THIRTY-ONE

Terra looked around at the ghosts of mansions around her. They were hazy in the rain, but Terra snatched glimpses of their size. The pathways were level and perfectly straight, creating a gridded system around the nearby residences.

A dog barked in a nearby house, its silhouette illuminated in the buttery light of the downstairs living room. In another house, the light from a TV flickered in an upstairs window.

Terra glanced at the ground and discovered that the footprints stopped on the marble pathways. The rain had washed away the traces of where they went. Terra squinted in either direction, trying to get her bearings.

"APRIL? A little help?" Terra muttered.

She braced herself, preparing for another glitch. Her mind cast back to the last time APRIL had failed her. Each instance happened when Terra was near someone who could control and affect the signals and frequencies inside her head. She searched for some other sign of humans or anyone who might be watching her but found nothing. There was no one.

This way. APRIL provided Terra with a set of arrows that led to her left. Terra followed the path cautiously, rifle in hand, skirting the edge of the island and occasionally glancing up at those metallic orbs. She could almost imagine a turret appearing from its surface and spinning in her direction, blasting her with a series of bullets.

That's one way to test this uniform...

She passed a series of manors, mansions, and villas. Many of them were several stories high, giving their residents a clear view over the ocean. Rain slicked the pavement, covering the world as if trying to silence any sign of human activity.

Eventually, Terra turned right, taking her first few steps into the heart of Liberty Crag. The place was beautiful, with ornate, perfectly groomed trees, hedges, and lawns. There were statues and ornaments of woodland animals and gnomes and trolls and falcons and every other animal and creature she could think of. Soon the curtain of rain hid the wall behind her.

An uneasy feeling settled in her stomach. Terra moved toward a large fountain set in a cross-section between buildings. The fountain was covered with a thin net and inside swirled koi of many different colors. She watched the fountain, her hair dripping from the rain, clothes sodden.

What the hell is this place?

A gunshot sounded in the distance. Terra spun, looking wildly around her. She asked APRIL to scan, but APRIL didn't offer any help. Instead, those same arrows lingered in her vision.

Movement came from her right. She looked through the rain and discerned the ghostly shape of someone walking toward her. Terra left the path and found a place to remain out of sight behind the thick trunk of an elm tree.

She peeked out and watched the figure grow clearer. Another appeared beside the first. They wore heavy black armor and carried assault rifles. Their helmets were low over their brows, darkening most of their faces.

They performed a lap of the fountain, faces grimly set, then walked off along another pathway.

Guards. The island is brim-full of defenses. Terra glanced back the way she'd come. *Well, apart from that door.*

She followed APRIL's arrows, keeping her wits about her. On a few more occasions she ducked out of sight of a set of guards until finally, she reached the back gate to one of the grandest manors she'd seen.

It looked like something straight out of a Bond movie, a miniature version of a stately British home. A double gate barred the way toward a long drive that swept along a lawn that could've been lifted straight from *Perfect Homes* magazine.

Terra kept her distance, examining the way ahead. A digital panel controlled the gate, and a series of cameras monitored the entryway. The arrow in her vision pointed straight toward the building.

Into there? Terra asked APRIL.

APRIL didn't reply.

Terra sighed. *You know, as useful as you are sometimes, you're a pain in the goddamn ass when I need you.*

Her vision momentarily glitched. Terra rubbed her eyes, then examined the wall that skirted the premises. She was about to head out and search for a way to gain entry when the gates *hummed* and swung open.

Terra paused for a moment. A game was afoot. She just didn't know the rules. She narrowed her eyes, then walked to the gate. She stopped briefly at the entrance, then walked straight through.

The gates closed behind her.

Terra drew a deep breath. *APRIL, you better be there when I need you.*

She strode along the long drive toward the manor. Several expensive cars sat in a neat line beneath a shelter. Strange and exotic flowers lined the way ahead. When she reached the back door, Terra was unsurprised to find it unlocked.

She nudged it open, glad to get out of the rain. Her hair dripped onto the hardwood flooring. She shook like a dog, removing the worst of the droplets, feeling the sting of the salt in her eyes. She examined the large kitchen and found it empty.

Lightning flashed outside.

Thunder soon followed.

Terra combed her hair back into a ponytail once more, making some effort to keep her vision unobstructed. The arrows in her sight pointed down at a pair of hiking boots that were caked with mud, sitting by the back door.

She was in the right place.

Cool determination washed over Terra, although her head began to pulse softly. She asked APRIL once more for help, and the cool sensation ran through her. She waited for the headache to clear.

It didn't.

Grimacing, she walked inside the manor, rifle raised and ready.

Sneaking through the house was difficult with her black boots *clicking* against the hard floors. Hardwood shifted to tiles, then back to hardwood as she checked the first floor and found it clear. The place was decked in the finest that the world had to offer. Trophies and trinkets filled cabinets, a cinema room held a screen that could've swallowed the house, and the bathtubs were the size of public pools. There were no photos or any signs of kinship to suggest who lived here.

Still, Terra had an idea.

She found the stairs and was pleased to see a carpet runner. It softened her footsteps as she climbed to the second floor and checked it.

All was clear.

The big surprise on the second floor was an armory and weapons storage. Whoever lived here clearly had a fondness for firearms, and that set Terra even more on edge. She tried yet again for APRIL's help and was pleased to receive thermal imaging of the floor above.

Where the hell have you been? Terra asked.

I am having difficulty...APRIL glitched. Terra screwed her eyes shut, bracing against the strange sensation. **Accessing systems... Trying master...override.**

Terra looked up at the orange mass of a person, seemingly asleep in a bed. There was only one someone in this place, and she made her way toward them, even after APRIL's imaging failed, and the orange figure faded into blackness.

The third story was almost barren. Several rooms were simply empty, unused, and untouched. Terra worked her way through the strange labyrinth until she eventually found the master bedroom. She laid a hand on the cool handle. Lightning flashed outside. More thunder followed.

Terra eased the handle down, then gently opened the door.

The room was mostly dark. Terra crept closer toward the darker shape of a four-poster bed. She skirted the side of it, then brought the rifle up with her finger on the trigger. "Whatever you do, don't make *any* sudden movements."

With her finger ready on the trigger, she leaned across to the bedside lamp and turned on the light. A soft yellow glow illuminated the room. Terra's eyes widened at the empty bed with the covers pushed back as if someone had recently abandoned it.

A sound echoed to her left. She spun toward its source. In the corner, along the wall where the door was, sat a man in a large leather armchair.

He had a cigar clamped between his teeth. His hair was tousled, and he wore a monogrammed silk pajama set that glimmered in a soft blue. A ribbon of smoke curled to the ceiling as he grinned through the haze.

"You're playing a dangerous game, Terra," the man crooned. Despite the rifle pointed directly at his heart, he seemed unfazed. "A very dangerous game, indeed."

Terra showed no sign of concern or fear. "Who are you?"

"Why don't you ask your friend? Isn't that why they installed them in your head?"

Terra remained silent.

"Oh?" The man smirked. "Are they not working?" He cocked his head. "How curious." He crossed his legs and settled back into the chair as though he didn't have a care in the world.

"You know who I am, Terra. You've known for some time. The name's Kravitz. Ludlow Kravitz." He chuckled darkly. "You've just met your maker."

CHAPTER THIRTY-TWO

Terra kept her gaze fixed on Ludlow, watching for any subtle movements.

"Talk," she commanded.

Ludlow lowered his cigar, hand draped lazily over the arm of the chair. "What do you want to talk about? Perhaps we can discuss the APRIL program and its integration with the AJS. Perhaps we could discuss how fortunate you were to survive your," he raised two fingers on each hand, "accident. Or perhaps we could discuss what's going to happen next, considering you truly have no idea what you've gotten yourself into."

"All of the above," Terra coolly replied. "How about you start though by telling me how you knew I was coming here."

Ludlow rolled his eyes, an impatient look a parent might give an insolent child. "You understand that you're on Liberty Crag? One of the most guarded and monitored locations in the entire world." He motioned around him.

"Only the best of the best of Atlanticans live here, isolated from the mainland with twenty-four-hour protection. There's more money invested in the security of this place than the combined budget of all the space programs ever launched from Earth. Of course, I knew you were coming."

"But you didn't only know I was coming," Terra replied. "You led me here. You allowed me access through the wall."

"Of course." Ludlow almost sounded insulted. "Why wouldn't I allow my greatest creation to grace my presence? Why wouldn't I enable her so I could finally see up close what I birthed?" A predatory grin crossed over his lips. "What a sight you are to behold."

Terra softened her shoulders although she kept her sights on Ludlow. The rain beat down outside, occasionally interrupted by a clap of thunder, though there were no windows in this room to see the lightning that preceded it.

"I don't understand. What was all of this for? Why me? Why all of this?"

"Because I can." Pain showed in Ludlow's eyes. "And because I must."

Terra raised an eyebrow. Ludlow pinched his brow, then rose to his feet. Terra tensed, tracking him with the rifle as he crossed to a chest of drawers and grasped a decanter filled with a burgundy liquid. He raised it and offered some to Terra. She didn't move.

"Very well," he muttered, pouring himself a glass. He returned to his chair, walking as if there wasn't an officer with a gun pointed at his chest. "When you reach the stature that I have, towering over many of the so-called 'moguls' who run around in this city, you begin to realize that protection is necessary to survival.

"This island offers some, granted. Well, it does an amazing job at keeping out the riffraff and protecting its residents, but it isn't foolproof. Money talks and loyalty is a commodity." He looked tired as he stared into his glass.

"I started my empire with good intentions, Terra. I was one of the bottom feeders of this place, crawling their way to something that others defined as 'suitable.' I fought for coin, networked with the right—and sometimes the wrong—people, until I had enough money to invest.

"Charity was my goal—still is. Much of my profit goes toward helping those on the island, injecting cash into places where it can benefit the sick and the needy. I'm sure Nora gave you some kind of overview of my background."

He shook his head. "I should have learned never to drink around colleagues. Even the tiniest mistakes can have cataclysmic repercussions."

He crossed his legs and rested his head against the back of the armchair. "You have to spend money to make money." He glanced at Terra.

"Do you know how many businesses I have out there in Atlantica? Operations that normal countries would define as 'illegal' and immediately shut down? I exploit the piss-poor systems on this island to make my coin, and I reinvest where I can. Does that make me a saint or a sinner?"

Terra didn't answer. Ludlow didn't expect her to. "Label me whatever you like, but such is the way of things. As my empire has grown, it only made sense to surround myself with further protection.

"I came here alone, finding the mythic Liberty Crag, an island surrounded by dangerous razor-sharp rocks and known to only a few. There is no public record of this place. Myself and the people who live here pay for silence. Those who aren't silent get extinguished, and we pay well to clear up their tracks. As I said, money talks."

He sipped his wine, then gave an appreciative nod at the flavor profile. "The AJS is the only weak link in the chain. So, we've taken care of this."

"Why?" Terra replied. "The AJS has been unable to break barriers for years. The whole system revolves around allowing criminals to thrive. What made you think the AJS would somehow unravel your scheme?"

"You," Ludlow replied dryly. He let the words hang in the air for a moment. "Oh, come on, Terra. Don't be so obtuse." He stood and walked around the room, the wine swirling in his glass, licking the edges.

"We at the APRIL program were looking to invest in the synthesis of biological matter and technology. The glasses were the first port of call, and it was our colleagues at the AJS who suggested that a maverick cop who had fallen from grace would be the best subject to control. If we could steer your direction, control elements of your biology, you would no longer be a problem for us."

Terra tracked him as he walked, always keeping him in sight.

"The first stage showed some modicum of success," Ludlow continued. "So when it came to embedding the technology *inside* a subject, you were the clear frontrunner. It was obvious that you would be a problem from the start. When my men failed to destroy you, we figured the next best thing would be to use you as a puppet in our trials. Cross did a great job implementing the technology while Nora watched from the sidelines."

He scoffed. "Pathetic bitch. She was with you in the operating theatre, monitoring our plans and watching over you, even then. I saw her through the lens of the APRIL tech as you were under anesthetic, glaring down at you from the balcony."

He sighed. "Then you managed to rid yourself of all technological ties, didn't you." He grinned, an impressed smile. "You sure have some contacts, Terra. The legendary mercenary, Valentina Winters, hacking into our tech and changing the wiring." His knuckles grew white, and the wine threatened to spill. "She freed you. Unlocked APRIL's power."

Terra stayed quiet. Sometimes silence was the best question when people were on a roll.

"Then you caught Garcia." He laughed, a strange, strained

sound. "He wasn't involved in the main plot, but he provided a nice obstacle, didn't he? He distracted you, helped us bide our time as we implemented the glasses AJS-wide.

"Now we have the AJS in our pocket, working to our every whim, blinding themselves to all of our misdeeds." He toasted Terra with his glass. "Not bad, eh? Executed to perfection. Now the final part of the puzzle is solved."

He held Terra's gaze for a moment, the pair of them staring at each other in the silence. "Hmmm…" he mused. "Now, what to do with you?"

Terra replied, "I'd recommend getting on your knees, putting your hands in the air, and I'll read you your rights. Everything you said, every word, every sentence, every syllable is recorded and synced to a secure server. You've revealed everything, and now there's nothing left but to send you down for what you've done."

Ludlow shook his head. He stalked closer to Terra, stopping only when the barrel of the gun pressed through his silk pajamas and into his chest. "Are you that blind?"

Terra pressed the rifle harder into his chest.

"You think I don't know that your system is malfunctioning? I know everything about you, Terra. I pay the right people, and I make what I want to happen, reality. Every move, every tiny change in your biochemistry, I know."

His voice lowered to a dangerous hush. "I know every move you make, so don't try to bullshit a bullshitter. I'm more powerful than you'll ever fucking realize."

He grabbed the barrel of the rifle in one shaking hand. "So if you're going to shoot me, do so. Because I'll tell you this for free: if I die, there's no way you're making it off this island alive."

Terra looked into the dark pits of his eyes, sensing the space that was devoid of emotion. Her lips peeled into a snarl as her sight glitched. Ludlow momentarily disappeared and reappeared.

He smiled. "Interesting…"

Terra growled. "What are you doing to me?"

"Nothing."

Terra glanced between his eyes, reading his intent. From what she could tell, he was telling the truth.

She glitched again.

He pulled the rifle, making her take a few more steps forward. She kept him at the danger end, ready to shoot if she had to.

"What's happening to me?" Terra asked.

Ludlow narrowed his eyes, calculating. "I did wonder..." He cocked his head. "You don't even realize it yet, do you?"

Terra grew impatient, raised her foot, and kicked Ludlow in the chest. Caught off-guard, he flew backward, sliding against the floor until he *thumped* into the wall. His glass fell from his hand and rolled along the carpet. Terra rushed toward him, fighting through a series of new glitches.

She loomed over him, trying to focus on the man who kept dancing in her vision. She aimed the rifle at his chest. "What's happening to me?"

Ludlow held a defensive hand in the air. "It's the Atlanticore..."

"What?"

"Your mind...it's powered by Atlanticore. It's the only efficient technology that could eternally power something like the APRIL technology once embedded in a person. Even a small core carries enough power to last years, maybe even centuries." His eyes narrowed. "It's the core that gives APRIL its energy, but the cores...they have limits when it comes to stability."

"I don't understand..."

Ludlow prompted, "Think of where you are. Think of what you know..."

Realization dawned on Terra. Her blood ran cold, skin stretching tight as she remembered the stories she'd seen in the papers, features that occurred at least once every few months. The Atlanticore was known as the treasure of the island, the energy source that trumped all other energy sources. It powered their bikes, buildings, manufacturing plants, and power grids. Atlantica had found a way to utilize this newfound clean, efficient technology for the benefit of its people.

Then some sought to gift the power to the rest of the world. Nobody fully understood it yet, but every time smugglers tried to run off with the energy cores, a strange thing happened. A few miles off the coast of Atlantica, the core destabilized.

In the oceans and the skies, on the very borders of Atlantica's territory, explosions were a common occurrence. The cores would cross a line and self-destruct, meaning that the rest of the world could only dream of such power.

Terra touched a hand to the side of her head. She had one of those cores beside her spine…a tiny one. Wouldn't that mean…

"It's not possible?" Terra breathed.

"I'm afraid it is," Ludlow replied. "If you want to remain in one piece, I suggest you don't stray too far from Atlantica. Even this island might be a stretch for your core. Perhaps that's the reason for your glitch, the destabilization process taking place."

Terra took a step back, the breath disappearing from her lungs. If she couldn't leave Atlantica without her core destabilizing, that meant she couldn't travel. She couldn't see the rest of the world, tour the popular attractions, experience different cultures. She'd known that but conveniently forgot, as she often forgot about her embedded core.

Because of this man sitting before her, she would be forever stuck on Atlantica, living her remaining days as a servant to the technology inside her head.

She growled, baring her teeth. Ludlow quivered under her gaze, his steely demeanor fading. He held out his hands.

"Terra, please. If you want to live, you have to let me go. Come with me, and I'll take you back to Atlantica. We'll pretend none of this ever happened. You'll live out your days on the force, and I'll live my days here. We can both survive this."

Terra shook her head. There was no other option. If Ludlow were permitted to live, then she, and the AJS, would forever remain a slave to his whims. There was no way she could let this go.

"I'm sorry," she stated with no apology in her gaze. "I can't."

She tapped the side of her rifle, the chamber mechanisms whirring as her firearm did its thing. She brought the scope to her eye and lined up the shot. "See you in hell."

The gun blasted. A blinding pain flared in Terra's leg. Her knee buckled. The shot went into the carpet.

Ludlow spun on the floor, then lunged forward. He barged into her, knocking her to the floor before fleeing for the door.

Terra snarled. She composed herself, then gave chase.

CHAPTER THIRTY-THREE

Terra tore down the stairs in Ludlow's wake. He hopped them two at a time. Terra went for three.

Her head pounded. At intermittent intervals, her sight glitched. She closed in as they sprinted toward the first floor, Ludlow expertly navigating his house toward a destination that Terra couldn't fathom. He couldn't be heading outside into the storm. Not dressed like that.

A fleeting thought whirled past. Why didn't he run to his armory? What was the point of all his weapons if he wasn't going to use them?

The answer was simple. On an island this protected, who needed weapons?

When she reached the first floor, he slipped out of sight. He dashed through a doorway, and it wasn't until Terra made her way through that she realized what was happening.

Ludlow stood by the wall, hand pressed to a panel on the wall. Green lights confirmed the command as a siren began to wail around them.

"I told you," Ludlow crooned. "You try to take me down, and you'll never get off the—"

Terra took her shot. Ludlow's eyes widened with surprise as the bullet tore through his pajama top. Rivulets of crimson stained the material as he clutched his chest and folded to his knees. His mouth silently flapped before he fell face-down on the floor.

The siren blared. Outside, Terra heard the commotion as the island's residents woke. She wondered how many guards a place like this needed.

She ran to the window beside the front door. A series of spot-lights were running back and forth, looking for the source of the commotion. Several guards in black uniforms raced toward the manor, moving into formation as they closed on the front door.

Terra saw a man throw something toward her. She stood back from the door.

The explosion sounded. Smoke seeped through the entrance. She ran to the back of the house as the door flew inward and several guards filed inside.

They moved toward the open doorway, finding Ludlow face-down on the floor. "Shit, they got him," someone called.

Another shouted, "I saw movement that way."

Terra sprinted for the back door. She threw her shoulder against it, surprised to find that it was not only closed but locked in place. She shot the handle, then charged again. This time, the door swung wide open.

A burst of fire flew toward her. Glass shattered. Terra sprinted into the rain.

She was out in the open, but she hoped that distance would help shrink her from sight. With the rain pouring as it was, as long as she could keep running, she might be able to escape them.

Flashlight beams searched for her. The guards piled out the back, running toward her in a hunting pack. Terra chanced a glance back and saw several flashlights in the manor's upper stories.

She sprinted, running across grass that was slippery and

treacherous. She slid, fighting to gain her bearings, leaving long brown tracks behind her. *Shit, shit, shit.*

Terra started as APRIL announced, **Caution, danger ahead.**

Her vision glitched.

Jesus, APRIL. Choose your moments.

Terra peered ahead as she found the wall bordering Ludlow's garden. She scrambled up, grabbing the top of the wall, feet slipping against the stonework as the guards closed on her. She was halfway over when someone shouted, and a burst of gunfire peppered the wall.

A handful of bullets hit her leg and hip. She grunted, uniform flaring as the protective material shielded her from their penetration. Still, the blow knocked her off and over the other side.

She crashed to the ground, the wakizashi pressing into her hip. She regained her footing on the sodden earth and ran the way she'd come, pleased to find APRIL's arrows appearing to lead her back to the secret entrance.

Terra pumped her arms. She spotted snatches of adjacent roads and paths, each one littered with flashlights and dark figures that searched for her and tried to close in on where she was.

"Holy fuck," Terra groaned. "Ludlow wasn't kidding."

A whirring noise came through the storm. Terra looked skyward, expecting lightning to flash and more thunder to sound. The whirring grew louder, like a monster emerging from the sea. It was only when the floodlights bore down from the helicopter that she realized what was chasing her.

She couldn't believe they'd send a chopper out in these conditions. The bird swayed back and forth, the pilot fighting against the storm as a gunman sat in the passenger seat and tried to aim at Terra. Bullets ricocheted off the walkways and thudded into the earth as she ran and zigzagged, closing on the wall.

Terra turned, aimed her rifle, and took her shot. She nailed the gunman. He flopped and fell out of the chopper, landing somewhere nearby that Terra couldn't see.

Terra ran.

She was almost at the wall, hope seeping into her before she noticed the shapes of several guards. She paused and aimed straight ahead. "Don't make me shoot."

In answer, the first guard fired. Soon they were all shooting at her.

Bullets crashed against her chest and legs, knocking her backward. Terra gritted her teeth as her uniform flashed. She ducked her head to the side to avoid fire, but a strange thing happened.

From her chest plate rose a thin mesh shield that guarded her face. She braced herself against the fire, feeling the bullets wear away at her uniform. She pulled her trigger and sent a spray of return fire at the guards.

One by one, they went down. When the gunfire stopped, Terra was gasping for air. Her body felt tenderized. She walked on, each step aching and exhaustive.

She stepped over the guards, aware of the cries of those behind her. She was tired. The rain dampened her spirits, but she knew how close she was to escape. She examined the wall, looking for the doorway, but nothing showed.

"Fuck, fuck, fuck..." She glanced to the side where the metallic orbs played sentinel. A *hum* sounded as a small turret worked its way out of the orb. It rotated, searching for its target.

Terra sighed, crestfallen. She tried the doorway once more, then ran back the way she'd come. Would she rather face the turrets or the guards?

She chose the guards.

More whirring came from above. More spotlights surrounded Terra. The light blinded her as several helicopters circled in the sky. Indistinguishable voices called over megaphones as guards surrounded her, guns all pointed at Terra.

This can't be how it ends, Terra thought. *Not like this.*

Terra spun slowly, looking for a way out. They'd blocked her in on all sides. She couldn't even see the helicopters above due to the bright light stinging her vision. Her vision glitched. Her head pounded. In a last burst of desperation, Terra commanded, *APRIL! Get me out of here.*

To her surprise, APRIL responded. **Affirmative.**

Terra had half a second to wonder what APRIL was going to do before the report of a gun sounded, and she collapsed to the ground.

The world went black.

CHAPTER THIRTY-FOUR

Something *beeped* in a regular, rhythmic sound.

Terra scrambled through the darkness, searching for its source. She tried to open her eyes, but failed. Her heart raced, memories of the last time she'd been incapacitated on a hospital bed filling her with dread. They had tried to remove APRIL, tried to cut it out of her brain.

"No…" she groaned weakly.

The *beeping* continued.

"Shhh… She's waking," a voice called. "Terra? Terra, are you there? Oh, please wake up."

Terra grimaced. She fought against her tiredness, peeling her eyelids open. The world was blurry and white. The shape of a pale face hovered over her.

"Mom?" Terra asked.

Marie clamped her hands to her mouth, fighting back tears. "Oh, Terra…" She reached forward and hugged Terra tightly.

"Not too tight," Terra croaked, her body hurting all over.

"Michael, she's awake," Marie eagerly stated. "Fetch the doctors. Quick."

A moment later, a doctor swept into the room. "Ah, Terra, it's good to see you up."

Terra grimaced and tried to push herself upright. She failed and flopped back.

"Don't try too hard," the doctor advised. "You've been through a lot. Your body needs to rest."

Terra looked around, confused. "This isn't a hospital."

"No," the doctor reported. "But you'll be treated like you're in one. Nora is very keen to ensure that you come back to full health."

Terra searched her brain, trying to understand what was going on. The last she remembered was being on the island, soaked to the skin, surrounded by guards and helicopters. How was any of this possible?

Her hand moved to her pounding head. She felt a bandage there. Panic welled inside her. "APRIL…they didn't…you didn't?"

The doctor gave a compassionate smile. "All in good time. Just take it easy, and I'm sure your parents can fill you in on everything. Lay where you are. We'll get you some fluids to help restore that strength." He motioned to a red button, not all that dissimilar from the one Ludlow had rung in his house. "If you need anything, buzz."

The doctor left.

Terra turned to her parents. Michael sat in the chair by her bedside while Marie stood by her, stroking her fingers through her hair. Terra wondered where Skooch was.

"We thought we'd lost you," Mary muttered.

Terra shifted and grumbled. "What happened? I don't understand."

"We don't understand all the details either," Michael replied. "As far as we can tell, you should've been left dead on that island. For all intents, you *were* dead?"

Terra frowned. "I died?"

"In a sense." Nora appeared in the doorway, her great bulk

blocking most of the light. She wore a warm smile as she approached Terra's bedside. "They said you were awake. How do you feel?"

"Like I've just risen from the grave."

Nora gave a sympathetic nod. "You did—technically." She sighed. "You did some great work out there."

"I did? I mean...I remember taking down Ludlow." She thought back to the moment she switched the setting on her rifle to "tranquilize" before shooting him in the kitchen.

Nora nodded. "Yes, we have him in our custody now. APRIL *did* record everything you extracted from him in the end, and we have a team compiling evidence to send him down for a long time. As far as I can tell, that will account for all the weak links in the APRIL program, and now we stand a chance of implementing some *real* change in Atlantica with the AJS."

Terra gave a weak smile. "That's great, but it doesn't explain my escape."

Nora raised an eyebrow. "Honestly, it seems ludicrous even to us." She drew a deep breath. "The AJS forces were on the Atlantican coast when Ludlow put them in place to try and block you. Your visit with Laura Nash raised the alert, which is why they attempted to stop you from getting to the island.

"When you got past them, they called over a team of helicopters to give chase. You were too fast for them, finding your way to Ludlow's place without incident."

"He let me come," Terra replied. "He made it easy, thinking I wouldn't be able to take him down."

Nora nodded. "Then came your chase." She gave an admiring grin. "You did well to fight your own."

"They had me surrounded," Terra replied. "There was nowhere to go."

"No," Nora replied. "There wasn't."

Terra waited, still not understanding.

"Who did you ask for help?" Nora prompted.

Terra thought about it. "APRIL was malfunctioning. The Atlanticore…" Hot tears pricked her eyes. "I couldn't…"

"But APRIL could," Nora interjected. "Sensing your predicament, APRIL did the only thing that it knew how. It shut down."

Terra's face fell. "Shut down?"

"Switched itself—and you—off," Nora continued. "You dropped dead on the ground. The guards closed in on you, checked for a pulse, and found nothing. By the time they declared you dead, the AJS had swept in and claimed you for their own. APRIL had sent the video footage of Ludlow to our team, and we were able to go in there and extract him before he woke up. We took you with us, expecting to begin arranging funeral arrangements when you gasped your first breath."

Marie silently sobbed, upset by the story.

Nora cast a pitying glance at Terra's mother. "You've been here ever since. We wondered if we'd ever fully get you back."

Terra let all of this sink in. Had APRIL been able to save her and help her call in for backup? She knew that the AI was built to protect her, but was it advanced enough to have planned all of this out to keep her alive?

Terra touched the bandage again.

Nora cocked her head. "What is it?"

"Did you…" Terra didn't know how to phrase the question. "Is APRIL still?"

Nora smiled. "APRIL is fully intact. Don't worry. We haven't separated you two." She glanced at Terra's parents. "I'd hate to separate best friends like that."

Terra let out a sigh of relief. "APRIL, are you there?"

Affirmative, Terra. I am present.

Terra let out a soft laugh, then flinched as her aching muscles protested. She glanced down at her body, seeing the shades of purples and yellows that littered her flesh from the bruises.

She placed a hand on her stomach. "How long until I fully recover?"

"Well, that depends," Nora replied. "With the aid of APRIL balancing your biochemistry and working on your innards, I imagine you'll be up and running again soon."

"You make her sound like a robot," Marie commented.

Terra smiled. "That's because I am."

EPILOGUE

Terra entered Corporal Black's reception and waited by the desk.

A young man in a freshly pressed suit worked behind it, searching the computer for something Terra couldn't see. When he glanced up at her, he asked, "Do you have an appointment?"

"Where's Gina?" Terra asked.

Black appeared in the doorway to her office. "Had to cut her loose. Turns out she'd been leaking information to people outside of the AJS." She shook her head. "Meet Peter Memphis."

"Hey, Peter," Terra offered.

"Hi," Peter replied.

"Come on through," Black instructed.

Terra sat across from Black, pleased to see the broad smile on her face. APRIL glasses sat on her desk, and even now, Terra couldn't help but cast a mistrusting glance toward the gadget.

"Glad to have you back," Black announced. "It's been a while."

"I'd hardly call two weeks a while," Terra replied. "Many people take longer to heal."

"Most people would take double the time to heal, at least," Black shot back. She studied Terra in silence.

"What is it?" Terra asked.

Black chewed her lip. "I'm trying to make sense of it all."

Terra rolled her eyes. "Here we go. Let me guess: if my end goal in all of this was to try and get myself back to my old precinct with Imani, why wouldn't I accept the promotion back to my old role?"

Black nodded. "Well, yeah."

Terra glanced at her hands clasped in her lip. "I guess the truth is that I feel there's more to give to this precinct. The hard work isn't over yet, and only in keeping my ear closer to the ground can I truly get the results I want. There's a long way to go until we can start to enact real policy change in this city, and I need to be connected with the *real* Atlantica, not the inner city Atlantica, to make that happen."

She blushed. "Besides, I've grown rather fond of the people around here."

"Did you really manage to get the AJS involved in an extraction on a private island?" Black marveled.

Terra grinned. "It was the first major AJS operation outside the public sphere in almost fifty years." She thought back to Ty Katakura and his stories of The Executioners. "It gives me hope that maybe we can work our way back there again."

"That would be a world I want to see. Speaking of..." Black took her tablet and tapped the screen. "I have an operation for you. Another one of Nora's protective bubbles where you can tread behind enemy lines without consequences. A real piece of work, it seems, multiple homicides, trafficking, the lot."

Terra examined the tablet. As she did, she saw Nora in her mind, promising Terra that no matter what happened on private property, she'd be able to pull strings to finally allow Terra to deliver the justice this city needed.

Terra finished reading the document. "On it, boss."

"Don't let me down," Black offered.

Terra stopped at the door and grinned. "Justice before mercy, my friend. Justice before mercy."

AUTHOR NOTES MICHAEL ANDERLE
AUGUST 20, 2021

Thank you for not only reading this book but this entire series and these author notes as well.

It isn't often Steve Campbell laughs at me, but he laughed HARD at me this morning.

More about STEVE laughing at me later...

So, I am in Cabo San Lucas at the moment, and I've shut down the account the company was using for a product called Virbela. (www.virbela.com)

It is a web-based virtual game-like software for business. That means you have these little 3D avatars that you use to run around a business-like environment that is located on an...island.

You read that right, *an island.*

(You can even take three business associates out on a small jet boat to chat while boating around. No drinking allowed.)

As a company, you lease offices (the LMBPN offices rented at $300 a month) that include multiple meeting rooms, multiple offices, and working areas.

My reason for doing this was to help during the rise of Covid and the meetings just...felt better.

LMBPN has never had any physical offices. I never wanted

any and felt that working from home was a fantastic business proposition. Why pay rent if you didn't have to? (Yes, why, when Slack costs hundreds a month already?)

Why be bound to an office in one city when I could work from any internet-enabled location around the world?

In short, none of us do or have ever worked from an office. However, there IS something to be said for having to do only Zoom calls.

They suck.

But, in an effort to streamline, we have reduced our meetings in Virbela significantly, and there just wasn't a need for the product. Thus, we decided to cancel the effort.

Then Facebook announced their VR Work Meetings product, and my imagination got all juiced up again. Not exactly on the meeting opportunity (well, that too) but on creating a 3D place for fans to visit that shares LMBPN in a way you just can't on a website.

STEVE AND HIS LAUGHING

So, I'm speaking to Steve in Zoom as I'm showing him some other technology, and I mention this long-held desire to create a fans' experience of LMBPN and our stories, technologies we have tried, our characters, etc. In an effort to conceptualize, I chose to liken the experience description…to a museum.

Not only a WRONG choice of words but apparently a ludicrous and hilarious comment. As in:

"I want to build a virtual LMBPN museum-like exper…exp… STOP LAUGHING, CAMPBELL! No, seriously…are you done? No??? Here, let me go BOIL A CUP OF COFFEE USING WOOD and let you get this out of your system."

I'm so glad I amused him so much. I suppose if laughter is the best medicine, Steve shouldn't need to go see a doctor for at least a decade.

>>Zen Master Steve™ Note: Here's the story from my perspective.

Whenever Michael travels, his mind shifts into hyper-creative / "here's a new idea I've been thinking of" mode. Usually, he doesn't share these thoughts until he returns, and I'm prepared for the tsunami of projects during our first call AFTER he's back at his desk. NOT during our first call WHILE he's traveling. Hence, the laughter. (Well, that and the words "LMBPN and museum," which did catch me by surprise. Anyway, it was an excellent laugh, and who doesn't like a good laugh!)

Anyway, stay safe and sane out there, and I look forward to talking to you in the next book!

Ad Aeternitatem,
Michael Anderle

www.ingramcontent.com/pod-product-compliance
Lightning Source LLC
Chambersburg PA
CBHW020411110726
47899CB00006B/1935